DISOBEYING HIM

M. K. HALE

Publication date : November 28, 2020

Font design by Maya Johnston

Cover Design by Meredith Hale

M. K. Hale

http://www.mkhale.com

Ebook ASIN : B08LKGR8HF

Ebook ISBN: 9781393610304

Paperback ISBN: 9798556336773

First Edition

❧ Created with Vellum

For my perfect and amazing mother, who wanted to clarify she never inspired the horrible mom characters in my stories.

BLURB

He craves control. She craves chaos. The only thing they might crave more is each other...

Nate

Allie Parser is driving me crazy on purpose and waiting for the moment I snap.

To say we are fire and ice would be misleading. We are mint toothpaste followed by a big gulp of orange juice. Pulp included.

I want to strangle her, and she wants to straddle me.

She says I need to stop living life by rules.

She doesn't want to know what I'll do to her if I break mine.

Allie

Nate Reddington, heir to his daddy's fortune and my RA, is cold, closed off, and a little obsessed with control (*hello, pair of handcuffs under his bed. How are you?*). But I can fix him.

He is used to women on their knees for him, but I'm more likely to kneecap him than obey.

As a psychology student, it is basically my job to "My Fair Lady" him and turn this icy man into a warm human being.

Maybe "warm" is the wrong word. Because Nate Reddington, red-faced and about to crack?

Scorching hot.

PROLOGUE

ate:

MY FAVORITE SECOND-GRADE teacher once said on a zoo field trip, "Most animals are more afraid of you than you are of them."

I never forgot because, the next day, I stumbled upon a hornets' nest and told the hornets, "Don't worry. I won't hurt you."

The hornet stingers and venom landed me in the hospital for a full day.

It was the day I realized it was correct to be afraid of things that could hurt me. Because even if they didn't mean to, even if they didn't dress in a devil's tail and sport a long mustache meant for twirling while tying someone down to a railroad track, even if they did not wear name tags reading,

"*Hello, my name is The Villain of Your Story,*" those people—who might appear utterly normal—could still sting you and infect you with enough venom to stick you in bed for days.

Unlike honeybees, humans had the unique ability to wish to harm someone and come back for more. People should have taken a lesson from the flower-loving, mild, and yellow form of hornets, and thought to themselves, "*Hmm, I am about to hurt this person either through my actions or words. Would I give up my life to harm them like this? Would I use this as my last stinger for the rest of my days if I had but one?*"

Humans hurt humans. Humans hurt bees. And hornets fucking hurt in general. Like, damn, the stings still ached over twelve years later.

And when *she* walked into my life—when this girl wrapped in a bright-red dress sparked some immediate, primal need in my body—deep down, I knew she would have the largest stinger of all. This was someone who could hurt me and come back for more.

This was the girl who could destroy me and everything I had worked so hard to become.

ALLIE'S #1 RULE FOR LIFE: THERE ARE NO RULES

*A*llie:

"ARE THESE...SPECIAL BROWNIES?" the girl asked me as I handed her one of the chocolate squares.

If by *special* she meant were they made to help me make new friends in my new dorm at my new university where I knew no one and was a six-hour flight and a two-hour taxicab ride away from my hometown, then yes, they were very special. My aunt had taught me from a young age that sugary baked goods were the quickest way to clog up a rich husband's heart or warm a stranger into becoming a close friend. I had no use for the rich-husband part as I was as single as a twenty-year-old girl could be: no crushes, no hang-ups, no nothing.

"The secret ingredient is love," I replied with a smile.

"*And?*" she prompted.

Did she want weed to be in my brownies? "And more love," I said.

"Isn't my roomie so sweet?" Marissa cooed.

After moving into the university dorm an hour earlier, I had met my roommate, Marissa—correction, the freakishly strong Marissa had strangled me in a death hug as she proclaimed we would become best friends who told each other our best-kept secrets.

This short, black-haired girl with an addiction to gossip could not fathom my secrets.

All she knew about me was that I came from a small town located somewhere in the South and I had spent a gap year after high school graduation to explore Europe. She didn't know why I had left my town and moved as far away as possible, working random waitressing jobs and learning new languages to survive abroad. She might have thought I was a tourist, but my experience better fit the label "runaway."

"Allie is sooo sweet," Marissa continued. "When I first saw her, I was like, wow, this girl is going to be so sweet, and then she said she made everyone in our hall *brownies*, and I was all, yup, I was so right. Allie is the sweetest."

"Eh." A noise came from me. "I'm not that sweet." After all, the brownies were bribery for friendship. "I just thought this would be the best way to make friends."

"Soooooo sweet."

As I went from door to door, knocking, meeting people, and giving them the chocolate dessert, everyone seemed to be discussing the same issue: a rule book had floated around to every room.

"Have you seen this?" a girl with bright blond hair, who

introduced herself as Jennifer, asked Marissa and me in the hallway, her roommates behind her. Jennifer held up some sort of manual. "It's ridiculous!"

One of the girls added, "No other dorm got a rule book. Just us."

Marissa sighed, full of knowledge over the situation. As a freshman, it came in handy to have a sophomore roommate. "You know it's Nate," she told them.

The mention of this unknown name brought new questions flying through my brain. "Who's Nate?"

"He's the RA. Resident assistant. The guy in charge of making sure we don't burn this place to the ground or throw a party." Jennifer flipped through the multi-page handbook. "This is crazy. Rule nine is no making popcorn in the hallway microwave."

I laughed, because how could I not? "What?"

Marissa took the booklet from her and read aloud, "No drinking alcohol in the dorms. No animals permitted. No groups of over five in a room. No smoking. No loud music. No posters. Jesus, how long is this list?"

"Fifteen pages. It's not even double-spaced."

"What kind of person writes a fifteen-page rule book and hands them out before the first day of classes?" This guy needed to check into a spa and spend some quality time with a mud bath and some hot rocks.

"Nate. That's who. No other RA does this." Jennifer crossed her arms. "He's got a power trip."

A brunette giggled and elbowed her. "You're just mad cause he rejected you."

She blushed. "I am not. He's crazy. This rule book is crazy. Some support here would be nice."

I saw an opening for friendship and jumped in. "She's right. I mean, this guy must have some serious issues. Whoever wrote this thing has not just a stick but a whole tree up his ass."

Instead of laughing, the girls' eyes widened. What? Was cussing no longer cool in college?

The hair on my neck rose at the sound of a male throat being cleared behind me.

"He's right behind me," I said, not needing to ask.

"I can promise you, nothing is up my ass," a dark-and-deep masculine growl sounded. "Unless you'd care to look?"

I laughed nervously, turning around and wanting the hallway to swallow me whole.

Holy mama mia.

He was... Wow.

Tall. So tall my gaze swung to his chest first before scanning up his neck to the rest of him.

A strong, tense jaw. Unforgiving cheekbones. His chiseled face resembled an old Greek statue, frozen in the same handsome expression of painful longing all the sculptures of that era emanated. The yearning to jump out of his stone skin and breathe as flesh.

Fiery bright-blue eyes mirroring the clear turquoise waters of the Perhentian Islands I had visited during my year abroad stared at me. My favorite color.

Under my gaze, he licked his lips, perusing me, and stared back. "Tell me, what are these issues you think I have, girl I've never seen or talked to before?" he asked angrily. My fingers itched to massage his tense shoulders. Or to tangle in his short, dark hair. Or touch him anywhere or in any way.

Don't back down. Your entire life, you backed down; don't fucking back down.

This was college. A new start. A new life. A new Allie. Being shamed or demeaned was no longer allowed. This was not the place I had grown up in and been ostracized into leaving.

No more being the bud for me. I was going to goddamn blossom.

Fighting the urge to look away from him and toward the ground, I stared him down and shot back in a matching angry tone, "Well, for one, it seems you have some serious control issues. Let me guess, something is spiraling in your life, so you've chosen to embrace rules and control the people around you?"

"*Ohhhhhhh,*" came from the shocked girls behind me.

His jaw dropped for a split second, as he did not expect me to fight back or tell him just what issues I thought he had. Well, he had unknowingly stumbled across a psychology major who loved diagnosing people, so the joke was on him. He wanted to open up a can of worms? Fine. *Let's do it.*

"From your dark clothing, I can assume you're more of an introvert than an extrovert. And by the way you look like your skin is crawling during this interaction, I would assume you're also more of a loner," I said. "You prefer to be by yourself, and instead of giving new things a try, you stick to a strict schedule because you'd rather be bored than disappointed or hurt by something you weren't expecting."

He blinked, his anger fading for a mere second as the shock ate away at the annoyance in his expression. "You can tell all that from me wearing dark clothes?" he sneered, but it came out disarmed rather than deadly.

"I can tell a lot about you from what you're wearing. Like your shoes."

I bent down on my knees in front of him to survey his footwear. He sucked in a surprised breath and asked, "What are you doing?" He stepped back, but I held on to his shoe. "Are you crazy? Let go."

There was a second where I absorbed the weight of my actions and how my face was now crotch level to sneak a peek at his groin. I tried not to, but I was only human. His pants seemed a bit tighter than before. Deliciously snug. *No, focus.* As blood rushed to my cheeks, I lifted his foot so I could see the bottom of the sole. He gripped my shoulder to stay vertical, risking his balance if he did not touch me. I struggled to concentrate with his hand on my skin.

"Looks new," I said. "That indicates you have a conscientious personality, which fits with the whole stick-up-your-ass thing."

"They are new," he said, tightening his grip on me. "Please stand up."

"Nervous to have a girl on her knees for you?" I asked, but instead of smiling, he locked his jaw. Hmm, maybe my position affected him the same way his fingers curling around my shoulder sent my heart into juvenile pitter-patter territory.

"They're just black shoes. There is nothing for you to read."

"Brand-new shoes can often be a sign of attachment anxiety."

"Excuse me?"

"Attachment anxiety," I repeated, babbling and revealing my obsession with psychology. "It often relates to separation

8

and abandonment. Do you have trouble building and maintaining relationships? Were you abandoned at some point in your childhood—?"

"Allie," someone—Marissa—gasped from several feet away from us, and I slammed back into reality. I had forgotten anyone else was listening to me other than Nate.

Embarrassed and angrier than ever, Nate pulled his foot from my grip. I stood on shaky legs, ashamed at how far I had gone in my analysis in front of the girls.

"Um," I started to apologize.

Nate moved forward so quickly he caused a small gust of wind to play with the tendrils of auburn hair hanging in front of my face. He leaned over, the strong scent of crisp apples and sweet soap flooding my nostrils, and he whispered threateningly in my ear, "You have no idea who the fuck I am." His warm breath bathed the side of my neck, each puffed exhale caressing the skin. "And you never will."

He spun around and strode down the hallway, away from me.

However, he piqued curiosity. "Well, now I'm interested."

NATE'S #1 RULE FOR LIFE: FOLLOW THE RULES

$\mathcal{N}$ate:

FUCK ME. It had to be her, didn't it? The girl I had watched wheel her four large suitcases into the dorm's lobby while moving in this morning—the girl who'd caused me a mini heart attack and a shocking, untimely erection in public—she had to be my next-door neighbor and the woman who had spewed out facts about me like she studied my journal and was completing an oral exam.

Shit, the image of her and the words "oral exam" turned dirty in my mind, and suddenly, I was sporting that same erection again. God, what was going on with me?

Keeping myself in check was my favorite hobby and best talent. Now, the back of my neck sweat, and shallow breaths moved my chest up and down. My body was freaking out about her. So was I.

She had no filter, considering she had listed out my every deep issue and insecurity in the public hallway while on her knees in front of me, holding my shoe. I mean, who did that? Who was she? Some secret stalker or reporter hell-bent on finding out what the wealthy Reddingtons were up to?

Whoever she was, she was dangerous, and I needed to stay away from her.

A knock pounded hard on the opposite side of my door. I sighed and approached it. *A Resident Assistant's job is never done.* The knocker seemed to rethink the heavy force put behind it and added a soft and delicate *knock, knock.*

I opened the door, about to introduce myself as the RA when I met *her* gaze. Red-dress girl.

Damn it, she was frustratingly gorgeous.

Her cherry-chestnut auburn hair was tied up into a long ponytail, triggering some deeper masculine instinct in me to pull on the strands. Wrap them around my fist as I tipped her head back and claimed those red lips. The tips of her locks were dyed a flaming red, as if I needed another sign of her impulsivity and sizzling potential for passion.

The strong cheekbones of her face screamed "confidence" and "queen." Then there was the red dress she wore, which dipped down into a "V" and revealed a hint of beautiful cleavage, causing a bit of my blood flow to change direction from my brain.

But she was off-limits.

The first rule of being a Resident Assistant: do not have a romantic relationship with one of the residents. Not an emotional relationship. Not a physical relationship. They caught George Lyell hooking up with a resident last year, and he lost his free housing, meal plan, and tuition scholarship. A total sum of over thirty-five-thousand dollars a year.

I could not afford to lose this job. Not with the money problems my family dealt with as of late. The world thought we were millionaires, and yet I took any side jobs I could find to send my younger sister lunch money.

This girl—my attraction to this girl—threatened everything. I relied on the money from my position as an RA.

Off. Limits. *It's just an itch. Scratch it with someone else.*

With a deep breath, I summoned all of my resolve, laid down fresh bricks for my emotional wall, and shot her my standard icy glare. "Yes?" I asked.

She peeked up at me from under her long dark eyelashes and smiled like the cutest fucking thing on the planet. "Soooo, I wanted to say sorry about the whole 'stick up your ass' thing," she said.

"I believe it was 'a whole tree,'" I quoted her.

Her adorable smile cracked into a full grin as she shrugged. "I mean, can you blame me? The rule-book thing is…a lot."

"Every rule has a reason to be there."

She clucked her tongue, and my eyes glued themselves to the little pink body part. My mind jumped to other reasons she might flick her tongue. "Agree to disagree," she said.

"You can't disagree with me. I'm your RA. I'm the one in charge."

"Tomato, tomato," she said them both the same way, ignoring how pronouncing one *"to-mah-to"* would enforce her ability to compromise. "Anyway, I thought I would bring you a peace offering."

She pushed her hand out between us and opened a napkin holding a single dark-chocolate brownie. The three-fourths baked kind involving an oozy, thick layer of pure fudge.

Fuck, I wanted the brownie.

I wanted her.

Apparently, my cock didn't care about what she said in the hallway earlier, because it rose with every passing second in her presence.

"You're not supposed to share baked goods in the dorm," I told her, looking away from the brownie to re-establish my resolve. "Someone could have an allergy."

"Are you allergic to chocolate, eggs, or nuts?"

"No."

"What about love?" She tipped her head to the side and stared me down with her dark lily-pad-green eyes. "Are you allergic to love?"

"Deathly."

She let out a small laugh but covered the brownie with the napkin again and started moving it away from me. "Well, I guess I better just take this, then...."

"You can leave it," I answered a little too quickly. "On the dresser. You can leave it there; I'll dispose of it later."

She was still grinning at me like we were best friends, giggling over a shared secret.

Danger, danger, echoed in my head. "Stop looking at me like that," I said.

She ignored me and plopped the brownie onto my dresser before she trailed farther inside my room, invading my space. "I'm Allie, by the way." Allie. My eyes followed her every movement.

Allie's legs made me forget to breathe. They were the things of fantasies. Bordering on the line of thick and thin. If I wrapped them around my waist, those legs would have the strength to latch on and stay there. I wanted to toss her on my bed, spread those legs, and lick her until she screamed —*No.*

Off. Limits.

She picked up my agenda from my desk, oblivious to my arousal from watching her breathe. "Wow, you already have the first month of assignments on this thing? Color-coded?"

"Not that I have to explain myself to you, but I like to be prepared."

She walked over to me and did not stop until her honey and roses scent claimed every particle of oxygen my lungs had access to. At every inhale, I breathed her in.

Up close, everything clicked. Allie was a provocative mermaid with her long reddish hair, her big seaweed-green eyes, her soft yet fierce face, and her succulent curves. A fucking siren.

The siren bent over and put her face close to my back-side. "I don't see anything stuck up there, but maybe—" I pushed her hand away when she went to cradle the back pocket of my jeans.

"No touching," I said, taking a few steps away from her.

She inched in front of me again. Her palm drifted to my chest, trailing down. A light caress, heavy with promises of loud whispers and soft skin. "You're *very* good-looking," she whispered as if *she* was the one entranced.

It was definitely me.

The warmth of her hand through the fabric of my shirt had my blood humming in my veins. When her nails dug into me, my blood switched from humming to operatic singing.

I did not have the willpower to take her hand off of me, but I managed to get out in a strained voice, "What did I just say about touching?" She disobeyed a direct order. No one ever went against my word. No one.

She pursed her full, succulent lips. "I didn't see a rule about touching in the handbook."

"Then you didn't read it." There were many rules about touching. Public displays of affection were frowned upon for multiple reasons. But public displays with the RA? Forbidden.

And yet, watching her stand in my room filled me with all the dirty thoughts of what else we could be doing in there. She looked so good; it was almost scary. I felt like a starving person smelling baked cinnamon rolls for the first time. I was already on edge, and she kept a constant push at my back to fall off the cliff of temptation.

Allie bent over again, surveying something in my room, and the back of her dress lifted, revealing more creamy skin.

I groaned and let my fisted hands drop in front of me, trying to block my rising erection from her gaze. She turned and stood close, her eyes focused on my face while my body focused on her proximity. How was I supposed to calm the rapid beat of my heart when she was still within touching distance?

"I don't have a habit of reading instructions or rule books," she said.

"Do you have a habit of diving into shallow pools and using power tools without safety goggles?" With the last ounce of my self-control, I moved backward to place more space between us. "Rules exist because they need to."

"Why are people not allowed to make popcorn?"

"Because it's one of the rules." And because the smell permeated the entire hallway and hung there like sweaty gym socks for two days before dissipating.

She tilted her head, exposing more of the neck I kept imagining kissing. A red mark caught my eye. Did she have a hickey? Why did that make me so fucking furious? Who was the guy she'd allowed to mark her, and what was his greatest fear so I could exploit it?

"But why?" she asked.

I had forgotten everything but the hickey. "Why what?"

"Why have rules? Life is short and full of uncertainties. Why not live every moment doing what you want to do?" she asked.

Because life was not about doing what someone wanted to do. It was about living. And living was about money.

She peered around my room again before jumping three fucking feet off the ground, backward, onto my bed. She wrinkled the sheets beneath her, making a mattress angel like a kid might do in fresh snow. "Comfy," she said, rolling around and covering my bed in her addicting scent.

I gaped. Half in medically diagnosed shock. "You're on my bed," I said like a genius narrator. What was I supposed to say or do? This woman tossed and turned in my bed, the same bed I would sleep in, dreaming about her at night.

A normal person did not jump onto a stranger's bed. Who *was* she?

Her dress rode up her legs from her actions as she tangled herself in my sheets. "Get off," I told her, my voice strained from shock and need. Typically, when I brought women to my room, my voice stayed cool and even. Typically, the women did not push back or give me lip the way Allie did.

She grinned; her hair sprawled over my pillow. Now it would smell like her. "Make me."

I wanted to. I wanted to make her moan, scream, come with my name on her lips—

Fuck.

She was wild. I did not *do* wild. "Seriously, get up."

"What?" she teased. "Am I breaking a rule?"

"Several."

"Good." She stopped rolling and sat up on my bed. "I'm worried about the way you're living. You seem to have an obsession with rules, and don't even get me started on that color-coded calendar of yours. I think we should go do something fun together."

I scoffed. "I have fun."

"You have every dinner scheduled at five o'clock. Elderly women eat later than you."

"Thanks," I mumbled.

"Look, Control Freak—"

"My name is Nate," I said. "Nate Reddington." I paused, waiting for her big reaction. But she remained silent. No recognition lit her eyes. "Of *the* Reddingtons."

"As I was saying, Control Freak, I, Allie of *the* Parsers, am a psychology major and, therefore, take responsibility for helping push people in the right direction. I think I can help you."

"Help me?" I questioned, and she nodded. "And what is it you think I need help with?"

"I think you need to throw out your schedule and live a little. With the walls you're putting up right now, I'd say you have some issues you need to work out. You also seem to be pushing me away for some reason."

"Get out of my room."

The change in my tone caught her attention. She got up from my bed and stared at me. "I think you're pushing me away because you know I see through that icy rule-abiding exterior you put up, and you're scared of living without everything planned out."

"I'm pushing you away because you just insinuated I need therapy." I opened my door for her to leave. "You don't even know me. Don't assume you know what's best for me."

Her cheery attitude slipped away, and now she stood there with an analyzing expression, trying to read me. "Fine," she said, finally making her way to my door. "I'll go, but I think I can help you."

"I don't need your *help*."

She grinned. "Oh, this is going to be fun."

DORM MANUAL RULE #5: NO LOUD MUSIC

llie:

"First day," I said to myself and pulled a yellow and orange dress from my closet. Bright colors were calming, after all. "You're going to be fine."

My roommate Marissa had slept at her boyfriend's house off-campus and therefore was not exposed to my rambling to myself. She said she would spend most nights with him. After asking her why she bothered to pay for a dorm room she wouldn't use, she just laughed, answering the question of whether she was a rich kid or here on a scholarship.

Anxiety nibbled at me as I walked to my first college class. In psychology; my favorite topic. This was why I was here. I wanted to get my degree so I could help people.

Walking into the lecture hall, my gaze zoomed in on an

open seat in the second row. I grabbed the seat and got out my notebook.

"Hello, and welcome to Introduction to Psychology," the professor said, her harsh eyes scanning the crowd. "If you don't find the scientific study of human behavior and the mind to be interesting, you are in the wrong class. If you are looking for an easy grade, you are in the wrong class."

A random guy next to me let out a deep sigh which I assumed meant he was not interested in psychology and was definitely looking for an easy grade.

Within the first ten minutes, we had a pop quiz.

The professor collected the quizzes with a smile that screamed, *I bet half of you failed this.* "I'll grade these by next class. Before we start the main lecture today, I also want to inform you about the final paper." Pens clicked and papers shuffled in a rush, as if the information on the final was the most important thing she would say all day. "You will choose someone you know to analyze. You need to describe their personality, what holds them back, what motivates them, what—using actual scientific terms from the textbook—they want to achieve, and how their mind works. This is not a fun, personality-and-background paper on a close friend. This needs to be a real, serious analysis. Don't choose someone you're not willing to dissect."

While other students in the class groaned, I smiled from ear to ear. This was what I already did in my normal daily life. Analyze, diagnose, and then find a way to help. I was Jane Austen's *Emma* but with more psychology, less match-making, and less delusion. I wanted to help people. The most recent subject of my attention? Nate Reddington.

Nate's extensive calendar agenda was a cry for help, and

my ear pressed to the floor, trying to hear what real issue laid beneath it all.

I knew it was rooted in fear. People pursued control over things when they feared those things could harm them. Or when they feared being controlled and thus attempted to control everything else around them. Either way, what Nate had was not permanent. I could fix him. Restoring his sense of control in his personal life would allow him to drop his need for rules and have some fun.

I would need to learn more, watch him, and be around him, but I could fight my attraction and be unbiased. Nate would be the subject of my science and not my affections. He was perfect for this paper.

I just had to get him to open up and be in the same room as me. Easy peasy lemon febreezy.

ᚦᚦᚦ

"So what do you guys know about Nate?" I asked the three girls who had complained to me about the dorm rulebook the previous day.

The blonde, Jennifer, had invited me to join them for dinner at the campus dining hall. I had maturely held back my scream of *"Yes!"* and settled for a *"Sure, that'd be great."* As much as I wanted to get started on figuring out Nate's real issues, I also wanted friends. Needed friends. Loneliness was the deadliest poison known to happiness.

"Other than that he's fucking hot?" Mackenzie, a redhead with a red-hot mouth who loved vinegar on her fries, snorted. Those were the few traits I picked up about her in the twenty minutes of knowing her.

Jennifer shoved her. "He's not that hot."

"Again, you're just upset he wouldn't go out with you," Sheila added.

Jennifer gave her a death glare before gazing back over at me with hesitancy. "Why do you want to learn about Nate?"

"I think he's going to be my new project."

She blinked. "Project?"

"Have you ever read the book *Emma?*" I asked her. "Or seen *My Fair Lady?*"

"You're going to Pygmalion him?" Sheila gaped.

Jennifer squinted. "What?"

"I'm going to study him for a psychology research paper. I mean, his control issues are..." I blew out a loud breath. "And while I study him, I'm going to get him to loosen up a little. Have some fun."

Jennifer still stared at me uneasily while stealing one of Mackenzie's fries. "Are you trying to date him or something?"

"Oh, no." I shook my head as fast as a wet dog drying off. "Our relationship would be professional as a psychologist and patient. I was going through a hard time last year and someone helped me through it. I want to be that person for him."

"But *why?*" Jennifer asked.

Why? I felt...connected to Nate. I saw myself in him. The difference was he embraced control, and I preferred chaos to distract myself from my issues. "Do you know anything about him I could use in my paper?"

"What is there to say about him?" Sheila sipped her coffee. "He's Nate *Reddington.*"

"Why do you keep saying his name like that? With more emphasis on Reddington?"

"Because he's Nate *Reddington*. You know, of *the* Reddingtons."

No bells rang. "I assume they're special somehow?"

"Have you been living under a rock? They're billionaires. Nate became a millionaire at age ten."

I did not follow money. In fact, I avoided any traces of it on purpose. "Hmm." A rich kid who feared being controlled or lacking control?

"He is honestly perfect: perfect GPA, perfect good looks, perfect income, and trust fund. I mean, damn, what I wouldn't give..." Sheila stopped when Jennifer again gave her a freezing and seething look.

"He's a jerk too," Jennifer added.

To me, his jerk-ness was not real and instead represented a wall he put up to keep others away. He had an air about him of cold professionalism, much like a bitter, old Wall Street businessman.

Sheila giggled at Jennifer. "Yeah, but that's his whole *thing*, you know?"

How did she know it was a defense mechanism? Reading people was my thing. "What do you mean?" I asked.

"He's a dom. Like the cold, self-centered, dom type. So hot."

Not what I was fishing for. Sheila took my silence as a question to know more about Nate's sex life.

"You do know what dom means, right?"

It seemed I was not going to get out of this talk. "Dominant."

"I heard he handcuffed this girl to his bed last year for a

full day. Every time he came back into the room after classes and such, he would fool around with her and keep her stimulated. Then, that night, they finally had sex, and she orgasmed for like an hour—"

"Ahh," I shrieked and put my hands over my ears. An immature move but, God, I couldn't hear anymore. Everything she said added to a fantasy I did not need in my life. I could not help but imagine being the one handcuffed to Nate's bed. No. *No, Allie.* He would be the subject of my paper. I had to stay unbiased.

"I know!" She took my discomfort to mean I wanted to hear even more. "A couple of us tried to get with him last semester, but he doesn't sleep with his residents. It's one of his rules."

Jennifer jumped in with more Nate knowledge. "You know how he handed out rules for the dorm? Well, he has a whole other list of rules for himself. I bet he has it printed on his walls somewhere."

She was wrong there. My eyes had taken in everything there was to see on the surface of Nate's room. Maybe I needed another visit.

"Do you know anything that's on it?"

Mackenzie snorted again. "Nate's a fucking mystery. The only rule we know is he never stays out later than ten o'clock at night."

"So he lives life like it's a planned calendar and never loses control." I summarized all I had gotten from them. "He sounds like a robot."

I would help him lose control and *live* life. I would not go near his sex life, but I could help him be a bit more spontaneous. A smile stretched my lips as I thought about making him lose control.

"Robot, huh?" Sheila giggled. "Well, I have it on good authority that the man is a *machine*."

❦❦❦

I SHOULD NOT HAVE BEEN GRINNING, but my lips refused to uncurl themselves as I turned on my music in my room that night. I wanted to draw Nate out. Mess with the bull and get the horns. I told myself it was because I needed to learn more about him for my paper. The loud knocking on my door a minute after the first song started playing made me smile so hard, it hurt.

I opened the door, feigning surprise. "Control freak."

He already pinched the bridge of his nose, a habit of his. Anticipating my difficultness? How interesting. "Allie."

His dark hair hung down in front of his piercing blue eyes, and I wanted to push it back, out of his beautiful face. His new black shirt fit him well. Really well. Still would have looked better on the floor, though.

"What brings you over, neighbor? Need to borrow a cup of sugar?" I walked farther inside my room, gesturing for him to follow. I bent over and cracked open the fridge. "Would you like a drink?" I listed what I had. "Coffee?" He glared at me. "Tea?" I could not help myself. "Me?"

"No loud music. Rule number—"

"Five," I finished for him.

His eyes widened. Impressed with my knowledge of the rules? "Look, apparently we're neighbors who share a wall, and I'm extremely busy and cannot even begin to focus when I can't hear myself think."

"Maybe that's a good thing," I commented. He appeared insulted, so I explained myself, "Sometimes it's good to not be able to think. There's a peace in silence and in chaos." *Don't worry, I'll show you.*

"Lower your music. This is the last time I'm going to ask."

"You've been asking this whole time?" A genuine chuckle rose from deep in my chest. "You do know questions and demands are two different things?" Maybe this demanding side also came from his wealthy background. A bit spoiled, Mr. Reddington?

A moment passed as he just stared at me like I was crazy. "Why are you not following the rules?"

"Why are you always enforcing them?" I stepped closer to him. *Okay, Allie. Time to learn some information.* "I've heard you even have rules for yourself. Want to share them?"

"Why are you doing this?" he rasped, frustrated. It appeared he had never had someone question his methods. He had probably also heard the word "yes," and never "why." Well, I would have fun teaching him. Poor guy.

"I want to learn more about you," I explained.

"To use against me?"

"No." I tilted my head and analyzed him. "Is that why you're so jaded? Someone once got close and learned too much?" He was in college; how could he have so much experience in being duped? A bit of guilt trickled into me as I tried to find out more for a paper. Then again, I did this to help him. Once both of us revealed his bigger issue, he could move on to live a happier and healthier life. "Oh, have you ever been blackmailed?"

"Stop it," he grated, his expression darkening.

"What?"

He stepped forward, closing in on me, until his breath caressed my cheek. "Stop trying to figure me out," he said against my ear, and little shocks of electricity shot down my neck. He smelled like apples. A sexy fruit salad. "I'm not some subject for your amusement."

"Good, because I'm not amused by you." I was aroused by him, but that was a whole other matter.

He leaned away from me and met my gaze. "Turn your music down."

"Tell me why you have so many rules."

He scowled, offering no response.

I turned down the volume on my speakers until it was audible as a low background tone. He nodded at my doing what he asked and spun around to leave.

"I did what you wanted. Aren't you going to answer one of my questions?"

He stood very still. With my music quieted, I could almost make out the sound of his breathing in my small room. Then he said, one hand on the doorknob, eyes on his exit, "Some things aren't meant to be broken."

DORM MANUAL RULE #8: BE FRIENDLY TO YOUR NEIGHBORS

llie:

"I LOVE YOU, ALLIE," Logan whispered in my ear, his arms wrapping around my waist. It felt so natural, so familiar, and yet so utterly wrong. "We belong together. Don't you see that?" I wanted to shout "no" but my mouth wouldn't open.

A noise erupted from the back of my throat as I fought to push myself away from him. My struggle did nothing. He held on tight.

"Just don't leave." His fingernails dug into my arms. "Please, don't leave. If you leave, I don't know what I'll—"

My body jolted awake from the dream. I blinked again and again until I saw I lay in my dorm room. *Deep breath.* The dreams had started again. Hadn't I locked Logan out of my mind? Four successful months of sleep without a nightmare. So why now?

I thought I had moved on. I thought I had adjusted. I thought I had healed.

Envisioning a safe in my mind, I pushed thoughts of Logan into it, locking it and throwing away the key.

Instead of dwelling, I rushed into clothes and speed walked to my first class of women's history. What I found there shocked me more than my reoccurring nightmare.

"No fucking way," he mumbled as I sat next to him.

Who knew Nate Reddington of *the* Reddingtons would be in my women's history class?

Talking to him served as the perfect distraction from my rough morning.

He looked *good*. His dark, form-fitting shirt stretched over muscles, firm pecs, and strong biceps. My mouth watered at the sight of him. His hair had a sexy disheveled look to it like someone had been running her fingers through it all morning. The thought of someone else touching his hair left a sour taste in my mouth.

I tried to suppress my smile when he saw me and glared. What was the first rule of college classes? Sit next to people, you know? I chose the seat right next to him. He was too fascinating to stay away from.

The way a vein in his forehead popped out in anger after I put my binder down was far too amusing. How was he so annoyed by me? Yes, I pushed his buttons, but for scientific reasons. Not that he knew that.

He drew me to him like a chemist to a newfound element.

I nodded at him. "Control freak." My relaxed state seemed to cause him more agitation.

"Red," he called me through his grinding teeth.

My eyebrows rose. "Red?" The tips of my hair were dyed

red, and I wore the color often, but was it enough to warrant a nickname? "Because when you see me your heart beats faster?"

"Excuse me?"

If I was "Red," then he was a bull, and I would have fun playing with him. "I'm trying to understand the nickname. A fact about red is that when people see it, it can often cause an increase in heart rate."

"That's not what I meant—"

"Or maybe you've taken Russian, in which case you would know that red contains the root word for beautiful, and you would be complimenting me on my physical appearance."

"Stop."

"Ah, you called me Red because it reminds you of a stop sign?"

"Got it, no more nicknames." He sighed and picked up his pen as if he were impatient for the class to start so he would not have to continue speaking to me. "I will call you Allie and nothing else."

I pouted my lips. His gaze dropped to them before meeting my eyes again. "Well, that's no fun."

"Neither am I. If you're looking for a more entertaining classmate to sit next to, I suggest choosing someone else."

"I find you very entertaining," I said. He shot me a look of disbelief. "I do."

"Sure." Nate sounded doubtful.

Interesting. He was insecure about his interpersonal skills? Was that why he continued attempting to push me away? "Do you have friends?" I asked.

He twitched in his seat at my bluntness. "Excuse me?"

I added, "I think you distance yourself from other people." I related to that.

"I have friends." He appeared offended. "More than you."

"I've started making some."

He huffed under his breath. "Jennifer and the others aren't good friends to make."

"What does that mean?"

"If you're smart, you'll stay away and find real friends."

What about Jennifer, Sheila, and Mackenzie was not real? "Are you saying that because being around Jennifer makes you uncomfortable after you rejected her?"

His fingers tightened around his pen, but no change occurred on his face. "I reject a lot of people."

"Not me."

I knocked my knee against him, and his body jumped at the small contact. He positioned himself away from me. "An RA can't be with one of his residents."

"If you weren't an RA, would you reject me?"

He cracked one of his knuckles. Trying to relieve some pressure? "I don't date."

"Is that one of your rules?"

He shook his head and glanced up at the ceiling as if God himself would help him deal with me. "Has anyone ever told you that you lack boundaries?"

"Why put your personality in a cage if you wouldn't put your body in one?"

He paused. This time when he looked at me, mild respect lit up his eyes. "That was deep," he complimented me, and a surprising rush of pride and warmth claimed my body.

"Were you expecting shallow?"

31

"I expected not to be asked twenty questions so early in the morning."

I held my coffee cup over to him. "Want a sip?" After offering, my heart did little pitter-patters at the idea of an indirect kiss with him touching his lips where mine had been.

"Coffee is bad for you."

"Everything is a little bit bad for you." I sipped from it. His eyes followed my action, focusing on my lips as I licked the traces of coffee away.

He tore his gaze away from my mouth. "It's important to stay away from things that are bad for us."

"You say that like you think I'm bad for you."

"You purposefully played loud music just to mess with me."

"It was a good song though, right?"

Nate rolled his eyes and, for some strange reason, I found the passive-aggressive action sexy. "For a sophomore, you're very immature."

"I'm a freshman," I said.

His eyes widened again and dipped down to my cleavage. A quick moment passed before he realized what he did, and his gaze shot back up to meet my eyes. "You look older."

"I am older." He arched an eyebrow, and I continued, "I spent a year abroad."

He let out a laugh. A real one. Deep and throaty and... Wow. I wanted to record it and listen to it on a loop like the unprofessional person I was. "Now it all makes sense. You're one of *those* girls."

"Ohhhhh, tell me more," I said, intrigued. He thought he could analyze me better than I could analyze him?

"You're a 'finding yourself' girl."

"Sounds kinky," I teased. His eyes darkened. "And what is a 'finding yourself' girl?" I asked.

"The same kind of girl who can't make up her mind on where she wants to eat dinner or what she wants to do with her life. The kind of girl who doesn't plan things the way things should be planned." He broke eye contact and spun his pen in his hand. "Let me guess, you went abroad for a year to soak up the culture and become more rounded, but instead just sharpened your edges with some nice photos for social media. You probably have some impulsive tattoo of an ex-boyfriend's name or a Japanese symbol you don't know the meaning of. You probably still use the word YOLO as an excuse to do whatever you want whenever you want. And you distract yourself by focusing on the flaws of others so you don't have time to see your own."

My mouth hung open. Nate may not have been able to guess what caused me to be all those things, but his accuracy was scary. Not only did I have a Japanese symbol tattoo, but I also had a YOLO tattoo. And now I couldn't stop wanting to show it to him to see his reaction.

Instead of dwelling on how he had summarized me in a thin nutshell, I changed the subject to his issues. "I bet you have the next twenty years of your life planned out."

He shot back with a small smile, "Twenty-five."

We exchanged a soft moment between us, where the lights in the room grew brighter and the air stilled. A split second passed where his expression remained unguarded.

His phone buzzed from his pocket, and he frowned, pulling it out. The screen flashed with an incoming call from

"Blueberry." Who the hell was Blueberry? Did she know her name was my favorite fruit and muffin?

His smile dropped, and he stood jerkily, getting up from the desk chair. "Take notes for me," he told me, about to press his phone to his ear and walk out of the class.

"I don't have a pen," I whisper-shouted after he hit the answer call button.

"One second," he told Blueberry over the phone and fixed his scowl of disbelief onto me. "You didn't bring a pen to the first day of class?"

"I'm a 'finding-myself girl,' remember?"

He tossed his pen at me and strode out. All I could catch from the phone conversation was, "Yeah, Blue, I'm here. Is everything okay?"

My new mission: to find out who this Blueberry was to Nate. My second: to stop feeling nauseous at the idea of him being with another woman who was not as lost as he was.

NATE'S #2 RULE FOR LIFE: BE FRIENDLY BUT NEVER FRIENDS

*N*ate:

IT WAS painful watching her look for a spot to sit for dinner in the dining hall. Jennifer and her posse had abandoned her the way I had seen them do with other freshman girls in the past. It did not help that her roommate Marissa was never around. The first week of classes came to an end, and Allie still sat by herself in the dining hall.

Watching her face crumple in hurt was almost enough to make me forget about why avoiding her was a good plan. I wanted to sit with her and answer her crazy questions and watch her grin like we had known each other our whole lives.

But I couldn't.

"Jeez, Nate, what's with the super angry face?" Joey, my

closest friend, asked me after stealing one of my mozzarella sticks.

"It's nothing."

Allie continued sitting by herself, looking like the poster child for loneliness. She was not only off-limits because I was her RA, but because she was my opposite in every way. We clashed more than we meshed. It was best to just stay away from her. *She's a finding herself girl.* I had no time for anyone who did not already know who they were.

Note to self: The goal for tomorrow is to not see or talk to or think about Allie. I had achieved harder goals in my lifetime. Going days without seeing people I knew was easy. Sure, Allie and I were neighbors who shared a wall and a history class, but that did not mean I had to see her every day. Not seeing her made not thinking about her easier and not thinking about her made everything else easier as a result.

But damn, her sitting by herself cut into me like a buttered up machete.

I needed to join her. My fingers grabbed my plate but, the next second I glanced back over at her, a guy sat down across from her. They talked, and she grinned like he was the funniest life form in the world. Who the hell was he?

"Seriously, what's up, man?" Joey broke through my inner turmoil. "You keep switching between sad and mad, and it's giving me whiplash."

"Do either of you know the guy in the checkered shirt?" I asked Joey and Ryan. Only then did Ryan look up from his phone and join our conversation.

The guy looked familiar and whatever he said caused her to laugh.

"I think he lives in our dorm," Joey said. Like me, Joey and Ryan were RAs for our dorm building.

"Better question: do either of you know who the girl in the red top is?" Ryan succeeded in making me more on edge than I already was.

"She's no one," I said.

They both squinted at her, and I ground my teeth, wanting to tear their gazes away from her.

Ryan shrugged. "Well, I think it's time I meet this Little Red Riding Hood."

Did he mean Allie? "She's not wearing a hood."

"Red top, reddish hair. It's hard to come up with nicknames on the spot. But damn, she looks good enough to eat."

"You need to move on to someone else." I warned him, "She lives in our building, and you know the rule about RAs and residents."

"I know that the taboo of it makes it hotter." Ryan nudged me with his elbow, and I scooted a bit away from him. He was a touchy person; I was not. "But I guess it's not as taboo if you're Nate Reddington. What does a millionaire care if he loses free housing and meals?"

Maybe the fact that *I* was not a millionaire. "Right." My father's current extracurricular was throwing out hush money like candy at a parade of people to keep the fraud, blackmail, and embezzlement rumors at bay. Being a member of the millionaire Reddington family was less glamorous than most thought. I had no money and one chance at escaping, and that was finishing school as an RA with all A's.

"Then again, you would never break one of the rules." Ryan sighed. "It'd make you too interesting." He stood up and took his half-empty plate with him.

"Where are you going?" I asked.

"I'm going to go talk to her."

Ryan walked over to Allie and the mystery guy, sat down, and had both of them laughing within seconds. A black hole formed in the pit of my stomach. How could he just start a conversation like that? Make her laugh like it was as easy as breathing?

Around her, even breathing was a difficult task to perform.

"What do you think they're talking about?" I questioned Joey, but he seemed uninterested.

I poked at the spaghetti on my plate, trying to eat, but my gaze kept falling back to Allie, Ryan, and the unknown male.

After about a minute, all three of them glanced over at me then turned back to continue their conversation. Alarm bells went off in my head. Were they talking about me? What were they saying? What was Allie saying?

My feet walked to her without my brain's permission. Joey's "Where are you going?" bounced right off me.

"Hey," I said when I landed in front of their table.

"Hey," they all replied.

Insert awkward silence here.

"What's up?" I asked.

"Eating since we're at a dining hall and all," Allie replied. "What's up with you, Nate?" *At least she stopped calling me a control freak.*

"You two know each other already?" Ryan asked.

I answered, "We met on the first day when she said I had a stick up my—"

"Up his ass," Allie finished for me, with no shame in her tone.

"You said that to him? To Nate Reddington?" Ryan's eyes went so wide, they threatened to fall out of the sockets. "Is this what love feels like?"

"I think you're my RA," mystery boy said.

Typically, I made it a point to know all of my residents. The fact that I could not put his face to a name showed how much Allie distracted me. "I'm Nate."

"Gavin."

Allie smiled up at me. "I followed your advice and made two new friends."

Male friends. "Fun."

"Why don't you join us? Four is a party after all," Gavin said.

"Do you party at all, Nate?" Allie cocked her head at me with a thoughtful expression. "What kind of drunk are you?"

"Excuse me?"

Ryan answered for me, "Nate never gets *drunk* drunk. I think once I saw him semi-drunk. He just went around dancing like a lunatic and kissing every girl he saw."

"Caveman drunk, huh?" Allie's green eyes sparkled with amusement. "Did he grunt a lot too?"

"Like tequila took away his whole vocabulary."

"This is not an appropriate conversation." I regretted my words when Allie appeared disappointed.

"You chugging gin that night wasn't appropriate either," Ryan joked. I elbowed him. She was going to think I was an alcoholic.

"Tequila and gin?" Her expression scrunched in shock. "Why did you drink so much that night?"

"He gets worked up every time his dad calls—" I elbowed

Ryan harder than before, knocking the air out of him. It was not his job to tell her my business.

"I've got to go—" The ringing of my cell phone cut me off. After a glance at the screen, I waved goodbye and answered it while walking away.

"Nate?" my twelve-year-old sister's voice was quiet over the phone. I strained to hear her as I walked through the loud dining hall toward the exit.

"Is everything okay? What's wrong?" Blue never called me. It was always the other way around.

"Yeah, you just didn't call yesterday, and I got worried," she said. "You call every day."

"Sorry, Blue, something urgent came up and once it was over, it was too late to call you." The warm August air wafted over my face when I walked out of the dining hall.

"Mom says hi," Blue lied to spare my feelings. Of the few things our mother said to her children, a "hello" was not one of them.

I changed the subject from our parents because, my, what a rabbit hole to fall down. "How did your math test go?"

"I aced it." Her smile was as audible as it was contagious. "Just like you said I would."

"You studied hard. You deserved it." She deserved everything. "What did you have to eat today?"

There was a pause. "Um, ravioli."

"Fresh or from a can?"

She hesitated again. "A can."

"And what did you have yesterday?"

"Ravioli."

Damn it. "What happened to the money I sent you to spend on fresh vegetables?"

"Mom found it in the mail before I could open it."

Damn. It. After the decrease in money coming in and an increase in money going out, the Reddington family was a mess. My mother had lost the maid and the cook, but she was not willing to learn how to do those household tasks herself. My father never visited the house anymore, so he was even more of a lost cause. Blue was stuck in that empty mansion for another year until I graduated, found a job, and sent the adoption papers in. I wanted to have her move in with me in the dorm, but if my boss found out, I'd lose my ticket to graduation and everything else would fall apart.

"I'll send more money soon, so make sure to watch the mailman. You need to start eating meals that don't involve a microwave."

"We had pizza last week."

Jesus. "That's not real food, Blue." My sister needed protein, fruits, and dark, leafy greens.

"I know." She let out a long breath. "I wish you were here."

"Me too." Even calling her once a day was not enough for me. She was the only person in my life who knew everything and understood. "I'd make you a grilled cheese and broccoli."

"I hate broccoli."

I chuckled. "You *think* you hate broccoli because it's been ingrained in you to reject anything healthy." A squirrel ran in my path, chasing another one up a tree. "Maybe you could try to eat dinner at a friend's house for the next few days."

"Mom doesn't like to be alone."

Mom did not like a lot of things. "You're too good to her." The woman refused to learn how to work an oven so her twelve-year-old daughter could eat. "Study hard for your history quiz next week, okay?"

"I will. Love you, Nate."

"I love you, Blue," I said, and she hung up.

I just had to graduate, get a job, and everything would fall into place after that. No more distractions. No more Allie.

❡❡❡

As I studied late that night, sound traveled through Allie's wall and into my room. She seemed to be talking on the phone, so I did my best not to listen and invade her privacy. Our dorm building lacked the normal cinderblocks, so the thin walls did nothing to keep noise out. That was half the reason Allie's loud music drove me insane. The other half was because it was *her*.

"...and new friend...Gavin...miss France and you..."

As I stared at the page in front of me, I willed myself to absorb the written words, but my ears kept honing in on her conversation. It was wrong to listen when she did not know, but I had no choice. From what I gathered of context clues, she talked to someone she knew from her time abroad in France.

"...RA...Nate..."

My head shot up at the words. Was she talking about me? Did it matter? Of course not—

"...he's so..."

So *what?* I put my book down and scooted my chair closer to the wall.

"...rules. It's annoying. He has some issues...help him..."

Excuse me? I was the one with issues? She was the one obsessed with me. How dare she judge me—

"…but so hot…"

I moved closer, not pressing my ear against the wall but also not *not* pressing it against the wall.

"…the kind of attractive…legitimately question whether or not he could be human…looks like a freaking Greek god."

This was wrong. I should not have been listening in like this.

"…Nate is hotter than a third-degree burn…but he's my… and he's frustrating." There was a sound like a laugh. "Yes, sexually frustrating too…Oh trust me, I'd love to jump him in the hallway, tear off his clothes, and—"

I slammed my book closed against my desk, and she stopped talking.

There was a brief moment of silence before she asked, "Nate, can you hear me?"

I knocked my knuckles against her wall, once for "yes."

"Oh, shit."

DORM MANUAL RULE #9: NO POPPING POPCORN IN THE COMMUNAL MICROWAVE

llie:

THE WORD *EMBARRASSED* DID NOT COME close to describing how I felt. Mortified came close, but not close enough. How much of my conversation with my French friend Eliza had he heard? The parts about his issues with control and pushing people away? My plans to help him? Or the small part of the conversation where I told her he turned me on more than anyone else I had ever met? Oh, God.

I buried my face in my hands. I had said things to make him think my mouth watered every time I saw him. Did it? Yes, but he still did not need to know that.

Wait.

Why was I so embarrassed? My thoughts were a natural reaction. Hell, being attracted to him was the most natural thing I had felt in a while. Liking—Finding Nate visually pleasing was healthy for me. I should not be ashamed.

This was ridiculous. I would not hide. The stuff Nate heard me say was not terrible. Well, not the end of the world at least. It would be fine. I would be fine. And he knew he was hot. He must hear it all the time. It was not like I *liked* Nate. I did not like him. He interested me because of his apparent issues. He was a psychological subject I was curious to study.

He is a frog. I am a dissector. I had no interest in kissing frogs, anyway.

I got up and knocked on Nate's door before I had time to think it through. I should have thought it through.

"Why were you listening anyway—" I cut off when he opened the door because his unarmed expression surprised me. Why did he look so...off balance?

His eyes dropped, and I looked down.

Ah, yes, my pajamas.

I had not been planning on seeing anyone else for the night, so I had slipped into my pale purple silk nightgown, which was a bit—a lot—more revealing than my normal pajama pants and an old T-shirt. The sheer material glistened in the dim fluorescents of the hallway.

A pained groan came from him.

The short fabric did nothing to hide the expanse of my bare legs, and a rush of warmth spread through me as his eyes locked onto them. Nate seemed to love my legs because he was looking at them like they were juicy sausages. *Let me find some mustard, and you can get set on devouring me.*

"A little under-dressed, aren't you, Miss Parser?" Was icy Nate teasing me? Interesting.

"I like nightgowns," I said, and his gaze still did not meet mine. I cleared my throat, and he blushed, looking up. "They're comfortable."

"Looks comfortable." The amount of mischief in his eyes shocked me. His mischievous side was a well-hidden secret. I liked it.

"Don't look so smug," I said, but I liked his smugness all the same.

"Being hotter than a third-degree burn shouldn't make me smug?"

His familiar words rang in my ears. Hotter than a third-degree burn. Those were the same words I had used to describe him to Eliza. I had hoped he had not heard that part.

"That was a personal conversation."

"About me."

Did he think this gave him power over me now? Screw this tension. "I find you extremely fucking sexy," I admitted.

His smirk fell off the face of the earth as he stumbled back a bit. This turn of direct honesty seemed to be the last thing he expected. "Um…"

"Is that what you want to hear?" I took a step into his room, and he inched back. Electricity sparked up my skin. I breathed in the new heavy atmosphere. "You want to know how I feel about you?"

"N-No." His gaze fell from my eyes to my chest, to my legs, before jumping back up again. "I didn't mean to eavesdrop."

"When I look at your hair, I want to pull it." A lion stalking in on a gazelle, I moved. The tip of my fuzzy slipper brushed against him, but I wanted more than a light touch.

"When I look at your eyes, I want to see them roll back, hazy with lust." His back hit his wall, and I stopped right in front of him. "When I look at your lips, I want to bruise them with mine."

He tried to keep his eyes off me by staring at his ceiling, but his control slipped. "Why are you telling me this?"

"Because I don't believe in keeping things inside," I said against his chin, unable to make contact with his lips unless he bent down. My lips brushed against his short stubble, like a sexy rug burn. "Keep things inside for too long and you'll explode." My hand settled over his chest. Over his fast-beating heart. "Do you feel ready to explode, Nate?"

His heavy breathing hit my forehead as his eyes zeroed in on my lips. His head tilted to mine but stopped before making contact. He hovered there. The smell of apples berating my senses. A moment of silence and loud blood rushed to my ears. One of his large, warm hands came up and covered mine on top of his hard chest. "You need to go," he said.

"But you don't want me to, do you?" I asked. His smug-ness vanished. I took it for my own. The sexual power felt incredible. It was the first time his walls experienced some crumbling. "I guess someone isn't the dom everyone thought he was."

He blinked, his tense expression turning to one of anger as he glared down at me. "What did you just say?" The new intensity in his gaze caused a slight tremor in my spine. The electricity in the air shifted. He had yanked the power from me and awarded it back to himself.

"I-I said I guess you're not the dom—"

My back hit the wall in a surprise turn of events. He had

somehow picked me up by my waist and pivoted me so I was the one trapped, with him standing in front of me, in mere seconds.

"You want me to dominate you?" He thrust against me, pressing me harder into the wall. His hands swiped down my arms, taking my fingers and pulling them up over my head. He planted a palm over my two wrists, holding them there. Caging me. Making me his prisoner. "Is this what you want?" The hot, straining bulge below his waist nudged my stomach, and I forgot any other reason I was there with him other than to feel this. To let my guard down and *feel*. "Is this what you want?" he repeated in a hard voice, matching the hardness grinding against me.

My jaw fell when my entire body went up in flames for him, and I strained to breathe out, "*Yes.*"

"You break the rules just because you secretly want to be punished, don't you? You want to drive me crazy. You want me to lose control with you?" he rasped, his eyes narrowed on my bottom lip, which I nibbled. "That's all this is to you? A game?"

His choppy breath wafted over my face, warming me. I craned my neck up to eliminate the distance between our lips, but his hold denied me the pleasure. "W-What?"

"I'm getting really fucking tired of you teasing me, Allie Parser."

The way he said my full name in his gruff, frustrated manner caused another full-body shudder. "Y-You cussed again."

"Oh, I can do more than cuss. And I bet you want to know what more I can do. I bet you didn't know you wanted to be pressed up against a wall until just this moment, did you?"

He was right about that.

"I bet you didn't know you wanted to be pinned and vulnerable to me, to whatever I want to do to you." He leaned farther down, dragging his lips against my chin just like I had done to his. When I turned my head to catch his mouth with mine, he pulled away just enough so I could not reach him. "I bet your nipples are puckering for my mouth right now. I bet if I suck one, your hips will start bucking for me. Me. Because you know I am the only one here who can give you pleasure like that."

Gain back your power. Your ground. "You're not the *only* one who can give me pleasure."

He straightened and moved my arms back down in front of us despite my protesting whimper. His hot lips brushed over my fingertips, burning the flesh. "Have you been touching yourself in your room, Allie? Thinking about me?"

Hell yes, I had been. "No."

"Because knowing you've been touching yourself in the room next to mine—a wall between us—would do some things to the remainder of my self-control. Some things that can't afford to happen."

"What kind of things?" *Be graphic, please.*

He grunted. "Get out of my room before I show you."

I tilted my head up, refusing to back down. "What if I said I want you to show me?"

"You don't," he replied, letting me go and taking a step back, away from me. Why? The heat from his expression faded as he tried to hide it from me, but his eyes were still as stormy as ever.

"I do."

"You need to stop teasing me, talking about me, and trying to figure me out," he said. "I'm getting tired of it."

"I'm not teasing you."

"Stop pushing me, Allie. I mean it," he growled. "You don't want to know what I'll do."

If I don't push you, who will? He needed a push; this interaction proved it. He had all that sensual energy locked up inside him, burning away? He needed an outlet. Not that I would be his outlet for him to plunge—plug—into. I just wanted to help him. Write a paper about him.

So why did it hurt not to kiss him?

He waved me to his door, escorting me out with a dominant, warm hand on my back. Sparks shot through my blood, hissing in my veins. "Try not to dream about me tonight."

When he shut his door behind my back, I whispered, "I'll definitely try."

☃ ☃ ☃

MY THOUGHTS REELED for days over Nate's hot words and even hotter body. Who knew I would be into being dominated? My personality was fire, not a malleable substance but one that burned if someone brave enough attempted to touch it. Nate seemed to know my needs better than I did.

Yet he was blind to his own. He needed to explode. Sexually and emotionally. I could help him in the emotion department.

No crossing the sexual line.

I wanted to touch him again, that was clear, but this was

practice for my future years as a therapist. This was for a grade in my psychology class.

"Where are you right now?" Gavin asked me. He had eaten dinner with me for the past few days after introducing himself in the dining hall. Now we sat for lunch.

Stop thinking about Nate and enjoy this new friendship.

Ever since being forgotten and dumped by Jennifer, Sheila, and Mackenzie, I had been craving companionship. A part of me blamed Nate for why I was not friends with the girls, but a deeper part of me knew he was right: I needed real friends. Gavin seemed like he could be a real friend. "So what did you do last night?" I asked.

His short blond hair hinted at his sunshine personality almost as much as his infectious lazy smile and dimples. His soft brown eyes focused on me as he replied, "Nothing. You?"

Other than embarrass myself in front of and then half-seduce Nate, only to be seduced by him? "Nothing."

We nodded at each other and ate more of our ham sandwiches. "Are we boring people?" I asked.

"What? No. We just don't party."

"Hey, I party," I defended myself, but it was a loose claim.

"New friends," a male voice shouted before Ryan sat next to me at our lunch table. "This should be a new eating tradition."

"It was a new eating tradition," Gavin said. "The tradition was not going to involve you."

The two teased each other with banter after finding out the day before that they had attended the same high school. "You think I'll let you keep Allie all to yourself?" Ryan asked. "I proclaimed my love for her a few days ago after finding out Nate is scared of her."

That piqued my interest. "What do you mean Nate is scared of me?"

"Don't take offense," Ryan said. "He's scared of most women."

"Yeah, why is he so…" Gavin started but did not finish.

"He's just strung tight. If you ask me, he needs a good fuc—" Ryan looked at me and backpedaled his sentence. "Fun. He needs some fun."

"I'm not a little girl; you don't have to edit yourself around me."

And I would give him a good fu—

"Nate is always telling me I need to cut back on the cussing," Ryan said.

Nate cusses when he is turned on. Hypocrite. "Cussing is healthy," I informed him. "It releases certain chemicals in the brain to calm people down."

Gavin grinned at me and said to Ryan, "She's a psychology major."

"Hot."

My friendships with Gavin and Ryan grew each day. We ate together, hung out together, and popped popcorn together. Ryan was an RA who lived two floors above us in the same building, and Gavin lived a couple of rooms away from me on the same level. They became the closest friends I had at Beckett University.

⚡⚡⚡

"Damn," Gavin yelled when his game character died for the third time. "Why do I keep dying?"

Both of us liked to distract each other from the other's

homework, so we had started visiting each other's rooms. We laid back on Gavin's huge beanbag chair as he played his video game and I ate his popcorn. "Because you lack the skill to pass the level and defeat that green man thing."

"Lie to me."

"The gaming system is cheating somehow. Everyone knows robots will always beat humans. Those *Terminator* movies are unrealistic."

He leaned his head onto my shoulder. "Have I told you recently how much I love you?"

I pushed him off of me, giggling. "You told me earlier when I volunteered to pop the popcorn."

My phone dinged, and I checked it while Gavin restarted his game. I had three new messages. All from Ryan.

"Allie, come hang out with me instead. Gavin is a hermit and I want to play Frisbee."

"I'm much more charming and good looking."

"If you don't respond soon, I will take it to mean Gavin has either murdered you or you two are having sex."

My jaw dropped, and I texted him, *"Ryan!"*

A ding came from my phone again within seconds.

"Give me attention. I need attention."

I laughed at it, and Gavin shot me a quizzical expression. "Sorry, Ryan keeps texting me," I explained.

"Tell him he's cutting into my Allie time. How are we going to become best friends if your boyfriend is always stealing your attention?"

"Ryan is not my boyfriend."

Gavin nudged me. "Does he know that?"

I nudged him back. "Of course, he does. We're friends. Just like you and me."

"I prefer to call us soon-to-be best friends. Once you finally trust me enough to tell me about your life."

"I've told you about my life." I had no clue he was so perceptive.

He paused his video game to give me his full attention. "It's okay that you don't tell me everything. I get it. I just hope you know I'm here when you're ready to."

I was silent for a moment before my arms wrapped around him in a hug. He laughed and hugged me back.

There was an abrupt knock on Gavin's door, and we separated from each other. The door burst open before Gavin had time to finish saying, "Come in."

Ryan stepped in and saw our close, intimate position on the beanbag. "You *were* having sex!"

I choked on the piece of popcorn I had just tossed in my mouth at Ryan's loud announcement.

"Excuse me?" Gavin questioned him and tapped on my back to help with my choking.

"I'm just kidding. If you haven't slept with me yet, you definitely wouldn't sleep with Gavin."

"Thanks, man," Gavin grumbled. I laughed.

Ryan strode into the room. "Can I hang out with you guys? I'm bored."

"You're always bored," I commented.

Ryan jumped down on the beanbag between Gavin and me, and we nearly bounced off it from the impact. Ryan's muscles now squeezed up against me. I had never realized he was so fit.

Still, not as hot as Nate.

"What were you guys talking about?"

"You mean before you so rudely interrupted?" Gavin asked. "Life."

"That sounds boring too."

"Let's do something fun," I said, and Ryan was already jumping up from the beanbag chair.

"This is why I've chosen you as my soul mate, Allie. What did you have in mind?"

DORM MANUAL RULE #21: NO WATER GUNS IN THE DORM

llie:

"This is completely against the rules," Ryan said. "I love it."

"Aren't you an RA?" Gavin questioned him.

"Yeah, for the hall two floors above us." He attempted a southern drawl as he held up his bright green water gun. "This ain't my territory 'round these parts."

I did my best impression of a cowboy and by that; I meant I did a mediocre impression of a cowboy. "I reckon somebody ought to claim this land."

Gavin rolled his eyes at us, refusing to play along with the accent. "I reckon you both are crazy."

"Partner, you thinking what I'm thinking?" Ryan asked, but I ignored his plan to gang up on Gavin.

I shot at Ryan with my water gun, soaking his shirt. He fell to the floor, faking his death.

"Why, Allie May?" He grasped at his wet shirt. "I thought we were in this together."

"The life of a lone ranger is the only life I know."

Gavin sprayed water at me and claimed the dorm hallway for himself.

We ran around, shooting each other, hiding behind doors or trashcans, using posters as shields, and pausing when people had to pass us in the hallway to get to their rooms. A couple of people looked annoyed, but most were amused and asked to join in the fun. After half an hour, we were a group of six, forming alliances and taking down other groups.

"All for one and one for all!" a boy named Anthony shouted, and we charged at the other team.

Then Nate walked into the hallway.

And everything fell apart.

I stopped running the second I saw him, but my sandals slid in the water on the floor, resulting in me falling hard on my back and landing on a harsh angle on my leg. "Ow!" My spine throbbed, but nothing compared to the searing pain in my calf and ankle. "Shoot."

"Allie!" I did not know who said it first, but Nate and Ryan bent down next to me at the same time. Gavin landed there a second later.

"What hurts?" Nate inquired.

"My leg and my ankle." And my pride. "Please tell me I didn't break something."

Nate trailed his electrifying hand over my leg. Though it hurt, his touch distracted me as tingles spread wherever his warm fingers met my skin. I sent a silent prayer up as thanks that I had shaved my legs the night before. "You didn't break anything," he said, caressing the red area and scanning every inch of it. "But you might have a sprain."

"Is it fatal? Tell me the truth."

Ryan and Gavin smiled, but Nate's shoulders did not relax. "I see you still have your sense of humor," Nate commented, his gaze flicking to mine. "You'll need that in the afterlife." Was he...going along with my joke?

"So you're saying I am going to die from this?" I asked, the small excitement of seeing Nate turn playful eating away at me.

"I'm saying if you ever do something like this again, I'll kill you myself."

My eyes widened at him, and a genuine laugh croaked its way out of my throat. Loud and awkward and real. At the sound of it, even Nate's teasing lips curled a bit at the edges. *Yes, please smile.*

Nate stood up and held his hand out for me.

Ryan mimicked his action. "Here, I can—"

I reached for Nate, but after putting a bit of weight on my leg, I sank back down in pain. "You know what, I'm just going to stay here until the Grim Reaper finds me. Thanks for all your help though."

"It hurts too much to stand on?" Nate asked, concern etched on his face, but some darker emotion lurked beneath his eyes. It looked like anger.

"What is standing if not tall sitting?"

"That made zero sense," Gavin said, betraying our friendship.

Nate bent down and scooped an arm under the hook of

my legs. "Put your arms around my neck." I followed his instruction, and he lifted me into the air. My side met the hardness of his taut pecs and warm chest.

Hello there.

"Um, I don't like this," I commented, but my nerves had nothing to do with the arousal pumping through my body at being held by him. People picking me up had never ceased to freak me out. "Please put me down."

"I'm not going to drop you." His serious eyes locked onto mine. With my ear pressed against his chest, his every heartbeat vibrated into me. Steady. Strong. Perfect. "I promise."

Every tense muscle in my body eased. How did he do that?

"I'm taking Allie to the health clinic," Nate told everyone. "Ryan, clean up this mess before someone else falls and hurts themself."

"I can take Allie—"

"What did I just say?" Nate's harsh voice took on a threatening tone. His entire face transformed into a menacing glare so deadly my pulse stopped at seeing it. "Clean this place up."

"I will, but I'll take her to—"

"How could you let this happen?" Nate questioned him. Loudly. Gavin and the few people still holding water guns flinched and had *retreat* written across their faces. "Water guns are against the rules. You know that. *You* are an RA."

"There are so many rules." Ryan shrugged. "We just wanted to have fun."

"Does she look like she's having fun?"

I opened my mouth, unsure of what to say.

"You're supposed to be responsible," Nate scolded him.

Ryan shot me a guilty expression before breaking eye contact and staring at the ground. "I'm sorry, Allie."

"It was my idea," I said, but Nate would not listen to me.

"Give me a reason why I shouldn't write you up for this," Nate demanded.

Ryan's eyebrows furrowed. "Because I'm your friend."

They stood there, Nate still holding me, and studied each other in silence. Then Nate turned and walked me to the exit of the dorm.

"Don't write Ryan up. It was my idea."

He did not look down at me as he carried me. Instead, he kept his gaze straight ahead. "Why is it you've been involved in every incident so far this semester?"

"That depends on your definition of an incident."

He stepped outside, and several people looked over at us. *Never seen a girl carried before?* Though, to be fair, they could have been gaping at Nate's muscles. I fought the urge to nibble on them. The urge was strong.

"I'm sorry about everything."

His arms tightened around me as most of the anger seeped from his face. "You do and say things without thinking them through. It's who you are."

"I'm still sorry."

"Thank you," he said, still staring straight ahead instead of at me. "On a scale of one to ten, how much does it hurt?"

I puckered my lips in contemplation. "I've always hated that question because it doesn't take into account that some people have never experienced level ten pain, so their eights are really fives."

This time he did look down at me. "Have you experienced level ten pain?"

"Level nine, sure. But who can say what a ten is before they've felt one?"

A wave of surprise and contemplation washed over his features. He closed his eyes for a second, then shook his head. A snort escaped him.

"What?" I asked.

"You do these wildly immature things, then say something deep and profound."

"I have layers."

"Like a taco dip," he said.

"But less cheesy."

"And a lot spicier."

A grin stretched my face until I winced in pain.

His good mood dropped, and he walked with longer strides after that. "We'll be there in two minutes."

"How can you carry me like this?" Sure, he had muscles to spare. I dreamed of worshipping his chest in just about every way possible.

"I go to the gym every day."

Note to self: *Buy more water guns. Get some taco dip. Go to the gym.*

The waiting room of the health clinic was full when we got there. Nate helped me sign in, then found me a chair to sit in, the last available one. He stood beside me as an awkward silence wrapped around us like a warm, itchy blanket.

Was he going to stay the whole time? What if it took hours? He could not stand there for hours. "You sure you don't want my seat to sit down?" I offered.

"Allie, you're the one who can barely stand. I'm fine."

"If you need a seat, you can have mine," a girl near us said.

She smiled at him; *"hi, handsome"* sparkled in her hazel eyes. "That way you can sit next to your girlfriend."

"She's not my girlfriend," Nate responded with cheetah speed.

The girl's smile grew. "Oh."

I did not like that at all. "He's such a tease." I placed a hand on his chiseled chest, which was an odd and difficult thing to do in my seated position. "He always tells strangers we're not dating." I patted his stomach, which was easier to reach than his heart. *Damn, now that is a hard, flat stomach. Bonjour, abs. Nice to make your acquaintance.* "This one likes to make me jealous."

The girl appeared as confused as Nate. "So, you two are together?"

"No," he said.

"There he goes again." I faked a laugh. "Sweetie, you're going to confuse the girl." I whispered over to her, "It's a game we play. He takes it too far."

"Um, okay." She gathered her belongings and stood. "You can just take my seat." She walked to the other side of the room, and I waved goodbye like a good Samaritan.

Nate narrowed his eyes on me as he sat down. His arm brushed against mine on the armrest before he shifted his arm off the armrest. "What was that about?"

"Just a bit of fun."

He nodded and picked up one of the magazines from the coffee table. "I think you were jealous."

Me? Jealous? Of her? Over him? I scoffed several times, one or two too many. "Just because I find you hot doesn't mean I would date you."

"Good, because I don't date."

"Like ever? Not even nonresidents?"

"Never."

So he did fear creating a bond with someone. Did he have a bond with anyone? "That's sad."

He flipped through the magazine on luxury living and shrugged. "It's the way it has to be."

"Why?"

He rolled his eyes. He hated it when I asked *why*.

"You know you don't have to sit with me the whole time. I'll be fine."

He did not respond. Instead, he picked up a magazine on fashion and handed it to me. It took an hour before the doctor saw me. Our arms touched on the armrest the entire time.

❡❡❡

"Did I mention how sorry I am?" Ryan texted me. *"I'll make it up to you at dinner. I saved you one of the last pieces of cheesecake."*

Me: *"It's not your fault I fell. Besides, I'm on crutches for like two days. I'm fine."*

By the time I limp-hopped my way to the dining hall, I found Ryan eating and walked—hopped—over. He saw me and grinned, then frowned with guilt as he saw my crutches.

"Hey!" I enjoyed talking to Ryan. Though his need for attention was evident, I liked that there was never a dull moment in the conversation. Eating with him and Gavin helped me feel more at home at Beckett University.

Ten minutes into eating, Ryan tossed a fry in his mouth and said, "All the female RA's have been bad talking you."

"Why?"

"Cause you're the only girl Nate has ever talked about."

I cough-choked on a sip of my soda. My raised eyebrows were enough of a question for him to continue.

"He complains about how you break the rules a lot but when they ask him why he hasn't written you up for it yet, he gets real quiet and changes the subject." I attempted to calm my throat as he went on. "They don't like you because they see the way Nate talks about you and they like him. It's all very soap-opera-y. If you get into a girl fight, text me the deets right before."

"I would not get into a girl fight over Nate."

"Shame."

"Why are all these girls so obsessed with him?" Like yes, he was sexy as heck, but he put up an attitude to be left alone. As a psychologist, I found that interesting, but why were other girls so into knowing him too?

"You tell me."

I blinked in surprise. Was Ryan insinuating I had feelings for Nate? "I'm not interested in him in that way."

Ryan smiled. "Did you know your lip twitches when you lie?" I was not lying. Nate was a project. A patient. I would help him, not be with him. "I noticed because I've been closely monitoring your lips. For scientific reasons, of course."

"Scientific?"

"From my knowledge of biology, I believe if we reproduced, we would create beautiful offspring."

I laughed. "You're not the best at flirting, are you?"

He shrugged, but his grin was full of mischief. "I haven't started trying yet."

DORM MANUAL RULE #14: ALWAYS LOCK YOUR DOOR

*𝒶*llie:

I screamed, but no sound came out. My therapist sat in his chair, calm, as I attempted to shriek with volume. He could not hear me. He never heard me. I was back in high school.

"A lot of girls have gone through what you have, Miss Parser," he told me. I tried screaming again. It did not work. "Don't expect things to go back to normal." He did not look me in the eyes. He stared down at his notebook as always, telling me what was wrong with me without even glancing my way. Without even seeing how ready I was to break. "You should expect to fall into a slight depression for a while." Check. "Suffer from lower self-esteem than before." Check. "And even problems with intimacy—"

I jumped up and ripped his notebook from him. When I glanced down at the papers, they transformed into pages from a textbook, listing long-term effects and symptoms as if everything I felt could be labeled or defined. As if I was a question on a test and not a person. I closed my eyes and tried to scream again.

When I opened my eyes, my mother stood in front of me as I laid on my bed. She wiped a stray tear off my cheek and picked up one of the fifty frilly pillows she had bought for my room. She shoved the pillow down on top of my face, muffling my screams until they were as silent as before, suffocating me. Suffocating me.

I woke up, startled in my bed. Sweat soaked my pajamas, and I took two deep breaths to calm myself down. That was not my normal nightmare. What was happening? Why was I having nightmares again? Hadn't I healed? I thought I was over it.

Distraction time. Find a distraction.

☝☝☝

MY LEG BOUNCED under my desk from excitement in my psychology class, eager for a distraction from my morning nightmare. With every chapter we read, I felt more prepared to write an amazing paper on Nate and help him work through his issues.

"Please come see me if you have questions about the first quiz. It will get harder from here," the professor told us as she passed back the graded quizzes and concluded class. Once mine dropped in front of me, my leg stopped bouncing.

I couldn't believe it. I had gotten a D on my first psychology quiz. A *D*. What. The. Hell. How? I knew psychology. I knew it better than anything else. It was what I wanted to do with my life. How could this happen? My chest tightened, and I took a deep breath and counted to ten. A D.

Waves of panic crashed over me. *Breathe.* A couple of minutes after the class ended, I approached the professor as she stood next to a teaching assistant at her computer.

"Hi, um—"

"I don't offer extra credit," she said.

"Okay, but do you have any advice on how I can improve my grade? I know there are only a few graded assignments in the class—"

"If you want to do well in my class, write a good final paper. In the end, the quizzes don't weigh much. Just the midterm and the final paper. Do you know whom you will write about yet?" She asked it like she knew the answer was no and that my last name was Procrastinator. Well, not in psychology. I did not procrastinate in my dream class.

"I do." I smiled when she seemed impressed. "I'm still getting to know him."

She spun around, facing me once she knew I was dedicated. "And what will be the focus of your analysis?"

"He has an obsession with control that I believe is due to a traumatic childhood experience." I did not know much but, from context clues, that was what I had picked up on. "He has a list of rules he lives by."

"Hmm, I'm intrigued." She leaned against her podium. "And you have this list of rules?"

Not exactly. "I know it exists."

"You'll need to know everything on it for an in-depth paper."

"I will."

❦❦❦

"*ALLIE, I don't think that's a good idea*," my best friend and past roommate, Eliza, from my time in France messaged me after I explained my plans for sneaking into Nate's room to find his list of rules for my paper.

"*If I find his rules, it will help me better understand how I can help him and also help me not fail the required class for my major*," I sent back. Jennifer, the blonde from my first week, had mentioned he might keep a paper with the rules in his room.

Eliza: "*I know you just want to help, but breaking into his room? C'est fou, non?*"

It was a bit crazy, but I needed to do it. Sure, I needed a good grade, but I also wanted to help people live their best lives. Nate closed himself off from people and as far as I could tell, he lacked strong friendships and relationships. He needed to let go of his control issues and do something unexpected. He needed to break his own rules.

If I could get into his room and find his list of rules, they would serve as the topic of my final paper and a to-do list for his breakthrough. In the end, he would thank me. Hopefully.

"*Helping someone who did not ask for help is dangerous*," she messaged.

When I had first met her in France, Eliza had been a shy girl with dreams of pursuing a career in performance. With my help, she had found the courage and taken the stage. Her smile under the spotlight gave me chills. She looked set free. Home. I wanted to do the same for Nate.

He would be upset with me trying to help him, but I saw myself in him as I was a year ago. I had pushed away everyone and everything. If I could help someone not go down that rough road, I would.

When he went to the bathroom, I sprinted into his room

and searched the place. Automatic signs that Nate was not the typical college boy: no clothes scattered the floor and the smell of sweat and Axe body spray did not pollute the air. The soft scent of apples and cleanliness lingered in the air. The smell of Nate.

I ran my hand over his bed sheets. No crumbs. He needed to explore the pleasure of eating food in bed. My mind took a dirty turn as I imagined lying back on the smooth mattress in nothing but whipped cream.

His lips would curl up in his rare mischievous smile. *"You look good enough to eat."*

"Then what are you waiting for? Devour me."

Focus, Allie. I moved away from his distracting bed and looked around for any piece of paper labeled "rules" or "why I hate fun." Instead, I stumbled across a photo on his desk of him kissing the cheek of a young dark-haired girl. Nate had a sister? My original assumption of him as an only child was proven wrong. Hmm.

"What more is there to know about you?" I asked and bent down to look under his bed. Nothing but books and a bin of microwavable noodles. A small black box grabbed my attention. I pulled it out and opened the lid. "Fuck." I shut it and shoved it back under the bed. *Stop thinking about Nate putting you in those handcuffs. This is not the time. And was the slip of silk a blindfold? Shit. Focus. Focus. Focus.*

"If I were a list of rules, where would I be?"

I opened a couple of drawers in his dresser. *Mm, a boxers man.* Jesus, now I was just being creepy. I just wanted to find a simple list of rules. The sound of heavy footsteps outside the door made my heart freeze in my chest. I stepped toward his closet.

No. No way he was back so soon. Did he remember to wash his hands? Of course, he did, he was Nate Reddington. I had gotten too distracted and wasted all my sleuthing time.

If he found me in his room….

The doorknob turned.

↑↑↑

MY HEART THUMPED SO HARD in my chest, I worried he could hear it through the door of his closet. I had jumped inside the second I saw him open the door. Since his closet door had not been closed, I left it cracked open a bit so it would not raise suspicion. That way I could see him and know when he left his room again.

Please, pick up a book and go to a class.

Instead of grabbing something and leaving, he sat down on his bed and let out a deep breath. A part of me wanted to ask what had him so stressed. The other part of me realized I hid in his closet. Like a stalker.

Oh my God, I had snuck into his room. And gone through his stuff. And now I was trapped here until he either found me or left. What if he never left? It was after five-thirty, so he had already eaten dinner. What if he stayed in here for the rest of the night? Would I have to sleep in his closet? What if I snored? Jesus, what had I gotten myself into?

I shuffled my phone out of my pocket and texted Eliza. *"Why did you let me do this?"*

Eliza: *"You are the most impulsive person I know. You would have done it no matter what. Did you get caught?"*

I did not know what would be worse: getting caught any

second, or waiting two hours and then getting caught. No, if I got caught, everything would be over. Nate would think I was a freak. An obsessed freak. Oh God, why couldn't I have just thought this idea through more? Why was I so stupid?

Through the crack of the closet door, I peered out, hoping he was finishing up with his bed wallowing. Instead, he had his phone pressed up against his ear. Jesus, what college boy called someone on the phone anymore? I found that kind of sexy.

"Hey, Blue." Who was this mysterious Blue? He listened for a bit. "You know I don't want to talk to him." Who? "Did you eat today?"

For an eavesdropper, I had bad luck in finding out anything interesting. As far as I could tell, the call was a simple "how are you doing." My heart did a funny flip when he ended it with, "I love you." Nate *loved* someone. So Blue was his sister in the photo? If he had a bond with her, there was still hope of him making bonds with other people. He did not completely isolate himself. I wanted to walk out of his closet and give him a medal. Then I realized I still stood in his closet.

"Hey, could you do something for me without asking any questions?" I texted Gavin.

After two minutes of watching Nate read from a textbook, Gavin responded, *"Oh man, what is it?"*

Me: *"Please find a way to get Nate out of his room for at least a minute."*

Gavin: *"Why?"*

Me: *"You promised you wouldn't ask any questions."*

Gavin: *"I did no such thing."*

Me: *"Please."*

I waited for a text back that never came. Instead, a light knock sounded at Nate's door. Gavin led him out with a fake problem, and I prayed my thanks to him. Slipping out of Nate's closet, I took one last look around the room and saw his dreaded color-coded calendar. Notes from colored pencils, highlighters, and post-it notes littered the days. It was insane. It was the root of his problems. I grabbed it before I let myself think it through.

Once I was back in my room, I laid the spiral-bound booklet of months down on my bed.

Shit, what did I do?

The sound of Nate's door shutting echoed through our shared wall. He was back in his room. No calendar.

My original thinking when taking it was, *you can't leave empty-handed.* My original thinking was stupid. I was stupid.

He would notice it was gone. What would happen then? Maybe the next time he left the room, I could run it back in.

A big shuffling noise came through the wall, followed by a "What the hell?"

He noticed. Within one minute of it being gone.

More noise came from his room. Things being moved around. His chair legs scraping against the tile floor.

He would stop looking eventually. He had to.

❦❦❦

TWO HOURS later of light cursing and loud sounds, he still searched for the calendar. The same calendar sitting on my bed. I wanted to bang my head against the wall and scream, *"It was me."* Guilt cut me up into little regret pieces with its shame fork and opened its remorse mouth to eat away at me.

No wait, Guilt did not need to bother with cutting me into small slabs. It had already swallowed me whole.

"*You've got to return it,*" Eliza messaged me.

The goal was to return it when he left again, but as time went on; I started to accept I would have to return it in person before he tore his whole room apart. Once he knew I had snuck into his room and stolen it...

I buried my face in my hands and groaned. I needed to swallow my pride.

My hand thumped against his door.

"Busy," he yelled, not opening it.

I knocked again.

"What is it?" He tore open the door, then paused. His gaze raked down my body. "Oh, Allie, hi."

"Hi."

He started, "Sorry, but I'm—"

"I found this." I pushed his calendar into his face.

He took it from me, and his shoulders dropped from their tense state. "You found it?"

Just nod and stick to the plan. "Found it in the hallway."

"You found my calendar in the hallway?"

Shoot. "I'm lying. That was a lie." *Deep breath.* "I took it."

"What?"

"I snuck into your room and took it."

"You *what?*" The raising of his voice should not have given me tingles the way it did.

"I also saw the handcuffs you keep under your bed. Very dom-y of you," I babbled. "Sorry, by the way. Didn't think you would miss the calendar that much," I jabbed him with my elbow in a joking manner. He was not amused.

He stood there with a stone expression carved by the

most talented of statue artists. Sculptors. *That's what statue artists are called.* The silence and stillness of his reaction scared me. Had I broken his brain? Was he also having a hard time remembering the word for sculptors?

"Are you going to stop staring at me anytime soon?" I asked.

"Are you crazy?" His voice came out as tight as the knots in my lower abdomen.

"Apparently, yes, since I snuck into your room and all."

"Breaking and entering is a crime." The familiar vein in his forehead came out to play. "An actual crime."

"You left your door unlocked—which breaks rule fourteen from the manual, by the way—so I wasn't breaking in. It was just your average entering."

His mouth opened. More silence. Then, "Why?"

The truth? "Someone told me you had a list of your rules in your room."

He still appeared confused. "For someone who asks 'why' so much, you sure don't answer the question very well."

I could not just open up and tell him it was for a psychology paper that would ruin any future analysis, so I went with the other half of the truth. "You shouldn't be living by a list of rules. When I couldn't find it, I took your calendar because I was trying to help you realize you don't need to follow a schedule. You can't let a clock or agenda dictate how each day will go."

He creaked his door open wider and pulled me into his room by the arm. His grip was the perfect mix of hard, soft, desperate, and calm. He closed the door behind me and stood with the tips of his shoes against mine. The scent of apples infiltrated my nose. A part of me wondered if he smelled liked baked apple pie when he got hot. "This thing between us, you wanting to learn more about me, it needs to stop."

"I just want to help you."

"You keep saying you want to help me. What does that mean?" he asked, narrowing his intense eyes on me.

Synonyms. "Help you. Assist you. Fix you."

"Fix me?" The low tone of his voice shot shivers down my spine. Cold shivers licked down every vertebra with minty saliva. There was a tremble in his bottom lip, which I noticed because his lips were close. So close.

"You need to stop relying on control to feel safe," I said. "I can fix—"

"Have you ever thought that maybe the reason you're so concerned with fixing others is so you don't realize *you* are the one who's broken?" He spat verbal poison at me.

The poison took root instantly. My breathing slowed. My heart halted. A coolness itched in my veins.

"I'm sorry." He tried to suck the poison out. "Allie, I'm sorry. That was—"

"I'm not broken," I whispered. I was a bee hovering over a dead flower. Willing pollen that was not there. Willing life to crusted petals.

"You're not." His fingers stabbed through the dark strands of his hair. "That was a horrible thing to say. I was upset—"

"I'm sorry I took your calendar."

He closed his eyes and released a frustrated breath. "Thank you for returning it."

"I'm going to leave now." The words came out with no emotion. I felt myself retreating. Laying the foundation for a nice, big wall to come shooting up. All my hard work from the past year crumbled.

"Wait," he said, but I disobeyed him.

I sprinted to my room and slammed the door closed, needing to hide. Needing to wrap myself in blankets until the ice in my chest melted.

Nate slammed a hand against our shared wall and cursed. I swore I heard him say, "I'm sorry."

NATE'S #3 RULE FOR LIFE: KEEP YOUR ENEMIES FAR AWAY AND YOUR FRIENDS EVEN FARTHER

*N*ate:

SHE HAD snuck into my room and yet *I* was the one who felt guilty? Damn it, how was she able to twist me up inside? I half expected her to shove a stick into my chest, spin it around, and pull out a cotton candy shaped dessert made of my organs. That was how messed up she had me. Like a sicker version of being wrapped around someone's finger.

I had pushed her away, but she saw my pushes as pulls. She infiltrated my senses. Pushing her away was an option that had jumped overboard and drowned. She was already inside of me. Like thick bacterial mucus during a bad cold. And no matter how much of her I got out of my system, more built up the next day. A gross comparison, but a valid one.

My claim: I needed to stay away from Allie. Evidence supporting my claim: Being around her led to feelings and words seeping out of me like blood from the gashes she had sliced into me. She picked and prodded at me like I was an experiment.

I was so damn tired of being treated as less than a person.

Over the years, I had a hard time separating pals from real friends. People who liked me versus people who liked the connections the Reddington family offered them. Allie did not seem to care about my last name, but she acted like the rest of them. Uncaring of my feelings and ready to do whatever she wanted to reach her goal.

But what was her goal?

To "fix" me?

I vibrated with anger; the fingers making up my fists twitching from tension. She had insinuated I was broken. Me. Broken.

Then I told her she was broken. And her face had crumpled. Crumpled. *Fuck*.

I fell back on my bed, letting the mattress springs creak as it moved up and down from my weight. She had broken into my room and stolen my calendar, and *I* was the one left feeling horrible about myself? That was so damn unfair. Everything about her was unfair. The way she looked, knowing she was off-limits to me. The way she made me laugh, knowing the emotional walls I built up had a weakness for strange humor.

How was I to be held accountable for my words when sleep evaded me for days? Mostly due to reoccurring images playing through my head of Allie in her revealing purple nightgown. She thought *I* was a Greek God? She looked like freaking Meg from *Hercules*. Her long, wavy auburn hair, and her silk purple nightgown covering thirty percent of her…. So thin it was almost see-through. Damn, I had wanted to rip it off and fucking pin her to the wall, take her right there in the hallway—*Jesus, Nate, stop.* Allie broke rules. She had snuck into my room like a crazy person. Why the hell was I still so attracted to her?

She was crazy. "Broken." I shook my head as shame tingled in my lungs. How could I have let something like that slip out of my mouth? I had no business or right calling another person broken. She had just…stabbed me. *"I just wanted to help you. Fix you."* Why? Why was she so obsessed with me?

Why did she think I needed fixing?

Was I broken?

I let out a frustrated groan. I was pissed at her, but I needed to apologize.

That crumpled look on her face flashed in my mind and froze me half to death in my temperate room. She was always so overconfident and smiley. Cocky and teasing. She sparkled in a dim room. But my words had snuffed out that part of her. She had looked at me like her soul was glass ready to break and I had just flicked my fingers against a crack.

"I'm sorry," I whispered, alone in my room.

How was I supposed to make her feel better when I needed to avoid seeing her?

Which one was more important?

☝☝☝

I HAD NOT SEEN Allie in three days. Some nights, I heard the door to her room open and close, but since it was after midnight; I stuck to my strict sleeping schedule and kept my eyes closed until my alarm clock tore them open the next morning. On the third day of not seeing her, I went to dinner fifteen minutes later than usual as if maybe trying to catch her, but she did not frequent the dining hall during the times I did.

She probably ate dinner around seven-thirty on most nights or something. Wild girl.

My goal to avoid her turned on its axis and became trying to find her. To apologize to her for being a dick. And maybe receive an apology for her insinuating there was something about me she wanted to "fix" as well.

My confidence spiked one night at the end of the week when I heard the door to her room open and close around six o'clock. *Time to get rid of this guilt.*

I knocked on her door and waited as some muffled sounds happened behind it. Was she tidying up? For me?

Her door opened just enough to show me half of her face. "Oh, Nate." She sniffled and wiped her nose. The green eye on display was puffy and bloodshot. She had been crying? Had I made her cry? The sudden urge to take myself outside and teach myself a lesson bombarded me. "Um, what's up, neighbor?"

I cleared my throat. To address her tears or not to address her tears. That was the question. "Um, I wanted to—"

A banging noise occurred behind her. I tilted my head to peer inside, but she moved and blocked me. Was she hiding something?

"What was that?" I asked.

"Nothing," she responded. "So what did you want?"

Right. The apology. "I wanted to say I was sorry about—" A louder banging noise came from the corner of her room. I squinted, seeing nothing over her head. "What is that noise?"

She sniffled again. "Things falling off my dresser, that's all."

"With no one touching them?" I questioned.

"Gravity is always touching them."

"Right." *Just move on and apologize.* "I'm sorry about what I said before about—"

And even louder banging noise.

"Okay." I pushed inside her room. "What is that?" I looked around, but nothing caught my eye. Then it sounded again from behind her closed closet door. "Are you hiding a man in here?" I asked.

A dead chill settled in the air.

She glanced from me to the closet with an expression of guilt. "Um, no."

Unbelievable. She was sleeping with someone? She could, obviously. She had the right to.

I had not had sex with anyone since meeting her.

"She is a single woman who can do whatever she wants. I have no claim to her," I thought at the same time I yelled at her, "Who the hell are you sleeping with? Ryan, is it Ryan?" I would kill him.

"Whoa, what? No—"

I lost it, rolling up the sleeves of my button-down shirt and fastening them over my thick forearms. "You think you can fuck someone in this room?" The room next to me. Next to where I could not sleep, because of thoughts about her.

She narrowed her eyes, anger trickling onto her puffy red face. And if the asshole had made her cry... *Oh, I am going to prison tonight.* "If I was, it wouldn't be any of your business. It's not in the rule book."

"I don't care what's in the fucking rule book." I strode up to her, and she tipped her chin up to match my gaze. "Make him leave right now."

The sparkle in her eyes, the one I had been missing, came back to life. "Maybe I want him to stay. Maybe he's going to stay all night," she said the words slow enough to punctuate each syllable. "I hope you have noise-canceling headphones."

"He is leaving," I grated. "Now."

She clenched her fists at her sides, but her anger just made her look more adorable and sexy as fuck. "Unlike you, I'm not an unfeeling robot. I have needs."

I looked down at her swollen lips. From being kissed? *No one sucks those lips but me.* "I know all about your needs." My hands moved up and settled on her hips of their own accord. My fingers dug into her sides, pulling her closer. *I hope he hears this.* "You don't need someone else to satisfy those needs, baby. Not while I'm fucking breathing."

Her pupils dilated, hopefully from arousal and not rage. "You couldn't satisfy me if you had vibrators for fingers."

How did she make me want to throw my head back and *roar?* "You want my fingers to prove it to you right now?" I pulled up the fabric of her dress, inching it up and revealing more and more of my favorite, smooth legs. Her tender thighs quivered as I bunched the bottom of her dress up to her stomach.

Black lace panties.

Like she was trying to kill me.

She succeeded.

"I see that little damp spot. For me," I muttered. "You want my touch right now, don't you?"

She whimpered before clamping down her jaw so no other noise would escape.

"You want my fingers pounding inside you."

She breathed out, "No, thank you."

"You want my thumb swiping over your swollen little clit."

Her eyelids hooded, and I stepped closer to her, absorbing her warmth and tripling it to sizzling heat.

My stiffening cock pulsed hard inside the confines of my pants. "You want me to own your wet little pussy—"

Another noise sounded from her closet, reminding me of why and how I had gotten to this point. I let her dress drop back down, shaking off my lust, and marched up to her closet.

She flung herself in front of it. "You can't do this. You don't have a warrant," she said.

I twisted the doorknob and pulled, her body being shoved into mine at my pulling open the door.

I blinked. No guy. "What—" Then I saw it. A cat. "What is this?"

"His name is Fluffykins and you will treat him with respect." She ventured inside and picked up the small feline, showing me her tight backside behind her dress as she did just that. The fluff of faded orange cuddled into her neck.

"You're not allowed to have a pet. No animals in the dorm. It's the—"

"Second rule in the book," she finished for me.

Dang, why did I find her memorization of the rulebook

just as sexy as her breaking all the rules in it? "You can't have it here."

"It is a him," she clarified, flashing his genitals at me for verification I did not need, nor had I asked for.

"You can't have him here."

"He's a stray, he has nowhere else to go."

"You can't just keep him."

"Why not?" she asked, but her voice cracked. She then sneezed three times in a row, holding the cat out, far from her body.

The red eyes. The sniffling. "Are you allergic to cats?" I asked, putting it all together.

"I wouldn't say allergic—" She sneezed. "Hmm. Maybe."

"Maybe?"

"I mean, yes, my body has a hard time functioning around cats, cat hair, etcetera. But really what's some sneezing, a runny nose, itchy eyes, and a closing throat compared to the love of a pet?"

I gaped at her. She was crazy. And sweet. She had taken a stray cat in even though his presence hurt her and messed up her ability to breathe? "Come on." I waved her out of her room, but she did not budge.

"What? I told you, I'm not going to leave him back on the street. He just needs some rest for the night and then I'll take him to a shelter, I swear."

"You can't sleep in the same room as that cat."

Her eyes widened. "So you want me to sleep in *your* room?"

"What? N-No." Interesting how her thought process landed her there. "I meant the cat will sleep in my room tonight, and then he is going to a shelter in the morning. Immediately in the morning."

She nibbled her lip. "I don't know. Cats can sense bad people. He might try to claw you in your sleep," she stated.

I fought off a smile. "Are you trying to say I'm a bad person, Allie?"

"Hey, I'm just saying animals can sense certain things, that's all."

I stepped closer to her again, my thoughts jumping back to the black panties I knew she wore and the damp spot on them. She was wet for me, and I hadn't even touched her. It was only fair considering I had been hard for her since day one. She sniffled as she glanced down at my lips.

I held out my arms, and she placed Fluffykins into them. "You can say goodbye in the morning," I told her.

"How do I know you won't throw him out on the street to protect your rules?"

Was that what she thought of me? That I would abandon a helpless cat on the side of the road on a college campus? "I'll take good care of him. Maybe we will even stay up late and watch an action movie together. You know, guy stuff," I cracked a joke and fought the instinct to slap myself on the forehead. *Nate Reddington* did not say bad jokes out loud. Or any jokes out loud.

But she smiled and released a little half-laugh. Even if it was a pity laugh, the sound of it on my ears... Magical.

My grin was unstoppable. *Focus.* "But um, before I forget, I wanted to apologize for what I said before. About you being broken. You're not."

She lost her smile but nodded, serious. "Thanks."

"You're not even close to broken. You're amazing, Allie Parser."

She nodded again.

Right. *Just get out of there.* Then I remembered, I expected an apology as well. "Do you have anything you want to say to me?"

Her eyebrows squished together. "Not that I can think of. Why?"

"Nothing about that night? What you did? Said?" How she was trying to "fix" me.

"Nope. Thanks for the apology, though. Take care of Fluffykins for me."

She closed the door on my face.

DORM MANUAL RULE #29: NO GROUPS OF OVER FIVE IN A ROOM

 llie:

"Do you have anything you want to say to me?" Nate had asked me. Did he want a love confession? What was he fishing for? I did not like him. Did he think I liked him? I mean, yes, I was attracted to him. Duh. Every girl with heterosexual tendencies seemed to be. But that was it.

Him pulling up my dress and biting his lip at the sight of my black panties? His whispered dirty words of *"You want me to own your wet little pussy."* It was the hottest moment of my damn life. But he was off-limits to me in that way until after I finished my paper about him. Maybe next semester. Once he was fixed.

He needed to cut loose and remove all those thick walls he put up.

Some muffled noise came from his side of the wall, and I leaned closer to make out his words. "Fluffykins...Stupid name...Mr. Orange Guy...Call you Crush."

Nate was talking to Fluffykins. My heart evaporated into a liquid, which dripped into my stomach and swirled around. I settled in closer to our shared wall.

"...Allergic to you but still took you in...Crazy." I frowned at his insult, but he added, "Cute."

He thought I was crazy cute?

"Need some milk." There was some shuffling as Nate opened his mini-fridge in search of a treat for Fluffykins. The bedsprings creaked, and I closed my eyes, picturing him cuddling up to the cat. It was hard to imagine due to my original thinking of him throwing it out a window and spraying everything clean.

Maybe this was what Nate needed. Something to take care of. Something to give him affection. Something he could talk to. Or someone. The cat would need to be gone in a day or two, but that did not mean Nate had to go back to being lonely.

What if I found him a girl?

The wave of nausea wracking me caused a bit of confusion. I would not be—should not be—jealous at the idea of him being with someone else. In my psychological expert opinion, he needed a bond with someone where he could be vulnerable and share his feelings instead of bottling them up. But who?

I tapped my chin in contemplation, still fighting back the uneasy feeling in the pit of my stomach.

If I let my jealousy win, that would make me selfish. He

needed this. A connection. His friendships did not seem as deep as they could be. He hid aspects of his life from people.

I would find him a girl. My business cards would require a larger size cardstock once I added "matchmaker" to my list of skills, but I was willing to do it.

The question was: what kind of girl did Nate want? Who was his type? Leggy brown haired girls with red highlights, obviously, but we could not have that kind of relationship while I studied him.

I wrote on a piece of paper: *Nate's Dream Girl*. Now I just needed to fill in the blanks.

❢❢❢

THE NEXT MORNING, I knocked on Nate's door bright and early, trying to catch him off guard. It worked because he answered, rubbing his eyes, shirtless and in nothing but plaid pajama pants.

In a hoarse voice, he rasped, "Allie?" Waking up in a split second, he glanced down and turned back into his room, searching for a shirt. "Sorry. Um, what's up? Is something wrong?"

"Nothing is wrong." *Other than you covering up those magnificent, edible muscles.* "Just checking in on Fluffykins."

"Crush," Nate called out, and the cat maneuvered out from under the covers, where he had slept in Nate's bed. Was I a little jealous over a cat? Maybe. "I renamed him. Calling him Fluffykins was just cruel."

"Fluffykins is an adorable name for an adorable cat," I cooed, walking toward Nate's bed and trying not to think about the time I rolled around on it and how comfortable those sheets were.

"If I called him Fluffykins, he would have killed me in his sleep."

I picked up the cat, but he craned his neck to keep an eye on Nate. "I think he likes you."

"He's cool." Nate shrugged, but the corners of his mouth tugged up. Ah, yes, he craved affection. Living a lonely life did that to a person.

Allie, you are going to find him the best girlfriend in the world.

Nate stepped forward when a disgusting noise came from my body. "Did you just gag? Are you sick?"

At the thought of setting him up with someone else? "What? No, I just coughed a little. In the middle of my throat."

My nausea when thinking about him with someone else was worrisome, but everything would be fine. I would help Nate get over his mystery issues and acclimate to life, get an A on my paper, and become a therapist after many, many more years of schooling.

"I'm driving him to a shelter this morning before my first class," Nate told me, with a drop of sadness in his dry eyes.

"You're going to miss him." I poked his side, painfully aware of the gorgeous skin laying beneath the thin T-shirt. "You could keep him you know."

He lifted Fluffykins from me and held him close. "No animals are allowed in the dorms."

"You're an RA, you could get away with it."

He pressed his lips together as the cat nudged its head into his chest, begging for some attention. Nate scratched behind its ears. "I can't afford to lose my job if I get caught housing an animal."

"I thought you were rich or something. What does a job matter?" Was he having money trouble? Was there something deeper going on with his family? He needed someone to lean on more than ever.

"It just matters, okay."

"Okay." *Time to do some recon.* "So you said you don't date. Have you ever dated? Like back in high school when you were maybe less jaded?"

He frowned. "Why are you asking me?"

"I'm just wondering what your dating history is like. I'm a curious person."

He saw right through me. "It's not an appropriate question for you to ask your RA."

I rolled my eyes. So far, the few times he lost his cold professionalism were when it became hot professionalism in the bedroom. "You're not just my RA." I gestured between us. "We're friends."

"No, we're not," he said.

A hard punch to the jugular may have hurt a little less than his words. "What do you mean?"

Nate sighed and placed Fluffykins back down on his mattress. "Look, Allie, I've let this go on long enough; that's my fault. I am your RA, and you are my resident. I'm responsible for you and your safety. You might think we're friends because I've been giving you leeway over stunts like the water gun fiasco and the cat, but it's over. If you break the rules again, I'm going to have to write you up."

"Write me up?" I was trying to help him. Anger flared inside me but doused itself. He was pushing me away because he knew I was finally cracking him. No one liked change, but it was better to accept it than ignore it. Nate was changing. He was realizing I was right about him. *Aww.* Patient's first denial.

"Trust me, I wouldn't find pleasure in it."

"No, you need something else to find pleasure in," I commented.

"What?"

"Blondes or brunettes? Does eye color matter to you? What do you look for?"

"Excuse me?"

"In a woman," I clarified.

He stared at me, concern lighting up his eyes. Clearly, his brain did not work as fast as mine. "Allie, again, I don't date. If this is some game—"

"Why don't you date? Will you tell me that?" *So I can correct it.*

"No, I won't tell you that." He scoffed, shaking his head at me in distaste. "You act like details about my personal life are supposed to be made available to you. We are not friends. We are not anything."

We were something. Therapist and patient. He just fought not to accept his role. "If you tell me why you don't date anymore, I'll leave you alone."

"Forever?"

"For a week. I'll leave you alone for a week."

He looked at the cat as if it could help him make sense of me. Admitting defeat, Nate answered, "I don't date because it ended badly the first time. Goodbye now."

Caught up on a long-lost love? I could help with that.

After some research. "Want to give me a name?" It would save me a lot of time.

"No."

"That's fine." I winked at him as he glared. "See you in a week."

♥♥♥

IT TURNED out social media trumped diamonds for being a girl's best friend. After I found Nate Reddington's account, I cyber-stalked him back to his high school years in search of his mystery girl. If she was the reason he needed control and distanced himself from people now, she also held the key in helping him move on.

Maybe he did not date because he was still stuck on her. Maybe I could rekindle something for him.

When I clicked on her profile, I gagged again, fighting back nausea. She was beautiful. Of course she was. All of her pictures featured her wearing a variety of colored bikinis. Tanned gold skin. His ex's dark black hair soaked up all light, making her the focal point in every photo.

She glowed.

Did I glow?

I brushed the bad, jealous feeling aside and dug deeper into her account. I did some Google-ing of both of their names. After two hours, I had all the information I needed.

He had broken up with her after she had told a magazine reporter about Nate's troubling past with his father, betraying his trust. That bitch. *Isn't that what I'm doing?* It was different, of course. Nate had opened up to her, and she had sold his secrets for money. No wonder he pushed people away and refused to date. He could trust no one with his secrets. As a part of a famous billionaire family, anything he had to say was worth more than a shiny penny to the press.

Poor Nate.

"He just needs to start over," I told myself. I would find him a trustworthy girl.

❦❦❦

THE NEXT FEW days were spent trying to find single girls on campus who did not have black hair—as I did not want to remind him of the girl who had gifted him his baggage—and were interested in a submissive and dom relationship. The best way to do that was to invite the girls who frequented a secret BDSM sex club on campus to my dorm room for a meet and greet mixer. Finding the secret BDSM club was easy, as they seemed happy to talk to a potential new female member.

I bought some cranberry juice and set up a punch bowl in my room as the girls arrived. My roommate again made no appearance in our room, so I had nothing to worry about. I hit "play" on my music speakers but kept them at the lowest volume, so Nate would not come over before I was ready.

It felt like I was forming him a harem. *Just got to narrow it down.*

"You would say you're trustworthy?" I questioned one of the girls. She was a year older than me and perfect for Nate. "Dating this guy means being able to keep his secrets. No matter what."

"Is he rich or something?" The light shining in her eyes at the prospect eliminated her from the list.

"Something like that."

Maybe searching for a girl without black hair and a submissive streak was not enough. Maybe she needed to be rich too, to understand the pressures on him.

"Are any of you from wealthy families?" I asked the room full of fifteen women. Most shook their heads. "Dang."

"When do we get to meet the guy?" a blonde asked.

"He is…hard to get through to. So I need to choose who I think he will open up to."

"I'm great at getting men to open up," one yelled, sipping the punch. "Opening up their pants!" She cackled, drunk, which surprised me considering it was eight o'clock at night and the punch I served had no alcohol. "Turn the music up," she yelled again.

The others started chanting.

"I don't think that's a good idea—"

"Do you have pictures of this guy?" one girl asked. "You were so cryptic in your message."

"He's hot, trust me." I had left his name and picture out of it because I did not want someone to show up with a *"Nate Reddington"* obsession. He needed someone who would treat him like a normal person. Though, no normal person ate dinner at five o'clock.

"And he's a dom? What level dom? Hardcore?"

"I don't really know," I said. "He has handcuffs."

"That doesn't make someone a dom."

"He's…got a controlling personality," I offered.

"Hot."

"Turn up the music," the drunk girl yelled again.

I walked over and guided her to my door. "I think you should go."

"But—"

Loud, passive-aggressive—or just aggressive-aggressive—knocking came from the other side of my door. Oh jeez. I had been hoping to correlate the meeting time with his shower time. He had been taking half-hour-long showers over the past week. Another sign he needed a woman.

"Did you just gag?" the drunk girl flinched away from me.

"No." I took a deep breath and opened my door. "Hi, neighbor."

Nate peered over my shoulder at the room full of gorgeous women and narrowed his crazed eyes on me. "What's going on here?"

"Just talking to some friends," I said.

"I thought Gavin and Ryan were your friends."

"They are my guy friends. I need some girl friends."

He glanced at my room full of girls again. "How many friends do you need?"

"Why, do you think there should be a maximum number?"

He tossed me his classic scowl. "You're breaking the rules again. No more than five people in a room."

"Who's this?" The drunk girl swayed beside me as she looked at him.

"No one. You need to leave." I shooed her out, and Nate made room in the doorway for her to slip out. "See? Now I'm down to fourteen people in my room. That's less rule-breaking than fifteen."

"Everyone needs to leave right now or I'm writing you up."

Oh, Nate, I am doing this for you, you dummy. "Sure, but

before they do, do you see anyone in here you might want to get to know better?"

His eyes did not leave mine. "No. No one. Now end this party."

"If this is what you think qualifies as a party, we need to get you to a real shindig."

His frown increased because he did not want me to see him smile. "Shindig?"

"That's right."

"Is this the guy you want one of us to hook up with?" a redhead called out, interrupting our private conversation.

Nate's expression changed as he absorbed her words. His eyebrows pointed down, his lips thinned, and his jaw locked.

"WHAT?"

NATE'S #4 RULE FOR LIFE: DON'T LIE UNLESS IT'S TO A LIAR

ate:

"Is this the guy you want one of us to hook up with?" someone had asked, and Allie's face went red and scrunched up with guilt.

"WHAT?" I had come over to tell her to keep it down and instead found a mini party in her room. And she was trying to find someone for me to hook up with?

What the fuck was wrong with this girl?

"You invited all of these girls here for me to hook up with?" I asked in a gritty tone.

"Not all of them. Not at the same time."

I threw my arms up in the air. "What is going on with you, Allie?"

She stood her ground and pointed a finger at my chest. "You need to start dating again. It's a step in your recovery—"

"My recovery?"

"You have all this baggage from your old relationship."

"My old relationship?" How did she know about Abigail? Did she… Had Allie Googled me?

"Now I know your issues come from trust. So I gathered these girls here to find someone good for you, who could help you—"

"You're the one who needs fucking help," I yelled at her.

She flinched, backing away from me. "I'm just trying to—"

"Stop. What more do I need to say? We are not friends. We are less than nothing. Stop thinking I'm something you need to fix. How messed up are you to do things like this? Are you focusing on me so you don't have to focus on yourself and your own problems?"

Her lily pad green eyes widened. "I—"

"Are you obsessed with me? A lonely stalker? What is it? Why won't you stop playing with me?" I knew I looked crazed, running my fingers through my sculpted hair, making it a tangled mess, but I did not care. I did not care about anything other than making sure Allie never came near me again.

"I'm not playing with you, I—"

"If I have trust issues, it is because of people like you." This time, I pointed my finger at her chest. Her perfectly curved, bouncing chest. I tore my gaze from her, hoping to calm myself. As I looked around her room, attractive women with curious expressions stared at me. "You wanted me to hook up with someone here?"

A part of me had thought Allie's interest in me was rooted in her attraction to me. That maybe she liked me and was drawn to me. But her forming a harem for me to choose from did not say she liked me. It said she pitied me. And pity made me so fucking mad.

"You." I met the eyes of a brunette in the corner of the room. She wore a red dress just like Allie had on the first day I had met her. I waved her over to the doorway. "Let's go."

"What?" Allie squeaked as the woman walked up to me without hesitation. "What are you doing?"

"You want me to hook up with someone else? I will."

"No, I wanted you to date," Allie said, her words coming out in a rushed jumble. "Have a relationship. You can't throw yourself into meaningless sex—"

"Why not?" I asked. "Who are you to judge me when I don't see you dating anyone?" Even though the suggestion came out of my mouth, I wanted to suck it back in. The idea of Allie with a boyfriend—with anyone but me—it made me gag.

Ignore her. Allie had crossed a line tonight and needed to be punished.

"Would you like to come to my room?" I asked the brunette, who stood beside Allie after approaching upon my request. I wanted Allie to hurt the way I hurt. Her betrayal cut into my spine like a jagged dagger of shark teeth stuck in my back. If I hurt her, she would never try to fix me again. She would give up on me.

It would be safer for me if she gave up.

"I'd love to come to your room," the brunette purred, but I never looked at her.

I searched Allie's expression for a white flag of surrender. Allie held strong. "Why are you doing this?"

"You wanted me to find someone. I now have someone. Thanks, goodnight." I waved, wrapped an arm around the brunette, and led her next door.

"No," Allie shouted, trailing me in the hallway. "This isn't how it's supposed to be. This won't help you heal."

She was upset because it would not help me "heal." Not because she cared about me. But because she saw me as some kind of project. A project she failed at. Good. Let her fail. She had made me feel inadequate for the last time.

I held my door open for the brunette as she walked into my room and slammed it closed in Allie's face.

"Nate, stop, I'm sorry," she called from behind the door.

I turned some light music on for the first time ever in my room. Anything to tune her out.

"What's your name?" I asked the brunette.

"Hannah."

"I'm sorry I pulled you into this, Hannah. You can leave if you want." I sat on my bed and put my head in my hands.

"I don't want to." She sat down next to me and my mattress moved up and down at her new weight. "What's the deal with you two?"

"She thinks she needs to fix me. I guess by finding me a woman." I blew out a breath. "It's toxic to think someone can heal someone else. Even I know that."

"What do you need to heal from?"

I hated questions. Especially after being questioned by Allie. "You should go," I told Hannah.

"If I go, she will know we didn't hook up," she said. "It seemed like you wanted her to think we did." She placed a hand over mine, and I removed it, sinking away from her touch.

"She wouldn't care." Allie would not feel the jealousy I wanted her to because she had been the damn person to find a group of fifteen women for me. She did not feel the same possessiveness for me I felt for her. Whatever. It was better that way.

"I think she would care," Hannah chipped in with her opinion.

"How did she find you?" I asked.

"EC," she explained. "Erotics club."

"What?"

"She said you were looking for a submissive."

Thoughts overwhelmed me until I threw myself back on my bed, the springs creaking. "That fucking girl." She had found a sex club on campus just to find me a potential girl-friend? Had she talked to any of the male members? Was she interested in any of them?

"You want her," Hannah said.

"Only in the sexual sense."

"Hmm." She got up on her knees, balancing on my mattress. "Let's make her jealous."

"I told you, she wouldn't be jealous."

"Oh, come on, you don't even want to try?"

I bit my lip. A deep, dark part of me wanted to see Allie hurt. Maybe even feel some of the humiliation I felt. And even though I told myself it was not the main reason, I wanted to see her jealous. I wanted to see her face go tomato red as she tried to stake her claim on me and failed. I wanted her to care about me. For real. Because being the only one with feelings after everything she had done was getting old.

"Moan," I told Hannah.

She blinked, a small grin stretching her delicate face. "What?"

"Moan. Now."

She jumped up on my bed, facing the shared wall where Allie lived, and moaned like I was fucking her.

"That's it, baby," I said loudly against the wall, making sure Allie could hear me. A loud thud sounded in her room, but that was it. "Just like that."

Hannah giggled, and I slapped the wall as if it was her ass. She stopped giggling. This time her moan was real.

I waited to hear Allie do something. Yell something.

Instead, a loud whack occurred from the opposite side of my wall. Did she want to start a slapping war?

I banged a hand at the wall again as Hannah moaned louder. "You feel so good," I told her. "Best I've ever had."

A yell came from Allie's room. Finally. *How much longer until she knocks on my door and kicks Hannah out of my room?*

"Close already?"

Hannah let out a low groan, grinning at me with two thumbs up. She probably thought this was some sort of romantic comedy situation. It was not.

It was punishing. For both of us. The longer Hannah and I kept up the act, the quieter Allie's room became. Sweat dripped from my forehead as I moved my bed and grunted, waiting for Allie to come and stop us. To come and yell at me. To show she cared.

She never came.

Neither did Hannah or me.

After ten minutes, I gave up and Hannah left with a sad, pitiful expression.

Allie did not care about me. So what? I did not want—need her to. I needed her to stay away from me.

After this, she just might.

⚐⚐⚐

IT WAS around nine o'clock the next night when a knock sounded at my door. A part of me wanted it to be Allie in her purple silk nightgown. Allie, the girl who wanted to fix me. The girl who did not care about me. The girl I had attempted to hurt but did not faze. I had not seen her since calling her a lonely stalker.

I opened the door, and it revealed a nervous-looking Ryan.

"What's up, man?" I asked, worried something was wrong. He never came to my room.

He shrugged and walked inside. He got right down to business. "What do you think of Allie?"

I had to organize my thoughts to not say something I would regret. "She's—" Crazy. Funny. Impulsive. Beautiful. Childish. Too hot for her own good. "—fine, I guess. What do you mean? Why?"

"I think I like her."

My body froze. "You're an RA." My voice was hard, and I turned to stone as he paced back and forth. My heart rate increased as I imagined the two of them together. So I could be jealous and she couldn't? It was so messed up. I needed to get her out of my head.

"I know. I know, and that's why I came to you. I mean, dating her... I don't think that would be breaking the rules, you know?"

"You're an RA; she's a resident. That breaks the rules," I reminded him.

"Yeah, but I'm not her RA. She's not a resident of my floor; she is just a resident of my dorm."

I absorbed his words, trying to find a flaw. He was right. The rule was strict when the RA had to report on or supervise the person he or she was romantically interested in. Ryan was not employed to watch over Allie. I was.

"I mean, do you think it'd be okay? I don't want to lose my job here. It pays for, well, almost everything."

I remained quiet as my thoughts tangled and crashed into each other in my mind.

"Nate?"

"It's dangerous. You shouldn't. I mean, she's...she's so different." She was wild and fearless and impulsive. She said what she thought always, with no reservations or hesitations. She did things without thinking. She hurt people without being hurt. "You're opposites. You need to think about this, there's no way it would work—"

"Are you sure you're talking to me right now?"

"Of course, I'm talking to you." Was he implying I was talking to myself? I would never go after Allie. My feelings of jealousy aside, she rubbed me the wrong way. She saw me as broken and a project for her to fix. Even without those problems, we were fire and ice. We did not mix. Apart from our evident attraction, which could be fought, we had nothing in common. Well, not a lot in common. And it would be against the rules. "Allie…is dangerous. If you're asking about the rules, I don't think they would fire you. But, if you're asking me, don't. Or at least wait until you know she'd be worth it."

"I think she is."

I did not sleep well that night either.

DORM MANUAL RULE #11: NO PDA IN THE HALLWAY

llie:

"You're asking me out?" I asked, shocked.

After eating lunch with Ryan, he had walked me back to my dorm room and asked, *"Will you go out with me?"* in the hallway before I could go inside. Ryan did not seem like the dating kind, but I did not either. I had not been on a date in over a year, not after Logan.

"You barely know me," I told Ryan.

"Well, you see, the point of dating would be to get to know each other." My stomach wrung into twisting knots from the nervousness on his face.

I grew quiet as I contemplated; my mind shot back to my fight with Nate. Nate's words rang in my ear. *"Are you focusing on me so you don't have to focus on yourself and your* own problems?" He had added, *"Maybe you should look for a boyfriend for yourself."*

Ryan asking me out served as the perfect distraction. I could stop thinking about my guilt and hurt feelings over Nate, and work on myself. In truth, dating was a huge part of my healing and growth process. I had put it off long enough, swearing to myself one day in the faraway future I would be vulnerable and form a genuine bond.

I needed to go out and get Logan out of my head. I wanted to move on and find someone.

My eyes raked down Ryan, seeing him again for the first time. He was attractive. Light brown hair and cheery hazel eyes. He also made me laugh, and I did not want to lose our friendship so close to it starting.

"Are you sure?"

Ryan huffed out a chuckle. "Am I sure? Of course, I'm sure, Allie. You're awesome. Hot, funny, a bit crazy—"

"Crazy?" I raised my eyebrows at him.

He bit his lip, smiling. "Sometimes you stare off into space while you're thinking or talk to yourself out loud by accident."

"I do?" I tried to mask my horror. What things had I said?

"Yeah, but don't worry, it's cute. I like it. I like you." Something in my chest warmed at his statement. He must have seen that he said the right thing because he continued, "Would you want to go bowling Saturday night?" Bowling? I had not been bowling since my third-grade archenemy invited me to her eighth birthday party. She had put mustard in my seat, long story.

"Yes," I replied with a smile. I was going on a date. Logan be damned. A stray, rabid thought of Nate popped into my head and how he'd had loud sex next door in his room just to prove a point.

"*Best I've ever had,*" he had groaned through my wall.

My only thought had been, "*But you haven't had me.*"

I cracked my knuckles and reminded myself that Nate was off-limits and now of no interest to me. I had a below-average amount of pride, but being called a lonely stalker and hearing a man have revenge sex through my wall was enough to convince me to call it quits.

Nate did not want my help. That was fine. I had crossed a line, and I knew that.

We were not friends. That was fine too.

It was not as if I had talked to him every day, and now my hours were empty without him. I was a busy bee.

I was going on a date.

"Great." Ryan became his normal, overconfident self again after receiving my positive response and leaned in to kiss my forehead. When he pulled back, I turned to open my door and saw Nate standing in front of his room a couple of feet away from us.

It was the first time I had seen him since the revenge sex. His blazing eyes locked onto us and narrowed. Was Nate's glare at Ryan caused by jealousy? Not that it would matter. No more Nate for me. And knowing him, he glared at me because that was just his way of looking at me. "No PDA in the hallway," he said, but all I could hear was his voice as he told the girl, "*That's it, baby. You feel so good.*"

Rage fueled my lungs as oxygen took a vacation. "Hmm, you're right," I responded and pushed Ryan inside my bedroom. "Thanks for the idea, Nate."

His flaring nostrils were reward enough.

❡❡❡

"WHAT IF I don't have what it takes?" I stressed to Gavin as we ate dinner together. I had gotten *another* D on a psychology quiz. Gavin did not know it, but I had also scrapped my paper on Nate after every analysis I wrote started with the words "asshole" and "jerk face McGee." Psychology was my major, and I was messing it up.

"You do, Allie. Everyone gets low grades in the first semester of college. Think of it as a warning. As long as you do well on your other assignments, you'll be fine." He changed the subject to calm me down, but he chose the wrong subject. "So, Ryan and bowling Saturday night, huh?"

"He already told you?" Surprised jabbed me. I thought the date would be informal. Ryan telling Gavin sounded a lot more serious. Ryan had taken my pushing him into my bedroom as a teasing joke, so I was hoping something casual was expected.

It had been a long time since I spent time on a "date" with a man that involved "feelings."

"I woke up to a text saying, *'I'm going to impress her with my fourteen-pound ball. Good luck next time.'* It took me a minute to realize what that meant," Gavin said.

"He sure is cocky."

"And apparently, bally." Gavin winked at me.

I threw a potato chip at him then grew serious. "I'm kind of worried about this date."

"You should be. This one college date is your one shot at finding your soul mate. If you mess it up, you'll never recover."

Gavin put me at ease. "I love you," I said.

"Obviously."

†††

I WAS STUDYING in my room the night before my date with Ryan when my phone rang, flashing "incoming call from *Birth Giver.*" Aka mom. *No. No. No.* Worst possible time. But inconveniencing and vexing me were talents of hers.

"Hello?" I answered.

"Your father misses you." Her *but I don't* sounded loud and clear from her tone. "It's been a year. You didn't have time to come see him before you moved into school?"

Considering I promised never to step foot in my hometown again after high school graduation... No. "I flew from France to Beckett, mom." After what had happened my senior year, being on the same continent as Meadowville was too much for me. During my twelve months abroad, I had not called or interacted with my family in any way, which was a major part of the tranquility and serenity I had experienced.

"Your father doesn't understand why you needed to go to a school so far away from home," she added.

How many eye rolls does it take to get to the center of a conversation with my mother? The world may never know. "I'm only a plane ride and a taxi cab away."

"You might as well still be in France."

I wish I was still in France. Talking to my parents reminded me of why I had left the country in the first place—*Don't think about it.* "It's not my fault you won't travel to see me."

"This was never the plan. You were supposed to go to school with Logan."

That name. *Don't think about it. Don't think about him.*

"Your father wants to know how your first couple of weeks were."

"You're not curious too?" I teased, but she stayed as cold as ever and did not respond. "They were fine." There was no way I would tell her about my first two failing grades from my major class.

"All right, I'll tell him. Also, I have something to talk to you about." *Good because I had no more ideas for topics of conversation to have with you.* "It's about Logan."

Now I was the one to become as cold as ice. "Mom." The tone of my voice should have silenced her. My warning should have been clear.

"He wants to see you."

"No," escaped my breathless lips as all the air was sucked out of my lungs. My body, my limbs, and my brain started to shut down.

"Honestly, Allie, how long are you going to give him the silent treatment?"

It had been a full year since I had seen or talked to him. That was not the "silent treatment." That was cutting someone out of my life.

"Honey? He says he is sorry and grudges aren't healthy. He was just a kid."

A kid? It was only a little over a year ago. "I don't care." I did not know what to say. It was hard to find words. It was even hard to breathe. God, I hated panic attacks. Why did talking to my mother almost always cause one?

"His mother told me he still loves you. He has been dating, of course, but she said he still has not gotten over you breaking up with him."

I hope he dies. I flinched at my own harsh thought and was glad I had not said it out loud by accident.

"And Allie, I know you still love him too—"

"I. Do. Not." The power in my voice was unmistakable. My anxiety faded as rage took over.

"Allie, if you just saw him again, I think you two would—"

"No."

"He wants to apologize and you will let him." My mother's voice became as hard as mine. "Don't be ungrateful. Your father has done business with his father for years now. You will do this for your family."

"How dare you?"

I hung up on her and turned off my phone.

Then I cried.

♀♀♀

AFTER CRYING for close to an hour, I pulled myself together. *No more thinking about Logan.* "I am ice," I repeated my mantra. "*Hard, cold, and unbreakable.*"

What Logan did to me was unforgivable, and the fact that my mother still wanted me with him made me ill. If my parents pushed for me to see him, after everything—after me seeing a therapist and after me leaving the country to go abroad for a year—they did not love me. How could they love me if they would willingly cause me so much pain? They were the ones to push Logan and me together in the first place. They were the reason I had been trapped in the terrible relationship for so long.

I wiped away my tears and changed into my pajamas, consisting of sweatpants and a loose V cut shirt. My cheeks were still red and my eyes were puffy, but I had to go to the bathroom. Hoping to not run into anyone, I ran. I sprinted right into Nate because my day was meant to be all bad luck and bad karma wrapped into twenty-four hours.

"Allie?" Nate's voice was softer than normal, like he knew I had been crying. I was an ugly crier, and my face would stay cherry red for at least an hour afterward.

I made a noise instead of asking "what" because I was afraid of my voice cracking.

"Are you... Is everything okay?" he asked. His attentive eyes widened when I gave a pathetic laugh.

"What does okay even mean?"

"It comes from the words 'all correct.'" Of course, he would know something like that. He loved the origin of words. The dictionary was probably his favorite book, the weirdo. Sexy weirdo.

"In that case, I am whatever means all wrong." I tried to pass him to slip into my room.

"Do you want to talk about it? I'm here."

I choked on a harsh breath. "You're here for a lonely stalker who means less than nothing to you?" I threw his words back at him.

He clenched his jaw. "As your RA, I need to be available in emotional situations. It's my job."

"Don't you hate me?" I asked.

Two long seconds passed before he answered, "I don't hate you."

"But you're annoyed by me."

He stood there, his eyebrows furrowed and his lips slanted down. He opened his mouth and closed it. His strained face reminded me of the zipper of my skinny jeans after a trip to a buffet.

"Nate, just say it. Jesus, you look constipated holding in whatever thought you're trying not to say."

My words made him angry. With a frustrated sigh, he said, "I'm...not annoyed by you."

"That wasn't all you were going to say." I crossed my arms and raised my chin. "Just say it." If he said something hurtful, it would bounce off of me. After all, sticks and stones might break bones, but words from Nate Reddington might keep me up at night for a year, replaying the critique until I cried myself to sleep as I planned to tonight.

"I shouldn't say it."

"Now you have to say it."

He scoffed. "I don't have to."

I rolled my eyes. "If you don't say it, you'll forever be known as one of those people who say 'I have a secret' and then never share it."

"If you share a secret, it's not a secret."

"Say it or I'll kiss you right on the mouth," I threatened.

His gaze dipped to my lips, and he swallowed. "I...I'm not annoyed by you."

"You said that already." My face hovered in front of his, proving my threat. The smell of crisp apples and toothpaste tickled my nostrils as my lips parted.

"I'm annoyed by how you make me feel."

"And how do I make you feel?"

He hesitated again. "Why were you crying?"

Right. I had almost forgotten in his presence. How cliché.

"I'll be fine," I reassured him, but he looked doubtful. Still, he did not un-tense himself or offer comfort. "I'm just tired."

I opened my door and was about to walk in the privacy of my own room when he moved closer behind me.

"Is it Ryan?" he inquired on a light growl.

"Why, are you jealous?"

"Are you jealous?" he asked.

"What?" Who did I have to be jealous about? The girl he had fucked next door to hurt me? Why would I be jealous of her? Because she had him? In the words and valley girl accent of the beautiful Cher—the one from *Clueless*, not the singer—*as if.*

Nate let out a heavy sigh and looked at the tiled floor. "Never mind."

"It has nothing to do with Ryan." My answer seemed to satisfy him because he nodded and moved back away from me.

"Just..." He appeared in pain to say, "Tell me if you need anything."

"Thank you."

There was a part of me—after everything—that wanted to tell him all of it. I wanted to tell someone, who appeared just as damaged as I was, what had happened to me. I wanted Nate to hold me and stroke my hair, whispering, *"it'll all be okay."* I wanted both of us to heal back into normal people with easy lives, who could interact without hurting one another. I wanted Nate to want me enough to break his rules for me.

But that would never happen.

☂☂☂

"A<small>LS</small>, what did I tell you last time?" Logan asked threateningly in my ear.

I whimpered on my knees in front of him as he pulled my hair into his fists. "I-I shouldn't look at anyone else."

"And what did you do today?"

"Please, n-nothing," I pleaded with him, but my words did nothing to calm him.

He slammed my head against the side of his car door. Something sticky started dripping down my cheek. Blood. Everything went fuzzy for a moment, and I only heard the end of his question when my ears stopped ringing.

"—at him! You think he's better looking than me? Huh? You want to go fuck him instead, you whore?"

Uncontrollable tears streaked my face. The skin on my knees stung against the sharp, uneven asphalt of the parking lot, and the side of my head hurt like never before.

"Answer me!"

"No," I shrieked before he could hit me again. He had a habit of staying away from my face, but I saw his fist rising toward my eye. "I love you! I would never be with anyone else. I never looked at him, I swear." I had just asked the older man for the time. Why was I so stupid?

Logan's foot connected with my stomach, and I doubled over at the force, trying to get oxygen back into my lungs.

"You know I hate this, baby," he said, suddenly calm and caring in my ear. He sounded like the old Logan again. "I don't want to hurt you; I'm sorry. I just need you to understand that you're mine. You need to feel how much you hurt me sometimes." His warm fingers cupped my cheeks, and he brushed away some still trickling blood. "I love you."

"I know," I tried to kiss him because kissing might make him stop hitting me. He pulled back before I could.

"I don't want to do this, but..." Logan grabbed another fist full of my hair, ready to slam my head against his car again.

I wish I could have blacked out from the pain, but I remember everything.

And I screamed. And I screamed. And I screamed.

NATE'S #5 RULE FOR LIFE: AVOID VULNERABLE PEOPLE AS THEY ARE CONTAGIOUS

 ate:

HOARSE, blood-curdling screams woke me up with a start. At first, it sounded like they were in my room, but once the cobwebs of sleep faded from my mind, I registered the screams were coming through my wall. Allie.

My shoulder hit my door so hard while I ran, I might have dislocated it. I rushed to her room. Luckily, she had not locked it—I would chastise her later—and I stepped inside without pause. The light was off, but small rays came through the blinds on her window from light posts outside. She laid on her bed, her eyes closed, her hands tangling in her hair, and she was still screaming.

Screaming.

My heart tripled its beating at her screams.

She shrieked, "Logan, please, s-stop."

"Allie." I bent down and shook her shoulders. I did not know if this was similar to not waking someone who sleep-walked. What were the rules for sleep screaming?

At my touch, her eyes shot open.

"It's okay," I whispered, trying to calm her down as I pulled her hands out of her hair. She yanked the red-brown strands so hard, I worried she would subject herself to early onset balding.

"What?" Her eyes were wide and terrified as she hyper-ventilated. I needed to calm her down. "Nate?"

"You were screaming. I came to check on you." My eyesight adjusted to the darkness of her room. Her inflamed cheeks were covered in tears. I wiped them off, and she sat up on the bed. "It's okay."

"Did everyone hear me?" Her voice rang full of humilia-tion and distress.

"No," I lied. Though maybe I had stopped her before she woke up anyone else. No one would know where the screaming came from anyway, and no one needed to know. My heart tightened as I stared down at her in her broken state, and one thought entered my mind. *Protect.*

"Oh, God." She put her head in her hands, and I sat next to her on the bed. A deep need to be close to her ruled my body.

Her treating me like I was broken now made perfect sense: it was how she saw herself.

No wonder she was obsessed with me. No one screamed in nightmares like that unless they had lived one. I had lived plenty. Even with my walls up, she had seen that. She knew I hid something, pushed something down deep inside of me. She had seen herself in me.

She had not been drawn to me because of my last name, but because of what she saw in me.

She had crossed the line plenty of times between us, but that was who she was. Allie had no sense of boundaries. Her trying to find me a girlfriend had pissed me off, less because she wanted to fix me, and more because I wanted her to want to *be* my girlfriend. Not that I wanted a girlfriend. I just…

I wanted Allie to want me the way I wanted her.

In this moment, I felt closer to her than ever before. Always, in our interactions, she claimed the upper hand, but now she was the vulnerable one. And I wanted to comfort the shit out of her. I wanted to buy different flavors of applesauce, soup, and tea, and line them all up as a *Feel Better* buffet. I wanted to wrap her in a cloud.

Instead, I rubbed slow circles on her back the way I did to Blue when she got failing grades or a stomach ache. "Really, it's okay."

Allie lifted her head to look at me again.

"It's not okay; nothing is okay," she whispered in a hushed tone. Her throat had to be sore from the screaming. "I thought I was over this."

"Over what?"

"The… My nightmares."

"It's natural to have nightmares—"

"They're not," she said. "They're memories."

Who the hell had caused her to feel so horrified and afraid? Her screams had sounded like she was being murdered. I wanted to ask her what her nightmare had been about, but the difference between us was I knew when not to cross a line.

"This happens a lot?" I offered an open question, which she could answer with detail or blow off.

She chose the blow off option. She pushed away from me. "Why are you here?"

"I already told you—"

"Just go, okay?" She wiped the rest of her tears off of her cheeks. "You don't even like me."

"That's not true." I liked her too much, that was the problem. Did she think I did not like her after the stunt I pulled with Hannah, the girl from Allie's erotic sex-club harem? I had been trying to hurt her and myself. I had wanted her to be jealous, but she was not. "Allie, you were just screaming and crying in your dreams. You need someone to talk to."

She appeared to be on the edge of breaking down, like her walls were too crumbled to come back up. "I'm fine by myself."

"I'm sure you are. You're strong." I placed my hand on her head as a small, comforting gesture. It came across more like a human patting the head of his four-legged best friend. *Why aren't you better at this?* "Who's Logan?" I repeated the name she had said in her sleep.

Before me the strongest, most impulsive, and wild girl I knew broke.

She broke.

Like a final explosion. Tears burst from her as her breathing roughened. She told me everything. She said she had been having reoccurring nightmares for a year now. They all related to her ex-boyfriend from high school. She did not tell me he hit her, but it was easy to figure out. I hated *Logan*. Who the hell could hurt Allie? She was a sunbeam or a little fairy. Pure, innocent energy. Well, not all innocent.

I wanted to kill him.

I wanted to hold her.

She clung to me, seeking comfort, as I stroked her hair and back. "Why were you with him for so long?"

Her back, which had turned to jelly, stiffened back into bone. She pushed away. "That's always the question, isn't it?" Her tone grew angry. "Everyone always wants to know why someone would stay with someone who hits them. Do they not realize a person who could hit a woman could kill one too?"

I pulled her back into a hug, and she sank into my body like she was made for me. Like maybe I was made for her.

"Fear. That's why I stayed with him. It's also why I left him," she said in a way that told me not to ask any more questions.

After what felt like an hour, she returned to her old self and put up her walls. I got up to leave, and her hand caught the back of my shirt.

"Stay." Her voice was so soft, I almost missed it.

She probably wanted someone to wake her if she screamed again. However, as I laid down next to her and let her put her head against my chest, I told myself she wanted me to stay because she wanted *me*, and because *I* made her feel safe. I wanted to be there for her the way no one had ever been there for me as a kid. It was obvious she put on an act around others to keep from breaking, and I related to that more than she would ever know. The difference was she acted a bit crazy and did whatever she wanted, and I lived by every rule and restriction possible. There are a lot of different ways to suppress bad thoughts.

Her breathing evened and her face relaxed as she fell back asleep. She looked angelic. Her hair spread out on my chest and her smooth legs lined up against mine. It had been a long time since I had *slept* with someone. I had a rule about people being in my space. Allie seemed to be able to break any and every one of my rules.

God, she was so pretty. Up close, I could see a few freckles on her cheeks. Her warm body pressed against me, reminding me of a blanket of security to my soul. Her lips were made of fairytales. Red and glistening for a happily ever after. All I wanted to do was kiss her. It was all I ever wanted to do anymore. Everywhere I went, she seemed to be there. And every moment I saw her, I fought an attraction boiling me from the inside.

She looked so peaceful and beautiful as she slept. But she was with Ryan. Her date with Ryan was tomorrow as he had made sure to tell me.

After learning so much about Allie, how could I let someone as callow and shallow as Ryan have her? He had no clue what she had been through. He could not relate to her the way I could. Damn it, she was everything dangerous to me. Off-limits because of my job; off-limits because of the emotions I felt around her. I was out of control. I had never been out of control.

One thing was for certain: I could not leave Allie alone anymore. Not now that I finally understood why she pushed me. She had pushed me so she would not have to push herself. She found "projects" in other people to feel less like unfinished work.

She could fix me any day of the week.

I knew too much after she had trusted and talked to me. Avoiding her would be malicious. She needed someone, and I wanted to be that someone.

There could just be no touching, no attraction, and no romance of any kind. She needed a friend; I would be a friend. Nothing more. I could fight the heat that flooded my body when I looked at her. It would be fine.

Everything would be fine.

❡❡❡

"I'M SORRY, sir, it's not working," the dining hall worker told me and handed me back my silver credit card. I was buying lunch, and I had already tried two of my go-to cards.

"Okay," I attempted to keep the worry out of my voice. Those credit cards always had money on them. They were linked to my father's account. "Can you try this one?" I handed her my debit card. It had money on it from my summer of working at a law firm as a file clerk.

She scanned it and shook her head. I was shocked. Something had to be wrong with the machine because I had not spent a dime of my money from my account; I was saving up to buy a place for Blue and me after graduation.

I handed some cash to the worker and exited the line after being embarrassed to hold up everyone behind me.

Walking over to the tables, I saw Allie sitting by herself. I had slipped out of her room in the morning before she had woken up. How would she treat me now, after I knew what had happened to her? Would she be friendlier? Would her walls come down again?

I put on a smile and sat down in front of her.

"Nate," she said in a surprised tone.

"Hey," I greeted her softly, and her eyes narrowed.

"Don't act differently around me."

I frowned at her. "I wasn't."

"You never smile at me. You also never eat lunch with me."

"I just didn't like you sitting alone." My tone became defensive, and she relaxed a bit. She read me so well, she was fluent. She saw through my fake smile and, apparently, preferred my normal colder voice to my nice, comforting one.

"Why?" she asked.

I got up. If she did not want me to join her—

"Not that I don't want you to sit with me," she added. "I just... Why?"

"RAs are supposed to sit with and talk to any residents who seem lonely." My words seemed to hurt her because the edges of her lips sunk in disappointment. An emotion flashed behind her bright green eyes before I could place it.

"I'm already sitting with someone." She said it like "so, bye."

If she needed space, I would give it to her. But we were linked now. She had to understand that. I got up and turned to walk to a different table. "Fine."

"But Nate?"

I glanced back at her. God, she was pretty. "Yeah?"

"Thank you."

❦❦❦

I WENT to the gym hoping to work out my issues, even though adding muscle to my arms would not make my home or school life any easier. I also wanted to work out, hoping to forget about how Allie was doing on her date with Ryan. Ryan made her laugh. What if she fell for him? What if she told him everything and she no longer needed for me to be a shoulder to lean on? What if they slept together?

I hit the punching bag in front of me with a loud *smack*. I needed to forget about Allie. I would be her friend, and as her friend, there was no reason for me to worry or think about her and Ryan.

I hit the bag until the skin on my knuckles bled. Damn it.

After an hour on the elliptical machine, I went to buy a water from the vending machine. When I swiped my normal credit card, it said, *"Denied."* I paused and frowned. There was no way. The cash register at the dining hall had been malfunctioning, so why the hell did it not work on this machine? I tried my gold credit card, and the machine flashed in red letters *"Denied"* at me again.

Taking a deep breath, I scanned my debit card. It had to have money on it. I never used it. It was my savings. There was no—

"Denied" flashed on the screen.

"Shit!" I shoved the machine. Why was this happening? Maybe my phone had messed up the magnetism of the strip. What other reason could there be?

As I walked back to the dorm building, I pulled out my cellphone and called my father.

A female voice answered, "Hello?"

"Who the fuck is this?" My frustration flared. Why was a

woman other than my mother answering my dad's private phone?

"No need to be rude." I heard a muffled sound from the phone and a lower volume, "George, I think it's for you."

"Hello?" My dad sounded as agitated as I felt.

"Who was that?"

"Oh, um, just a new secretary. Training her on the new phones and such." I heard a light giggle through the phone speaker, and my stomach twisted.

"Do you let every new secretary answer your non-work phone?" I held back on also asking if he slept with all his secretaries.

"Why did you call, son?"

"My cards keep getting denied."

"Yeah…about that, I've been meaning to talk to you. We're having some money problems at the moment. I think you should try to decrease your spending for now, son."

"*My* spending? I'm not the one who always takes a limo and eats nothing but lobster while my family sits at home eating microwaved ravioli every night." I let out another heavy breath. "My debit card got denied too, though. What's going on?"

"Well, I may have taken some money out—"

"What?" The rage in my tone rang clear. "Those were my savings. How could you even do that?"

"My name was still on the account from it being joint when you were a minor, so I had access—"

"I wasn't asking you how you were able to. I was asking how you could do something like that without telling me or even, it seems, without remorse." Without access to my money, I could not send my sister, Blue, cash for food.

"It's my money too."

"No. No, it's not. I've worked every summer since I was fifteen for that money. It was all *mine*."

"And you're *my* son."

I ran my fingers through my hair, frustrated. "If I called your driver, would he tell me you're still paying for a limo to drive you everywhere?"

"Nate—"

I summoned the confidence of the girl with auburn hair and red tips. The girl who stamped her name on each of my thoughts. The girl whom I had called crazy when she was one hundred percent herself with no remorse, even though at some points—specifically, the harem—she should have felt some regret. "Transfer my money back to my account, dad. I need it; you don't. Oh, and maybe send some money to your wife and daughter so they can eat some real food."

It was the first time I dared to hang up on my father. It felt good.

DORM MANUAL RULE #30: NO ROMANTIC RELATIONS WITH YOUR RA

llie:

RYAN WAS AMAZING, he was. Funny and charming. But even as we bowled together on our date, I could not get Nate out of my head. The way he had held me, his eyes full of familiar pain. After having told him almost everything about my past, I felt linked to him.

What if only broken people can fix each other?

But it bothered me when I had asked Nate why he wanted to sit with me and he had said it was his job as an RA to comfort lonely people. It reminded me of him calling me a lonely stalker. I was not lonely. In fact, I was on a date...and I was also thinking about a different man. Welp. *When in doubt, figure it out.*

My therapist in high school had told me a side effect of

being in an abusive relationship was problems with intimacy, so I had started having one-night stands as a *"Ha! I'm
fine."* In reality, I had just messed myself up worse by separating sex from feelings.

There was no magical fix for what I had been through,
but I had grown and dealt with it. I knew who I was now.

And I did want a real relationship again, to prove it to
myself and because I had not realized how much I missed
someone rubbing my back until Nate did it after my nightmare. I had run to myself enough. I wanted to find someone
else to run to.

❡❡❡

THE NEXT MONDAY, I saw Nate again in our history class. He
no longer frowned when he saw me. In fact, I swore I saw a
bit of a smile. It eased some of my caution as I slipped into
the seat next to him.

"Hey." Post-him-comforting-me-and-watching-me-fall-
apart-in-my-bedroom, post me-being-rude-in-the-cafeteria-
after-he-made-it-sound-like-it-was-his-job-to-comfort-me,
and post-my-date-with-Ryan, I was unsure how to proceed
with him.

He now knew more about me than anyone. And though
that should have disturbed me, it felt right.

"How was your weekend?" he asked.

Were we going to act like small talk with each other was
normal? Was I supposed to tell him about my date with Ryan
like we were friends? "Good, actually," I responded. "How
was yours?"

He hesitated before saying, "Fine."

"And by fine, you mean?" I prodded him.

"It was...stressful, I suppose." He faced the front of the classroom again like he expected me to drop the subject. He should have known me better than that.

"Why?"

"Just some stuff with my father."

The rough draft of my psychology paper had focused on him and his father, citing the article his ex-girlfriend inspired when she gave up Reddington family secrets for cold, hard cash. She had told the press Nate's relationship with his father was worse than rocky and qualified as neglect. She said his father used to lock him in the closet as a kid when he had business calls. "Want to talk about it?" I offered.

"No." His gaze remained focused on mine, and I could not tear myself away. "Do *you* want to talk about it?" He hinted at knowing my secrets as well.

"No." I did not want to talk about or even think about Logan. Nate turned away from me again, and I took a deep breath. "But I do want to talk to you about other things. I want us to be friends."

He stared at me. "Me too."

"Good," I said and smiled.

Now I just needed to stop thinking about him naked.

⚑ ⚑ ⚑

NATE WAS FUNNY. I had no idea Nate could be funny. I laughed so hard; some of the soda I drank at lunch came out of my nose. Our mutual jagged pasts made talking to him feel right. Open.

"You would really never go skydiving?" I asked him, still smiling at his story of him jumping out of a tree as a kid, thinking if he tried hard enough he would fly.

"Skydiving literally has *'die'* in it," he replied.

"It has the *sound* of 'die' in it," I defended.

He shook his head. "That's enough for me."

"But it feels like you're flying. I think you would like it."

"It doesn't just feel like you're falling to your death?"

"No. It's magical. With the adrenaline pumping in your veins and the wind slapping at you—you feel..." My heart beat faster as his gaze intensified on me. "This will sound weird, but you almost feel like a God."

"How can a girl who is brave enough to spend a year abroad alone and go skydiving be so afraid of cockroaches?"

That morning I had screamed at finding the bug in my room, and he had rescued me, complaining about how I should not eat and leave crumbs in my room.

"Bugs creep me out." I shivered from just thinking about them. "They make me think of coffins." Ever since the funeral of my great aunt when a maggot crawled over her face, anything in the realm of creepy crawly terrified me.

"So, what you're really scared of is death," he said. I was surprised at how well he analyzed me while I still struggled to figure him out.

"Isn't everyone afraid of death? It's a cliché at this point."

"Are you more afraid of death or the idea of not living?" His question shook me to the bone. I had not expected something like that from him. My idea of living was distracting myself to not think about my past.

"I almost died once." I tended to block out the memory, but for some reason, I felt no need to hide from Nate.

He hesitated before asking, "When?"

"Around a year ago." I prayed he did not do the math. I had told him about my breaking up with Logan a little over a year ago. Nate could guess something dramatic had given me the courage to leave him.

His angry eyes told me he understood. As did his flaring nostrils and tightening fists. "He fucking didn't."

"Well, as you can see, I'm alive, so correct, he didn't."

"I'll kill him," he growled under his breath, and the fierceness of it distracted me from noticing Ryan until he sat next to me.

"Kill who?" Ryan blinked, shocked to see Nate so riled up. He placed his lunch tray down on our table slowly, as if he was trying to figure out the aura of our conversation. "Is someone messing with you?" He turned to me and sat up a bit straighter, as if to show he could fight whoever it was too. Men.

"No, we were talking about…"

Nate saved me. "A cockroach in Allie's room."

I did not want Ryan to know anything about my past, especially Logan. My growing relationship with Ryan was light, bubbly, and nice. I wanted it to stay nice. Everything involving Nate was, well, intense.

"Oh." Ryan accepted it. "So, what's up with you two? I didn't know you ate together sometimes." There was a jealous ring in his voice.

Nate said, meeting my gaze, "We're friends."

My smile was infectious. Nate was contaminated instantly.

♟♟♟

"ARE you trying to be a terrible daughter or does that come naturally?" my mother asked me on the phone the next day.

I was so mad, my voice cracked. "Like mother, like daughter, right?" I hated how it sounded like I was crying. I would not give her the satisfaction of hearing me cry ever again.

"I just don't understand you. Why won't you let Logan come see you?"

My bitter laugh croaked. How could she not understand? He had almost killed her daughter. He had beaten me every month for two years. The little advice she had offered me was which shade of makeup best covers a black eye. I hated him. I hated her.

"I told you he wants to apologize," she said after I did not respond to her question.

"And I told you I never want to see or hear from him again."

"If you would just cancel the restraining order—"

"Cancel it? Really?"

"You two belong together." Her voice became dreamy, as if it was a fairytale to her. But Logan was a dragon instead of a prince, and I was far from a princess anymore. He had hardened me. I could no longer watch Sleeping Beauty without thinking about the coma he had put me in, without thinking about the kisses he stole without permission.

"I'd rather die." I hung up on her and let out a deep breath. I allowed a loud, tortured yell to escape my throat, to push out all my oppressive and negative feelings.

My fingers twitched as I craved a distraction from it all. It was the same feeling I got before obtaining a random tattoo or going skydiving or skinny-dipping in the middle of the winter. My mantra in my head turned into: *forget, forget, forget.*

"Are you okay?" I heard Nate's voice, and my head snapped up. How had I not noticed him entering my room? Was I so lost in my thoughts? "I heard you yell," he explained.

He sat next to me on my mattress with the ease of a normal friend, while my mind was infiltrated by treacherous thoughts of all the other reasons for why he could be on my bed. An image of him on top of me, pinning my arms behind my head burned into my brain, and I gave an awkward cough before I said anything to him.

"The walls are that thin?" I asked.

"What's wrong?"

I settled for being dramatic. My body dove into his chest, absorbing his heat and releasing a content sigh. "My birth giver called me again."

His strong arms pulled me in closer to him. "Who?"

"That's what I call my mother."

"Well, I call my mother 'mom' like a normal person," he teased me, his arms tightening around me for a moment.

"I hate her," I mumbled into his chest as I buried my face farther into him, using him as a shell of protection.

"Do you really?" Nate had problems with his parents, but he had never said he hated them. "Why are you so upset with her? What did she say?"

"She wants me to see Logan."

His body tensed under me. "What the fuck?"

"You took the words out of my mouth and my diary."

"What do you mean she wants you to see him?" He sounded as angry as I felt, and nothing had ever comforted me more. He was what I had needed. After Logan and what he had done to me, everyone had treated me like a fragile flower, like a single breath or comment would make me fly away. It was why I now kept it a secret wherever I went. I liked how Nate was as fiery as me. Every one of his reactions felt similar to my own. "What does she expect? You to take a break from classes, drive down, and visit him in jail? After everything he did?"

"Well—" I hesitated. "That's not—I mean, what she wants is for me to withdraw the restraining order and for him to come see me."

He was quiet at first. I could see the machinery of his mind working to understand what I said. "What do you mean him to come see you? He's locked up." Now I was the quiet one. "Allie, tell me he's locked up."

"I can't."

His shaken expression matched mine when the judge declared Logan innocent for attempted murder and guilty for mere light battery. "Didn't you testify?"

"I did."

"And the jury still let him off?"

"He got community service."

"What. The. Fuck."

The intensity in his eyes melted me. I should not have been feeling so at ease while talking about something continuing to haunt me, but I felt safe and understood around Nate. No one had cared for me this much in so long. No one had stood up for me or protected me.

His face was so close to mine, his warm breath hit my cheek, grazing the skin like a teasing thumb. My gaze locked onto his full lower lip. I wanted to kiss him. I wanted to kiss him so badly. I just wanted to feel *something*.

I leaned in and closed my eyes, but right before my lips could meet his, he pushed me away.

He shot up and off of my bed. "Allie."

I flinched at the pain on his face. "I—I just…" What could I say? I was weak, and I wanted him? I was feeling things I had not felt in so long?

He shut it down, rejecting me. "We can't."

Why can't we?

💧💧💧

"HOW COULD YOU?" Logan screamed at me, the agony in his voice matching the pain I felt as his grip tightened on my throat. The gaudy, fake-jeweled necklace my mother had bought me to match my dress cut into my neck. My perfect curls were ruined, and my mascara ran from my watering eyes. Prom had never sucked more. "I know it's not mine."

I sucked in a harsh breath. "It is yours. You're the only one—"

He let go of my throat and pushed me away from him. "Who else have you been fucking?"

I stumbled back in my high heels, almost falling onto the pavement of our high school's parking lot. We had danced for an hour before I built up the courage to tell him something that scared me worse than anything else. He had pulled me from the decorated gymnasium and outside to his car.

"No one. I told you, it's yours—"

"I always use condoms." The way he worded it instead of "we used condoms" made me even angrier. My anger, however, lacked the strength to drown out my fear.

"One must have broken," I said softly, in hopes to calm him down.

"You're cheating on me, I know you are," he yelled.

He opened his car's trunk. Inside it was a baseball bat—the bat he had used in the high school championships—and a spare tire. When I saw him reaching for the bat, I ran.

I ran back to the gym where the prom still went on. He would never hurt me in front of other people. He could not afford to get in trouble when he had to maintain his golden boy image. The mayor's son.

I ran and ran and ran. We had parked far away, and my heels limited my speed. I would have kicked them off, but Logan would catch up to me if I stopped to do so. Tripping on my long ball-gown shaped dress, I fell forward and caught myself with my hands. I cursed my mother for making me wear a princess dress.

"Oh, Allie." I turned my head to see him swing his bat up and, without hesitation, swing it back down to connect with the back of my knees.

I screamed like I never had before. This was the first time he had ever hit me with a weapon. My bones snapped under the impact. I couldn't stand up or move my legs, so I started crawling, pulling myself by the strength of my arms closer to the gym entrance and a street lamp. If I could get someone to see me, to see what was happening, they could stop it and help. Please, God, let someone help.

"Honey, you can't crawl away from me." His words chilled me, but I continued with haste to pull myself along the pavement. Luckily, my dress covered most of my skin so the harsh ground did not cut me up. Then his bat connected with my right arm, and I saw it break before my eyes. The burning pain blinded me.

He was going to kill me.

"P-Please, just put the bat down. Please."

He did not listen to me. He did not listen to me when he shat-

tered my ribs. He did not listen to me when he slammed my head into the pavement again and again. He did not listen to me when he left me for dead, bleeding in front of the gymnasium in my four hundred dollar prom dress.

My last thought before I slipped into the coma was a part of me had died that night and so had the baby.

"Allie." Nate shook me awake as hot tears clung to my cheeks. I must have woken him with my crying again. "It's okay." He cradled me against him and stroked a hand through my hair. "It was another nightmare."

My laugh was as bitter as a lemon, and his look of concern became even graver. "It was *the* nightmare."

"What happened?"

"Prom night. The night he put me in the coma." I hugged myself even as he hugged me. "I'm sorry I woke you up again."

"Don't be sorry. Ever."

"What would Hannah think of you coming over here?" Did he say, *"We can't,"* because of the girl he hooked up with? I had all but thrown my lips on his mouth. *I* had been the one who said I wanted us to be friends. Friends. And then I had tried to kiss him. Was my body incapable of convincing Nate I was not a lonely stalker? The embarrassment was a fresh wound.

His eyebrows furrowed. "Who?"

Evil little tingles sparked my skin at him not recalling the name of the girl he'd had revenge sex with in his room. Maybe she meant nothing to him. "That girl you…slept with." *"Best I've ever had,"* he had said.

"No," he said. "I was trying to—No, nothing happened with Savannah."

"Hannah."

"Right." Nate pulled on a strand of my hair. "Allie." He hesitated. Was he going to admit his feelings? That he wanted me— "I think you need some help."

Not what I had wanted to hear. "I've had help."

"There are some therapists on campus in the health center. I think maybe—"

"I've seen therapists. They all say the same thing and treat me like something out of a textbook." It was why I wanted to be a psychologist: to help people, rather than make them feel inadequate and easy to define.

He played with my hair for a moment before asking, "What do they usually say?"

"That I should expect to suffer from poor self-esteem, depression, and problems with, um, intimacy." One-night stands held no problem for me, but trusting someone with my feelings? No, thank you. But wasn't that what I did with Nate?

"And do you?"

"I hate how they think of it as a prophecy, like everyone doomed to one fate will be doomed to another. Everything I do is to try to be the opposite of what they tell me. Poor self-esteem? I get dressed up every damn day. Depression? How can someone be depressed if they go to parties, explore the world, go skydiving, and climb mountains in their free time?"

"So, no therapists." Nate nodded and bit his lip. I loved how he tried to think of ways to help me heal. "What about group therapy?"

"Like people with issues all coming together to sing 'Kumbaya My Lord?'"

"It may not be as cheesy as you think it is."

I snuggled closer to him at his comforting tone. "Would you go with me?" I did not want to go open up to strangers all alone.

His silence scared me until he said, "If you want me to."

"I want you to." Or more truthfully, "*I want you.*"

NATE'S #6 RULE FOR LIFE: FUN IS FOR PEOPLE WITH NOTHING BETTER TO DO

 ate:

"GOLDY WAS two years old when he died, and he was my best friend. Whenever I fed him, his tail would move faster and his big eyes would look up at me..." A boy who looked too young to even be a freshman held back tears.

Allie's hands were pale as she clenched her fingers into tight fists. I put my hand over hers to soothe her, and she glanced at me. Ignoring the sparks radiating from where our skin met, I squeezed her to remind her why we were here. She had been having nightmares every night, and I had thankfully convinced her to go to group therapy. So far, however, everyone's issues could not even compare to Allie's.

"I still remember the cute little bubbles he used to make,"

the boy finished his story, and everyone glanced around, confused.

"Bubbles?" The group therapy leader questioned. How did a dog make bubbles? Wait. "Goldy was…a fish?"

The boy nodded and made a sad noise. "Goldy the goldfish."

I knew what Allie was thinking when she sent me a distressed look. How was she supposed to feel comfortable enough to come forward and share with the group all the horrific things she had been through if their issues scaled from a dead fish to gaining ten pounds of the normal freshman fifteen? Most tortured people must not have wanted to talk about their issues and come to share their feelings.

"Next, let's talk to our newest members." The group leader looked at Allie and me. "Please share your names and something that's been bothering you."

Allie squeezed my hand, so I went first. "My name is Nate and I'm an alcoholic." Allie hit me hard, but it was worth it to see her frown turn even a little bit upside down. "Sorry, that was a bad joke, I'm nervous. I do think I sometimes drink alcohol to escape, though. Um, something that has been bothering me, uh, I've been having problems with my father and money." After my argument with him over the phone, my money had turned back up in my savings account. The credit cards still didn't work, though.

"And how does that make you feel?" The leader sounded like every stereotypical therapist in a movie.

"Definitely not good," I remarked, and Allie hit me again for sounding insulting.

"And you are?"

"Allie," she answered in a low voice beside me, and I squeezed her hand again. "And I, um, I…" She took a deep breath. "I've been struggling in a class." Something sank into my chest when she did not open up, but I also understood. It was the wrong environment.

"Which class?"

"Psychology, which is also my major, so it has kind of been freaking me out."

"And how does that make you feel?" she asked her the same question, like every problem was the same. I now understood why Allie disliked therapy. But not all therapy was as bad as this.

"It makes me feel like if I can't pull up my grades, maybe I don't have what it takes to fulfill my dream." Her words rang so full of emotion, I realized this problem was a real one, not one she made up on the spot. She was struggling with grades? I tutored people all the time; I could help her. Having trouble in classes during the first semester of college was normal. Everyone had an adjustment period.

Once the group therapy session ended, Allie all but ran out of the room. Thankfully, my long legs gave me the ability to catch up with her before she left the building by herself.

"Allie," I yelled after her.

She stopped her speed-walking until I made it to her side.

"I'm sorry," we said in unison and both cracked into a smile.

"I didn't think it would be…like that," I commented and ran a hand through my hair. I had been trying to help her and instead I had shown her how she had gone through more trauma than the typical college student, making her feel more isolated and alone. "Not all therapy is like that, though. Our school might just be cheap."

"I'm sorry I couldn't try to make it work, but I already know how to deal with things. I don't need group therapy."

"How do you deal with things?" Maybe she could give me advice on handling the problems I had with my family.

"I stop thinking," she answered as if her statement was not impossible.

"You're a psychology major, you know people can't just stop thinking."

"Have you ever done anything crazy that forces you to live in the moment and forget everything else?" The fire and animation in her eyes shook me.

"No. I prefer being in—"

"Control," she finished my sentence. "I know. But that hasn't exactly been working for you, has it?"

I frowned at her, and she smiled, putting her hands on my face and pulling it down closer to hers. My heart stopped beating, my body pausing, waiting for her kiss. I had no strength in me to reject her. God, I had wanted that kiss so badly. But she made no move to press her lips against mine the way I had imagined her doing for months now.

"So how about we try it my way?"

"I'm not going skydiving," I told her.

She grinned at me. Damn, up close like this, her smiling, she was stunning. "Okay, scared-y cat, we'll start slow."

⚲⚲⚲

"This is as close to climbing a mountain as we're going to get while we're in school."

"*This* is your idea of starting slow?" I adjusted the strap on my protective helmet as if re-doing the Velcro could save me in the end if I fell to my death.

"Oh, relax. It's just an indoor rock wall, and it's not even that tall." She pulled on her vest, which connected to the ceiling by wires. "It will be fun."

"Our ideas of fun are very different."

"Are you two ready?" The worker questioned us and led us to the base of the tall rock wall. "Even though you are wearing safety equipment, we always ask that you be careful. If you fall, let yourself fall, and don't resist or jump off the wall. Safety rules include keeping all your equipment in the right position and trying your best!" His over-friendliness was off-putting to me when I relied on him to keep me safe.

"Come on!" Allie pulled my arm until we were in front of the wall. She placed one hand on a red-colored rock ledge and grinned. "Let's go."

I took a deep breath and stepped up onto it, reaching above me for the two blue rocks to pull my body up higher.

As I stood off the ground, I thought back to how I would have never done this in my four years of college without having known her. This girl was a life tornado. Who knew I had been living in black and white Kansas until she had thrust me into colorful Oz?

Allie slowed down her climbing until I caught up to her. She was already one fourth done. While climbing, the fake mountain wall seemed taller.

"I would have thought someone with so many muscles would be a faster climber," she said, her words thick with snark. Her snarkiness was one of the sexiest things about her.

"Are you seriously challenging me right now?" I increased my pace and got closer to her level, but she was still up higher than me by about four rocks.

"It seems that way, doesn't it?" She climbed faster now. A flutter tickled the inside of my chest at the thought of proving myself to her.

We both began finding rocks and pulling ourselves up at a quicker pace. I almost passed her at one point, but she sped back in front of me when I had trouble choosing which rock to step up on. The higher we climbed the wall, the fewer rock ledges there were until we started having to fight and beat each other to the next rock to continue our journey up. Her body now above mine, her magnificent backside filled my immediate line of vision. A big, big distraction. Climbing was hard with an erection. Literally.

One of my feet slipped a bit, shifting my concentration to the rocks instead of her terrific ass. I mean damn, the curve of it—*No.* I was lucky she wore shorts and not her normal dresses, or I would have happily fallen to my death from such a distraction.

"I see you." I heard her, and my gaze lifted to see her face smirking down at me. She curled her head back, catching my ogling. "You sure that's the best thing to be doing right now?"

I focused on placing my hand over the rock she had just stepped off of. "I have no idea what you're talking about."

"So you weren't just staring at my ass like it was a juicy apple you wanted a bite of?"

My jaw dropped at her bluntness, but I should have been used to her straightforwardness by now. I played along because she craved someone to play with her. Joke with her. I wanted to be that person more than I wanted to get off this damn rock wall. "Less like an apple, more like a pair of plump persimmons," I referred to the juiciness of her ass.

She was stunned for a moment, and I grinned at surprising Miss Constantly-Surprising. "Did—Did you just compare my butt to persimmons?"

"Correct."

She laughed and continued climbing. "Only you could think of the most pretentious fruit."

I followed her, not allowing more than a foot between us. "How are persimmons pretentious?"

"The word persimmon makes me think of spoiled, rich people." She stopped moving above me and looked down again. She did a terrible British accent. "'Ello, me mum says to eat a persimmon a day to keep the ole poor man away." Her British accent lost power as it switched from English to Irish to Australian. "If I don't eat a persimmon in the morning, my parents will only let me eat the non-brand name caviar."

"You are ridiculous." I chuckled at her. "First off, never do an accent again. Second, why British? Do you also assume all British people are pretentious?"

She paused in her climbing as she thought, then resumed. "I think the Queen is pretty cool. I like her corgis. They're super cute."

"They are dogs."

"Are you a dog person or a cat person?" she asked. We looked to have about a fourth left of the wall to climb. She was still above me because there was no way to get around her when the rock ledges became so scarce. "I already know you're not a person person."

"What makes you say that?"

149

"Well, you know—" she cut off when her foot slipped, and she started to fall.

I raised my right hand off a rock and caught her by her bottom. My grip supported her, but I almost had a heart attack when I realized the exact position of my hand. My fingers cupped the warm, plump cheeks of her ass as my hand bent back. The heel of my palm pressed between her legs; my thumb aligned with her swollen clit. *Fuck.*

She let out a light moan and bucked her hips at the impact of where my hand was, grinding down on me. I wanted to take my hand away, but she still had not put her foot back on the rock.

"Um, Allie?" My voice came out rough and husky as I fought off my stiffening erection while keeping my grip on her so she wouldn't fall. She let out a light squeal as a response to my questioning her. "Um, could you put your foot back on one of the rocks?"

She shivered but moved up, off of my hand, and pulled herself back into position. "Y-Yeah."

I wanted to bang my head against the wall to stop the steamy thoughts bombarding my mind. *Repeat after me: she is with Ryan.*

Had the dampness between her legs come from the sweat of my palm or was she wet—*Fuck. Fuck. Gah.* How was I supposed to concentrate on climbing after that?

I liked her. I liked her sense of humor, her fearlessness, and how I felt different around her. I *got* her. Ryan did not get her. He could never understand what she was and how she had become it. Plus, she had trusted me with it all. Me. There had to be a reason for that. She tried kissing me before, and on multiple occasions, she gazed at me with the same passionate heat I felt for her. She liked me too. But that could not matter.

There were too many reasons for us not to be together. It was against the rules, she was dating Ryan, and we were too different. Why did it not matter to me? All of those things should matter. Why did I keep picturing us doing way more than kissing?

❦❦❦

PASSING ALLIE'S room on my way to mine, I heard two voices coming through her door. They both sounded alarmed and a bit hectic, so I stopped and knocked. The other voice did not belong to her roommate; it was a low male one. Gavin? Ryan? Why the hell did no one come to the door after I knocked? Instead, the voices stopped as if they hoped I would go away.

"Allie?" I asked through the door. I did not want to open it if she did not want me to. We had talked about barriers and us becoming friends before treating each other like RA and resident.

I heard a muffled statement, which I assumed was "who was that?" I opened the door because Ryan and Gavin would never sound so angry with her.

I stepped into the room and saw Allie standing behind her bed like she used it as a defense barrier. The guy glared at me, but I had never seen him before. His bright blond hair appeared almost white, and his body was one of an athlete.

"Who the fuck are you?" he questioned me.

I stood straighter as he took on an offensive stance. "I

could ask you the same thing." My remark seemed to bother him because he took another aggressive step toward me.

"Logan, don't!" I heard Allie say, and every muscle in my body tightened.

"Logan?" I growled, anger dripping from my voice.

All I saw was red.

DORM MANUAL RULE #32: NO VIOLENCE IN THE DORM

llie:

AFTER HEARING a knock on my door around six o'clock, I had assumed it was Nate or Gavin. Opening my door only to see the boy, whom I had spent every minute of every day for a year trying not to think about, froze me to the bone. My lungs quit without handing in a two weeks' notice when I saw Logan's face. At first, I thought it was another nightmare but when he shot me a small smile, my stomach twisted into nauseous knots. He looked the same. Handsome, smug, and dangerous. Had my mother told him where I was? How did she even know my room number?

"What did you do to your hair?" was the first thing he said to me. The last time I had seen him was when I testified at his trial, and yet those were his first words to me since the night he had almost killed me.

"Dyed it." He would have been used to seeing me with shorter hair. When we were together, I had it cut, so it was harder for him to grab and pull. "What are you doing here?" I asked in a calm voice. I did not know how his temper was anymore.

"I had to see you." He walked into my room as if he had every right to come into my personal space. He also surveyed every inch of it.

"I still have the restraining order."

"I want you to get rid of it." Logan plopped down on my bed and bounced twice before moving his gaze back to me. "Your room is small."

What was I supposed to say to that?

"You should move back home." He continued telling me things I did not want to hear. "You don't need to be here."

"I like it here." I became a bit more daring. "You're the one who shouldn't be here."

"I needed to talk to you."

"About what?" I inched to my desk where my cell phone sat. If I could just call someone—but who would know to come to check on me? They would just call me back and Logan would realize what I had done.

Nate. Nate would know to come over.

"I'm sorry about what happened."

A bitter laugh slipped out of me. "You're sorry?"

"Yeah."

"You almost killed me," I yelled. The constant anger bubbling beneath the surface came out with a vengeance. My anger triggered his. Fantastic.

"You cheated on me. I loved you, and you cheated on me." Logan standing with his hands clenched into fists and fire in his eyes used to scare me, but there was nothing left to fear. What more could he take from me? He had already taken my life.

"I. Did. Not," I said. The chill in my voice was enough to startle him. He had never heard me speak to him in such a way before. "That baby was yours and you fucking killed it."

He was silent. He stared at me with wide eyes and sat back down on my bed.

"You're not a part of my life anymore," I said, trying to revive a calm exterior. "I want you to leave."

"We belong together. You calm me down—"

"Get. Out." Once the words came out of my mouth, there was a knock at my door, and Logan and I paused. I could not breathe.

"Allie?" Nate's voice cut through the door. Upon seeing Logan's reaction, fear sliced into me, shattering my armor.

"What guy is visiting you so late?" Logan asked me, and I again struggled with my words. "Are you dating someone? Who?"

Nate opened the door and came in. He narrowed his eyes on Logan.

"Who the fuck are you?"

"I could ask you the same thing." Nate's tone held a challenge, and when Logan took on his *I'm-going-to-hit-you stance*, my blood turned cold, freezing into red ice in my veins.

"Logan, don't!"

"Logan?" Understanding flashed in Nate's eyes, and rage overcame him. Everything happened in a blur.

Nate ran at Logan and tackled him to the ground. Logan was strong but Nate seemed stronger. The first two punches were hard and fast into Logan's jaw, and it disorientated him enough to prevent him from blocking the next hit, which broke his nose. Logan let out a loud bellow and rolled both of them around, resulting in Logan being on top. This did not bother Nate because he pushed his knee up between Logan's legs, and, at that painful distraction, Nate escaped from underneath him. He shot back up while Logan knelt, holding his groin and glaring.

"What the hell?"

"You like hitting women but can't take a man hitting you?" Nate asked.

"Who is this guy, Allie?"

My hero? I again was shocked silent. Seeing such fighting from Nate should have been scary, should have triggered old fears, but instead…. Damn, how was he so fucking sexy? He accomplished what I had always wanted.

When Logan first started hurting me, all I wanted was my father or an imaginary big brother or a guy friend to stand up for me and protect me. My attempts at holding Logan back or getting violent with him always ended with one of my bones broken. I had never dreamt of being a princess, but Nate "saving" me was, well, hot. A steamy image of him in nothing but shiny knight armor flooded my mind.

"Let me make one thing clear." Nate pulled Logan's head up, forcing him to meet his gaze. "You will not talk to Allie. You will not look at Allie. From now on, you never even knew her."

"Who are you?"

"I'm the guy who can make you disappear. I don't care

how popular you are in your small town. I don't care that you come from money. I come from more money than you will ever see in your lifetime. I care that you hurt *her*." Nate's face moved so close and threatening to Logan's, I worried they might bite each other. "Don't ever come near her or try to contact her again. If you do, I will break you. Do you understand?"

"You don't even—"

"Do you understand?"

"Yes."

Nate pulled Logan up and pushed him toward the door. Logan spun around and appeared as if he was going to say something.

"Don't say bye," Nate told him.

Logan stepping out and closing the door allowed oxygen to once again fill my lungs. I knew I gazed at Nate like he was a rock star and I was not worthy of being in his presence, but I did not care. Someone had cared enough about me to help me, to defend me from Logan. Not even a jury had done that, let alone my own family. They had found out and told me his abuse was a phase and to stay with him because we had a "future together."

"How long was he here? Are you okay?" Nate rushed over to me and inspected every inch of my body. "Did he hurt you? If he did, I can still catch him and kill him."

A sound closest to a laugh jumped out of my mouth. "Nate."

"Are you in shock?" The concern on his face made me want to thank him and hug him and kiss him even more.

How had he become so important to me in such a short amount of time? How did he make me feel things I thought I might never feel again? Not to mention, the new ways he had me feeling too. I wanted him all the time. I thought about him all the time. I had been kidding myself by saying my fascination with him was for a mere paper. God, how blind had I been? The moment I met him was the moment I realized I could give no one else my attention.

"Nate," I repeated, tears prickling my eyes and blurring the magnificent view of him.

The worry lines on his forehead deepened. "Allie, the way you're looking at me—"

"How am I looking at you?"

In one smooth motion, he bent down, cupped my cheeks, and pressed his lips against mine. I nearly blacked out in the process.

Heat.

Chills.

Apples.

His lips moved against mine, claiming me, aching for me, and causing an ache inside me at the same time. The passion of it, the contrast of his gentle thumb stroking my face as the kiss became ravishing and ravenous. Perfection.

He was perfection. I felt the kind of sparks and tingles I had only read about. Ryan was a good kisser but after this how could I—I could not even think about Ryan. Nate filled up all of me with his kiss. Even his homemade apple pie scent intoxicated me.

One of his warm, demanding hands stayed on my cheek while the other traveled to squeeze my hip. He pulled me to him, his hot and hard body pressed up against mine in the most delicious kind of way. My fingers explored his hair, tangling in the dark tresses. When his devious tongue came into play, I almost fainted.

His tantalizing lips sucked mine, slow, and fast and full of cinematic potential. It felt like a romantic, passionate kiss in the rain, but we were dry and inside, and wow nothing would ever feel so good.

My breathing came in ragged heaves as he gripped the back of my tender neck, supporting my head to deepen the kiss. I did not know how long we stood there, making out, but when we needed to breathe again, he pulled back and held me close in front of him. The heat from his body radiated into mine. My personal heater. My favorite flame.

His face still appeared pained but his eyes were dark with arousal. "Allie."

"Nate." I loved his name. I could have said it or sang it from the rooftops all day. Nate, Nate, Nate, Nate.

"Allie. We shouldn't have." His words were like ice down my panties.

I hid my flinch but my voice cracked, revealing my hurt. My pain. "What?"

He stared at me with more concern but this time it felt more like pity. I hated pity.

"I'm sorry," he said.

"You are sorry?" Humiliation colored my cheeks. This man—who had just done more for me than my own family—had kissed me out of pity. My hurt sparked my anger. "Get out," I said.

His addictive lips separated, but they could say nothing I wanted to hear.

"I just kissed you because you were here and my adrenaline is high," I told him, trying to save my pride. "I would rather be kissing Ryan."

Nate jerked back, toward my door. "Okay."

"He's a better kisser, anyway."

Nate remained silent. His hand curled over the knob of my door.

"Bye."

❡❡❡

"So you and Nate—" Gavin started, and my head snapped up so fast my neck muscles suffered a twinge. Did the neck have muscles?

"What?" Gavin's eyebrows shot up, and his eyes narrowed at my immediate reaction. Great, now he was suspicious.

It had been a day since I had kissed Nate and snapped at him. I felt as guilty as ever. I had never cheated. Even though Ryan and I were not serious enough to qualify a kiss as "cheating," finding out would hurt Ryan. I could let no one find out.

I could also never kiss Nate again. Even if the kiss had my blood boiling and my body waking up for the first time in a long time. Last night, trying to fall asleep had been almost impossible. Every time I closed my eyes, I was kissing Nate and his hands were running over me and we were about to—

"I was going to say, so you and Nate have been hanging out lately." Gavin cocked his head to the side like a polite mother interrogating a child who drew on the wall with a marker. "But is there something else you want to talk to me about?"

"I can't think of anything," I answered faster than I should have.

"You're a bad liar."

"I'm not lying." I attempted looking insulted, but he saw right through me.

"When is your next date with Ryan?" He nonchalantly sipped from his milk carton, but his words held gravity. I needed to focus on Ryan. Nate would not have me, and I still had my goal to be with someone. I liked Ryan. I could love him…eventually.

"Soon," I said.

"Do you want to go on another date with him?"

"I feel like I have to," I admitted.

"Incorrect. According to the Declaration of Independence, you don't have to do anything you don't want to."

"I think actual history would disagree with you."

"What do you know about history?" Gavin laughed at me, but I had learned a lot from being around Nate. He was full of random facts.

"Well, I am in a women's history class with Nate."

"Ah, bringing up Nate again I see. How close are you two? Does he know the role of your best friend has already been filled?"

"I'll tell him next time I see him."

"And when will that be?" Gavin's voice became a bit more serious. Gavin was friends with Ryan and my liking Nate could have bothered him too.

I hated myself. Nate had rejected me multiple times already. Why could I not just let it go? Why did kissing him have to be more than anything I had ever experienced?

"Probably in class."

Nate had not talked to me since the kiss. It had been just

a day, but eating breakfast without him felt lonely.

Gavin thought about it for a moment. "*Nate* is taking women's history?"

"Yeah, so?"

"That's just kind of funny to me."

"Is it funny to you how the United States wasn't even one of the first fifteen countries to grant women the right to vote? Or how from the early nineteen hundreds to the eighties, women who went to the hospital were sterilized against their will because of their race and class?"

"Whoa, whoa, okay. I get it." Gavin laughed again. "I didn't mean it's weird for guys to take women's history. After all, girls have to sit through men's history from kindergarten to high school. I was just wondering why Nate would take it." Gavin contemplated, "I mean, I guess it could be a great way to meet girls. The gender ratio of the class must be pretty bent."

"Guys are not stupid enough to take women's history just to meet girls."

"Have you met us?" Gavin joked.

"Met who?" I heard Ryan's voice from behind me, before the chair next to me pulled back and he settled down onto it. "What's up?" He nudged me, flashing a playful grin.

"Nate is taking women's history," Gavin told him.

"Huh. I bet he could meet a lot of girls that way."

A ding came from my phone.

"Who texted you?" Ryan asked.

"*Nate*" flashed on my screen. "No one."

Gavin and Ryan frowned. Gavin said, "That's the most suspicious thing you could have said."

"I-I just mean, it doesn't matter. I'm hanging out with you

guys right now."

I did not get to read or respond to the message until I got back to my room after dinner.

"*I'm sorry about what happened,*" Nate had sent me.

Me: "*Don't be. It's fine.*"

"*It was not fine. I shouldn't have done that,*" he texted me back, fast.

Me: "*Logan deserved it.*"

Nate: "*Don't act like you don't know what I'm talking about.*"

The kiss. "*I know,*" I texted.

Nate: "*It can't happen again.*"

I read his message, and a pang settled in my chest. "*I know.*" As long as I was dating Ryan, I could not kiss Nate. Yet, it bothered me so much how he seemed fine with that. It was as if kissing me had been a mistake *and* meant nothing.

Nate: "*But I can't stay away from you.*"

My phone buzzed with another message following it.

Nate: "*I like hanging out with you.*"

I sent back, "*Me too.*"

Nate: "*We need to be friends.*"

Me: "*Okay.*"

Nate: "*Just friends.*"

His need to clarify annoyed me. Did he think he was so irresistible? He was attractive, sure, but it was not like all he had to do was look at me and I would fall on his lips. He was so smug.

Yet, I somewhat wished he was smugger. There was so much more to him than what he let other people see. His struggle mirrored my own and, dammit, he had fought for me. *Fought* for *me*.

Walking to the dorm bathroom an hour later, I was

surprised to see him coming from the men's showers. He carried a blue shower caddy and wore nothing but a white towel.

He had to have planned this. Fate could not have hated me that much.

His wet, dark hair shined, and the clean, fresh smell of him hit me like a paint grenade. The neon blue of his eyes shined brighter than normal, but I could not keep my eyes on his no matter how hard I tried. As my control slipped, so did my gaze. It followed a runaway water droplet from his slick hair, down his neck, sliding across the sculpted muscles on his toned chest, down to the light, happy trail of hair before reaching right where his—

It went under the towel.

Shit, was I drooling?

"Fuck," came out of my mouth before I could pull it back in.

I shivered at the heat in Nate's eyes after watching me all but devour him. He put the shower caddy in front of him, blocking any view of what I could make out through the thin towel.

"I don't think friends say 'fuck' when they see each other."

"I don't think friends see each other practically naked," I shot back. "Aren't you breaking the 'no indecent exposure' in the hallway rule?"

Nate noticed I was not going to pass him so he walked around me to get to his door. Still frozen in my spot, fantasies invaded my mind. My body was on fire. Why the hell did he have to seem so calm and unaffected? I wanted him to lose control. I wanted to melt him.

He said over his shoulder, "It should not happen again."

DORM MANUAL RULE #16: STAY AHEAD IN YOUR STUDIES

llie:

"WHAT'S WRONG?" Nate asked me after I sat next to him in class. I loved and hated how he knew me and my facial expressions so well.

"I got a C on my third psychology quiz." I let out a loud, disappointed and angry sigh. "I studied. So. Much. I thought I could pick up my grade, but no."

"A C isn't that bad."

"Oh, don't pull that shit on me." It was my grade. I was allowed to be worried. I had been a great student in high school. It had been rare for me to get a *B*. "I know you get all A's. You hate it when you get a ninety-one. And here I am, with my lousy seventy."

Every day in psychology scared me more and more. What if I

could not do what I had always wanted to do? What if my plans for the future were ruined before I had the chance to get started? And then there was the final paper, which I had trashed about Nate but still had not found a new subject to write about. The closer I came to the deadline, the more tempted I was to open the Word document on my laptop and finish the one about him.

"If you want, I could help you," Nate offered.

"What?" I picked my head back up. "What do you know about psychology?"

"I took the class a year ago because it filled one of my general requirements, and I've tutored people before."

"How much do you charge?"

"You don't have to pay me, Allie." The tone of his voice was sad.

"Oh, yeah, I forgot." I poked him. "You're a millionaire."

"But most importantly, I'm a tutor."

An image of him wearing a casual suit, carrying a ruler, and pointing at a chalkboard consumed my thoughts. He would make such a sexy teacher. Detention would never be so hot. Him leaning across my desk, telling me I needed to focus. Me dropping a pen and him bending down to pick it up, leaving him on his knees in front of me, my legs open in my dress, him seeing and moving forward to—

A small moan escaped the back of my throat when I got caught up in the sexual daydream. Nate's gleaming eyes widened before narrowing on me. His lips thinned, and he looked angry.

"What were you just thinking about?" he growled his question.

You giving me an A-plus plus in every possible way?

"Nothing."

†††

I DID NOT REALIZE I zoned out until Ryan's hand squeezed mine.

"It's your turn again." He pulled me out of my thoughts. "Do you not like pool?"

"It's okay." I stepped closer to the table and re-aligned my pool stick with the cue ball. I hoped this time I would hit a ball with a number other than eight on it.

"You just seem somewhere else today," Ryan said.

The loud ringing from my phone interrupted us, and he scowled at my device as I took it out of my purse to answer it.

"Fantastic," I murmured once I saw who called me.

"Who is it?" Ryan sounded as annoyed as I felt. I supposed he had a problem with our date being interrupted, while I was more upset over the person who called.

"My mother. Can you give me a minute? I should answer." I had already ignored three previous calls. Ryan nodded.

"Hello?" I answered the phone.

"Where are you?"

"Like in my life? I think I'm in a good place."

"You're not in your room."

What? "Excuse me?"

"Your father and I are outside your room, and it is locked, and we have been knocking."

"My room at school?"

"Yes, your room at school. Get here now." She hung up on me.

I took a deep breath to make sure I did not start panicking. "I have to go," I told Ryan, frowning. I both did not want to end our date early, and also I had no interest in seeing my parents. Why were they here?

"Really?" Ryan pouted his lips.

"Really."

"Am I—" he started before I walked away. "Am I doing something wrong? You've been in your head lately and now you're cutting our date short."

It's not you, it's me. "My parents are here, so I have to go find them before they break my door down. You're doing nothing wrong." I was the one doing wrong.

By the time I got to my dorm room, I had mentally prepared myself to see my parents. My father was in his typical expensive suit, and my mother wore her designer-of-the-week dress. She stood tall with an expression as sharp as the stem of her high heels. Once they saw me, they frowned, and my father checked his golden watch.

"We've been standing here for over an hour," my mother grumbled.

"I doubt that's true," I said.

I moved in front of them to unlock my door and waited until everyone stepped inside before I closed it. Thankfully, my roommate, Marissa, was not in the room again. Otherwise, it could have become awkward. More awkward. My mother scanned my room with the same distaste Logan had. My father sat down in my chair.

"Why are you here?" I asked them.

I had not seen them since my high school graduation day

a year ago, and I preferred it that way. My parents were not my parents. They had stuck me with Logan and had done nothing to help me afterward. My dad had taken Logan's side because of his business dealings with his father. My mother had used her tingling money-senses to choose Logan and his inheritance over my claims of assault and battery. She wanted me to marry him, even after everything. I still could not believe she had told Logan where I was when I had the restraining order.

"Logan's parents said you had him beaten when he showed up to talk to you." My mother's harsh voice could make an innocent victim feel like a guilty villain.

Did I regret Nate hitting Logan? I tried to find some sympathy for him, but nothing came to me. After all he had done to me, him being hurt and humiliated felt like justice. He had not gone to jail. He had lost none of his great prospects for colleges or jobs over it. Was I a bad person for *not* thinking what Nate had done was wrong?

"I did not have him beaten." I sighed. "You make me sound like a mafia lord."

"He had two black eyes when he got home. Not to mention, the other bruises on his body." They were concerned about his bruises? After he had hurt me for two years? After he had broken almost all of my bones and put me in a coma?

"Poor him."

"You ungrateful girl. How will he take you back after this?" my mother asked.

"Um, he won't?"

"You sound as if you don't even care."

"Um, I don't?"

My mother huffed. She had talked to me on the phone, but she had not seen me in a long time. I was stronger now, and I would not let her push me around.

"George, say something," she prodded my father.

My dad stared at the ground. My father had never called me when I was abroad, or even after I had come back. Between the two of them, I had always been closer to him. It had broken me when he had allowed me to continue dating Logan after he found out about the first time he had hit me. I had wanted him to stand up for me the way Nate did.

There were bags under my father's eyes. He looked much older now and thinner under his suit, causing my thoughts to turn to his health. As much as I wanted nothing to do with my parents, I still felt something for them. They had raised me. Yet, I did not know if I loved them anymore. Relationships with parents were complicated. They were supposed to stay your parents when you needed them, but once you were old enough and close enough to them, they were supposed to become your friends. I could not be friends with someone I could not trust. I also could not love someone who was not my friend.

"What do you want me to say?" my father questioned my mother in a sterner voice than he had ever directed at her.

"Tell her what she's done," she exclaimed. I hoped Nate was not home or he could have heard her through the wall. "Tell her we will have the boy arrested who did that to Logan."

"No."

My mother shrieked, "No?"

"Stop yelling."

"I'm not yelling," she yelled.

"Allie." My father finally looked at me. He had been either staring at the ground, his watch, or glaring at my mother this whole time. But now he focused on me.

"Yes?" I waited for the critique, the scolding.

"I—" His lips curled into the most heartbroken smile I had ever seen. "I like your hair."

My lungs wrung themselves inside my chest. I did not know what to say other than, "Thank you."

"You've stopped wearing gray too."

"Yes."

"I'm glad."

"Why are you talking about her looks?" My drama queen mother continued to announce, "We're here because of Logan."

"You're here because of Logan." My father's smile dipped into a frown when he switched his gaze to his wife.

"Then why are you here?" I asked him.

"I wanted to see you."

There was a moment of quiet before my mother broke it again with her shrill tone. "Tell me the boy's name who hurt Logan. That's why I'm here. We're going to report him to the police."

"No."

"No?"

"He defended me. Something you never did. You don't have the *right* to know his name."

With the terrible timing Nate always had, he opened my door and stuck his head in my room.

"Hey, Allie, ready for tutoring?" Nate's voice cut off when he saw I had visitors. "Oh, um."

"Nate." I motioned to them. My mother's glare lessened, and my father stood up to greet him. "These are my parents."

"This is a friend?" my father questioned.

Nate took it as an invitation to venture inside my room, regardless of the crackling tension awaiting him there. "Nate Reddington, sir." Nate shook my father's hand and nodded at my mother.

"R-Reddington?" My mother's glare disappeared and replaced itself with a look of awe. "Of *the* Reddingtons?" I had not known their family but, my mother did. I could see her money-sense tingling.

"Yes, ma'am."

"Wow." She appeared proud of me for knowing someone of such status.

My parents asked him a couple of questions about how we had met and his major. My father seemed less interested in him and more interested in asking me questions, but my mother would not let the spotlight leave Nate. She seemed shocked to learn Nate had been the one to beat up Logan and very conflicted about how she should feel about it. She was probably torn because Nate also had much more money than Logan or his family.

"That was you?" Flustered, she fanned herself like a Southern Bell stuck deciding between marrying a soldier or a businessman. "Really?"

"Yes, ma'am. I just hope he stays away from her from now on."

I laughed at my mother's confused expression. Her thoughts must have been in a storm, figuring out who would be best to support. I assumed Nate won in the end because when she said her goodbye to him, she winked at me as if to say, "*you can marry this one instead.*"

When they left, I launched myself into Nate's arms and he chuckled, hugging me to him.

I waited for him to push me away and say something like, "*We can't,*" but instead he tightened his grip on me.

"You okay?" he asked the same question he seemed to ask me every day, but this time it seemed heavier. All the more complex. All the more meaningful.

"Yes."

❡❡❡

NATE'S TANTALIZING lips moved against mine, teasing me. Offering a morsel of what I wanted, but promising a feast. He rolled me over on the firm bed and aligned our seeking and bucking hips. He knew I wanted him, hard and heavy against me. He knew me.

As he loomed over my body, his fevered lips never left mine. Our heat did nothing but build. His wide hand slipped down my neck and settled on the side of my rib, just below my aching breast. A whimper escaped me, and he groaned against my mouth before surrendering. His warm palms cupped my breasts, kneading the flesh, and his thumbs swiped over where I burned.

I moaned again, and he swallowed the sound.

"Allie," he whispered, pulling his lips away from mine to erotically nibble on my sensitive earlobe. "You've been a bad girl. Getting a C on your quiz." He moved his head down and pushed me all the way back on my bed, pinning me there. "You want to be a good girl, right?"

"Yes, yes, please."

"Then pay attention to your lesson." He kept his blazing eyes on mine as he licked the skin between my breasts, his thumbs working my nipples. As he sucked one tight peak into his hot and wet mouth, I let out a loud yelp. He alternated with suction, nipping, and soft licks, knowing just when to up his game.

"Nate!" My throat was hoarse from lust.

"I know." Nate gave a dark and sexy chuckle. His right hand trailed down my body until it stopped to make circles on my quivering inner thigh. "I know what you want." His hungry kisses moved to my neck as my heart decided to work in triple time. "Because I want it too."

"Nate," I cried out again and moaned. If his stroking got any faster, I would—I would... I was so damn close. Close to—to— "Oh, God!"

"That's it. Be a good girl for me." He licked the side of my throat as he thrust two fingers inside of me. The pressure, the speed, the pure fervor of it all ate away at me.

I felt ready to explode.

Any more and I would...

"Let go, Allie."

"Ahugh!" I woke up from the best sex dream of my life. Sweat soaked my sheets. I caught up with my breathing, and my muscles started to cool down after I calmed from my release.

I could not believe I'd had an orgasm from a sex dream about Nate.

But more than that, I could not believe the tortured moan cutting through my thoughts and sounding from Nate's side of the wall.

NATE'S #7 RULE FOR LIFE: ALWAYS BE THE ONE WITH THE LEAST KNOWN ABOUT YOU

*N*ate:

MY HAND WRAPPED around my throbbing cock before I could stop it. Her yells had woken me up first, but the moaning told me it was not another nightmare.

"Nate," she cried through our shared wall as if she was right on the edge. On the brink.

Shit. What was I supposed to do? Wake her up? It was obviously not a nightmare, and she sounded like she was enjoying herself. The tight pressure of my erection was painful enough to tell me another cold shower would not solve my problem. *Damn.* This girl drove me insane. All I ever wanted to do anymore was either talk to her or touch her, and I was not allowed to fucking touch her. She was still going out with Ryan. She was still kissing Ryan. Damn it, why did I want to kill Ryan?

"Nate," she moaned again.

I couldn't take it anymore. I squeezed the reddened head of my cock, trying to get back any sense of control, but only pleasure seeped into me. She was dreaming about *me*. Not Ryan. She felt like this because of *me*.

"Oh God," she yelped, and any resistance I had left dissipated.

My grip tightened, and I jerked my hand up and down my aching length while I listened to her through the wall. I knew it was wrong, but hearing her moan and whimper my name was just too much. I felt close to coming already, and I just started touching myself. It had been longer for me than usual. I used to bring girls to my room, but after meeting Allie, no one set my body on fire like she did.

Her sexy sounds became louder, and as a result, my stroking became faster. I could barely breathe, but I had to keep going. My chin fell as I squeezed shut my eyes and focused on the sounds of her moans and the slick sound of my stroking.

Pre-cum rose to the tip of my shaft and dampened my hand, making the sensation feel even better. Stronger. Mind-melting. My knees inched up as my stomach muscles rippled.

I could not stop pumping as I imagined Allie's soft hand giving me such ecstasy. How did this feel so fucking good? Was it being able to hear her? Was it because it was my name she yelled? Or was it because I had hit my maximum of cold showers, and now I could do nothing but work out my lust for Allie this way?

My heart thundered hard in my chest as her gasping and whimpering increased. Was she about to... Was I about to...

So. Close. Tingles tickled my balls and the base of my cock. I jacked myself harder, faster. *Allie*. Allie. My hips bucked forward, off the mattress, into my fist.

Allie's lips on mine.

Allie's hand on me.

Allie.

Allie.

Colors appeared in my eyelids, and I threw my head back, whacking it against our shared wall. She screamed her climax and, a mere moment later, I released a loud, strangled moan as I came too.

Shit.

I pressed my lips together as my cock twitched in my hand, shooting my release.

Staying quiet was impossible, and the moan slipped out of me before I could do anything to muffle it. Had she heard me? Was she still asleep? The only sound I made out from her side of the wall was heavy breathing. Maybe she was still dreaming and had not heard me.

It would be easier to stay away from her if she did not know I felt the same fiery attraction. If she knew my blood flowed south from just seeing her, she might make a mistake. I might make a mistake. We had already kissed, and I knew she felt guilty about it. She wanted to continue dating Ryan and, hell; I had told her to do so.

Friends. Friends, friends, friends. It was all we could be, and I would take friends over nothing. But damn, hearing her moan my name just now as I stroked my hard, throbbing cock—*No.*

Friends.

⚡⚡⚡

"HOW DO YOU NOT UNDERSTAND IT?" I sighed impatiently. Getting angry with her was easier than trying not to kiss her.

Tutoring Allie proved harder than I thought it would be. Not because she was not smart; she was very smart. It was more because both of us were having trouble focusing. At least, I had trouble thinking about anything other than the sounds she made when she came. Damn it.

Had she heard my moan through our shared wall? Did she know I had come harder than ever before, just from my hand and her sounds? Had I ruined our chance at friendship?

Did. She. Know?

She blushed when she met me in the library study room, but it could have been from embarrassment since she was a proud person and did not like how she needed my help to do well in the class she had been most confident about. She stressed over her grade, and I wanted to help her. But, damn, I also wanted to grab her, and kiss her, and hear every sensual sound I could squeeze from her as I devoured every inch of her body.

Focus.

Tutoring her did not help my lusty thoughts. She looked up at me with big, green eyes, and I imagined her as an innocent school girl ready to be corrupted. Which did not fit us at all. If anything, she was the one corrupting me. A lot of our hanging out was her saying, *"let's do something crazy,"* to forget about Logan, her parents, her grades, or whatever else was going on. She liked living in the moment so she did not have to deal with and live in her normal life.

I worried about that.

It was not healthy to deal with things by running away, but I ran too. She went rock wall climbing and out drinking at parties, and I shut out everything if it did not fit within my schedule or my rules. We were opposites, no wonder we were so attracted to each other.

"What do you mean how do I not understand it? If I understood it, I would not need your help," she replied. We were both a little snappy. A mixture of strong sexual tension and a lack of sleep caused our agitation. "Sorry, I don't mean to sound ungrateful. I'm just a little tired."

I sighed again. "Me too."

"Didn't sleep well?" she asked.

Was she hinting she knew I had stroked myself to thoughts of her and her soft moans? It was hard to find equal footing when I was not sure where the ground was.

"You seem…frustrated," she added.

I tried to push every thought of naked, moaning Allie out of my mind. "I am."

"Something keep you up at night?"

Did she remember the erotic dream she had about me or not, damn it? "Yes," I answered, wondering if she expected more from my response.

She shifted her chair closer to mine; she preferred sitting next to me instead of across from me when we studied. God, she smelled like roses. Roses and honey. It would have been so much easier if thorns covered her too. The fluorescent light of the study room illuminated her hair, making the red tint fiery. Strange how she could look like a devil and an angel at the same time. Beautiful. Dangerous.

She wore another dress today. This one was green like her eyes, and the sides were pushed down, leaving her shoulders bare. The lack of visible bra straps made my mouth drier than my father's sense of humor. Was she not wearing one? All I would have to do to see the body I'd been dreaming about was pull the material down and—

"Did you ever think about becoming a teacher?" she asked, oblivious to my naughty thoughts. "Since you tutor people a lot."

"I've always wanted to be a lawyer," I said.

She raised her eyebrows at me as her beautiful green eyes sparkled with amusement. "Always?"

"Yes."

"Straight out of the womb you were like, 'I'm going to be an attorney.'"

I cracked a smile. "I guess the first couple of years I wanted to be Superman."

"You still could," she joked, but the amount of caring in her voice was clear. She believed in me, which was more than most people. God, I wanted to kiss her.

"Let's get back to you." I flipped the page in her textbook and resumed quizzing her. "Name three internal mental processes."

"Memory, perception, and learning."

I ignored the flutter of pride in my chest at her being correct. "Good girl." I patted her head in hopes to calm down my need to touch her. It was either patting her like a dog or tangling my fingers in her hair and pulling her to me to crash my lips against hers.

"Jesus," she said, breathless.

Did I do something wrong? "What?"

"Just—Just hearing you say 'good girl' was a little weird for me." Her face was now completely red.

"Um, why?"

"Uh." She bit her lip. "You know."

"I know what?"

"Because you're a...you're into...you know." She made a face as if I would be able to translate it.

"What?"

"Dominant." She spoke faster than an auctioneer, "Which is why hearing 'good girl' from you just kind of made me think... But anyway, being dominant is cool, you know, for you. It fits you since you love control and all. No judgment here. Hell, everyone fantasizes about handcuffs at one point in their life, right?"

She had brought that up before when she tried setting me up with a woman from the campus erotica club.

"It's not like I'm into whips and chains." I hated talking about my sex life and it was awkward discussing it with the girl I fantasized about who also had a boyfriend.

"I never said you were."

An awkward silence settled between us when she leaned closer and asked, "What *are* you into?"

My fingers tensed around my pen. To tell her or not to tell her, that was the question.

She has a boyfriend.

She's with Ryan.

Fuck Ryan.

I looked into those lily-pad eyes and saw her pupils dilating, no doubt as she fantasized what I would tell her. "I'm into you."

She scrunched her nose, thinking I was trying to be cute. "Seriously."

"I'm so fucking into you, it's insane," I said, letting my hand fall under the table to squeeze her knee. Her leg jolted under me. "You want to know why I haven't been sleeping well?" *Fuck it.* My breath played with soft tendrils of her hair. "Because I can't stop thinking about you—in the biblical sense, if that wasn't clear." My lips trailed over her smooth jaw as my lungs fought to take in another deep breath of her roses and honey scent. "You want to know what I'm thinking about right now?"

It was the first time I had seen Allie so breathless. Hard to believe she could be breathless when she always took the air from my lungs. "Mmhhm."

"I'm thinking about how you're not wearing a bra under that dress and how easy it would be to pull the fabric down and suck those pretty pink nipples until they turn red and then suck some more."

She gasped at my words, which made me want to say even more.

I lowered my head, whispering in her ear. "I think about kissing you up against a wall, on a table, on a bed, on the floor. Whenever I look at my fingers now, I think about ramming them inside you until you squeeze them so tight, they go numb." I stopped talking just long enough to give her an example.

Allie cursed and bit her lip as my hot hand trailed up her skirt, my fingers inching closer and closer to those little panties I saw when she bent over in front of me earlier in the day.

She rasped, "How can you act like life is a boardroom and then say the sexiest shit like that?"

"You bring something out in me I've never felt before," I admitted. "It's scary."

"How is it scary?" Her eyelids lowered as my palm moved up between her soft thighs, connecting with her damp lace panties.

"It's scary because you make me forget about things I've worked hard to make everyone else remember. You have me sitting in class with a hard-on pressing into my jeans because I can't stop thinking about you." My fingers fanned out over her, caressing her soft skin and watching it jump and ripple at my touch. "You have me rereading textbook chapters because I find myself smiling and daydreaming in the middle of a paragraph, unable to remember what I just read."

"Smiling does not sound like a bad thing—Oh, Nate, yes." She bucked her hips up at me when my fingers slid behind the fabric of her panties.

So. Wet.

My fingers dipped into her, stirring her. "You have me smiling and jacking off every morning and every night to thoughts of you. It's distracting like nothing else."

"Some distractions are good."

I inhaled more of her rose-honey scent. She was a warm, comforting tea, except in this moment she provided no comfort. But damn, she got me hot. "And are you good, Allie?" My fingers stroked over her, finding her tight, slick bundle of nerves. "Are you good for me? Because sometimes I can't tell."

She lifted a shaky hand to the side of my face. "I never want to be bad for you, Nate."

I circled her clit fast, thrumming it, and she sucked in a sharp, broken breath.

"I don't want to be bad for you either," I said, my cock pulsing as my fingers played with her beneath the table.

"But—" She grabbed my wrist, and my fingers paused. "This is bad. There's Ryan, and the rules, and the fact that you keep pushing me away. If we do something now and you push me away again—"

"What if I didn't?" I asked, pinching her swollen clit and watching her chest shake. "What if I didn't push you away?"

But I had to.

It was more than obeying rules because I liked them. I could not be with Allie because I could lose my position as an RA and not be able to save Blue from my parent's neglect. I needed to remain platonic with Allie for my sister's sake. For my future's sake.

"You're about to push me away right now, aren't you?" she asked.

I slid my devious hand out of her damp panties and wiped my fingers on my pants. "Yeah."

The rest of the time we were in the study room, I could not get out of my head the image of Allie spread across my bed, handcuffed to the headboard, and bucking her hips up at me with unadulterated need.

❡❡❡

A KNOCK on my door that night surprised me.

"Nate, hey, sorry. Um, I just..." Ryan shifted his weight

and looked down. "I need to ask you something. Sorry for intruding and just laying this on you, but I need to know."

"What's up?"

I knew what he was going to ask. I knew it, and I dreaded it.

"I really like Allie, so I need to know—is something going on between you two?"

I should have told him yes. I should have told him something had been going on since the moment I had first seen her, first talked to her, first kissed her. I wanted nothing more than to have "something going on" with Allie Parser. I fucking dreamed about her. *Breathed* her. She understood me, and I understood her.

But that's not what I said. I lacked the bravery to tell the truth.

Is something going on between you two?

I regretted it the second it came out of my mouth. "No."

DORM MANUAL RULE #3: NO INDECENT EXPOSURE IN THE HALLWAY

llie:

I HAD RESUMED WRITING my psychology paper about Nate after we had become friends because it was already so close to being finished, and whenever I thought about analyzing anyone else, no one as complex and fascinating came to mind. I had learned a lot about him, but I still needed to know more.

My paper focused on the troublesome and complicated relationship Nate had with his father, but I needed more to accomplish the level of analysis my psychology professor expected. I *needed* a phenomenal grade on that final paper.

Guilt still pained me for choosing Nate as the subject of my paper while still trying to be a real friend to him, but I would tell him. Sometime. He would understand. If anything, it would be a compliment, right? That I had chosen him?

Damn it.

I felt guilty about Ryan because of Nate. I felt guilty about Nate because of the paper. I felt guilty about Gavin because I had lied about my messed up, complicated romantic feelings.

"Roommate!" Marissa cheered as she stepped into our room for the first time in a week and took me from my thoughts. I still could not believe her parents paid for a dorm room she did not use. Her boyfriend must be used to her living with him every night. "Oh my God." She stopped and fanned herself. "Why is it so hot in here?"

"I think the heater is broken," I explained.

I sat at my desk in nothing but short shorts and a thin black camisole, and even I was sweating. The building had switched from air conditioning to heat with the start of the fall season, but now our room boiled and bubbled and toiled and troubled. For the past three nights in a row, I'd had steamy sex dreams about Nate with no way to cool down since the room was ninety-five degrees. The lightheadedness affected my ability to do homework.

"This is terrible," Marissa complained. "It feels like a sauna in here."

"Saunas sound enjoyable. I would say it feels more like the evil witch's oven in *Hansel and Gretel*."

"Did you tell Nate about it?"

"What?" Seeing Nate only ever made me feel hotter.

"He's the RA. He's supposed to deal with problems like this. He'll fill out a report and call the maintenance man for you and everything." She picked up a folder on her desk and resumed fanning herself. "Dang, I was thinking I would sleep here tonight, but this is unbearable." *Fantastic, leave me to myself to deal with it. Not like it's your room too.* Great, now the heat was making me bitter. "How have you been able to sleep with it this hot?"

"I haven't been sleeping well, I guess."

"Do you want me to tell Nate—"

"No, I'll do it."

❢❢❢

THE ROOM BECAME EVEN HOTTER. By six o'clock, I was strutting around in a sports bra and the smallest pair of shorts known to man. The heat exhausted me so much I did not think to care about walking out of my room and into the hallway in so little clothing. I did not think about it until I heard Nate's shocked voice stutter at me.

"Allie." His bright, sky-blue eyes ate me up. "What—What are you wearing?"

I cut right to the chase. "My room is a toaster."

His gaze still worked down my almost bare body. "What?"

"If I spend longer than thirty minutes inside of it at a time, I'll burn to a crisp."

"I don't understand." He was surprised again when I grabbed his hand and pulled him to my room. "I don't think this is—Whoa. It's so hot in here."

"Tell me about it." I let out a deep sigh and leaned back on the wall. The heat and lack of sleep due to the heat made me so tired; my eyelids shut of their own volition and opened when he broke the small silence.

"Is your heater broken?"

"That would be my first guess."

He strode over to it and examined the knob and buttons. "How long has it been this way?"

"Um…three days, I think?" With my sleeping problems, the nights were blurring together.

"Your room has been this hot for *three days?*" Anger claimed his face. "How have you been able to study or sleep?" I swayed against the wall when my head went a little dizzy. "Whoa." Nate caught me before I even realized I was falling. "Allie?" He raised a hand and put it on my forehead. "Jesus, you're overheated. You must be completely dehydrated."

"I guess I should drink some water."

"You realize you can't even stand up on your own?"

"What? That's crazy." His hands left my waist, and before I knew it, I slid down to the floor. "Well, darn."

Nate caught me again, and this time scooped me up into his strong arms. "Allie, you can't stay in this room tonight. Even if I call someone to come fix it, it would still be too hot until it airs out."

"Where else am I supposed to go?"

He was already carrying me to his room. My side collided with his hard muscles and my dry mouth still watered at his strength. Once we were inside, he sat me down on his chair in front of his desk.

Nate leaned close and scanned my every inch. "Your face is red."

"Psh, your face is red," I shot back and realized it was the worst comeback of my lifetime.

"I think you're suffering from exhaustion and dehydration."

"Sounds bad."

"You need water," he said. He grabbed a bottle of ice-cold

water from his fridge and threw it at me. My vision blurred, so I missed, and it fell to the floor. "Sorry."

I picked up the water and opened the lid. Taking my first sip, I misjudged how far away it was from my mouth and spilled a decent amount of the water down my chest. I would have blushed if the blood had not already been pounding in my cheeks from heat exposure. Nate probably thought I looked like a mess. More skin showed than fabric; my hair was up in a messy bun, my body slick with sweat, and now water soaked me.

"Really?" I asked God. Everything embarrassing always happened to me in front of Nate.

"I have a towel you can borrow," he used such a low voice, it took me a moment to decipher whether he had said anything at all.

I followed his dark gaze to my soaked sports bra and realized the cold water had hardened my nipples through the material. I crossed my arms over my chest and glanced around the room, refusing to make eye contact with him.

"Thanks." I was uncomfortable. Recently, every dream I'd had was an X-rated film starring Nate. I had to keep telling myself that Ryan was the one I was dating, and just friendship was allowed for Nate and me. Nate made it clear again and again how he wanted to be friends and nothing more. So why was he looking at me with enough heat in his eyes to warm Canada in the winter? "Maybe I should go—"

"Allie, you can't go back in that room. It's dangerous to be in dry heat for so long." He frowned. "Why didn't you tell me that was happening?"

"Well, the first day, I thought it would stop; and then the second day, I thought for sure it would stop; and then today,

I decided I would just physically melt into a puddle and escape all my problems."

"I think your plans had some holes in them." He smiled at me before becoming serious again. Classic Nate. "Allie, why didn't you tell me about it?"

I sighed. What was I supposed to say? *I like being your friend, but the more we are around each other, the more I feel things I know you don't feel and don't want me to feel. So, I just thought it would be easier to deal with it myself first if I could because even though I love how close we've become, it is getting harder to be around you and not want to jump your bones.*

"I really should go," I said and stood up, trying to escape the situation. Pausing after a wave of dizziness flooded me, I stumbled to his door to leave.

"Sleep here." His words almost made me faint.

Had I misheard him? "What?"

"You should sleep here tonight." Still, he would not look at me. His burning eyes were glued to the ground, and he appeared...nervous. "You can't go back to your room, you'll pass out."

"Maybe Gavin—"

"Gavin has a roommate; there would not be room for you. My bed is bigger than the normal ones because I have a single."

"Ryan has a single too. I could—"

"No."

"No?"

"No."

"He's my boyfriend," I said both to remind him and myself. Sleeping with Nate? Was this moment another realistic dream? Would this end the same way those had? No.

Ryan deserved better. This was just Nate being his version of a gentleman and looking out for my well-being.

"I know." He met my eyes, this time with a tortured expression on his face. "You're staying in my room tonight. End of discussion," he said.

"So fucking bossy." It made me want him even more.

♀♀♀

"So…"

"So."

Saying we would sleep together, in just the strict dictionary's definition of "sleep," was easier said than done. We stood on either side of the bed staring at one another as if waiting for one of us to chicken out. I could not make Nate sleep on the floor in his own room, but no way was I lying on the tile. My exhausted body needed a comfortable bed more than oxygen.

I sank onto his mattress and swallowed a moan when his cool sheets met my warm skin. All the muscles in my body relaxed. Damn, how was his bed so soft? I wanted to lay in it forever.

"Ar-Are these silk sheets?"

He continued to stand at the side of the bed, watching me roll around in comfy delight. "Yeah."

I stretched and threw my head back against a pillow he had let me borrow. "This feels so good."

A quiet noise came from him in response.

"Are you going to come in?"

"Come in?" he croaked. I felt bad for drinking so much of

his water. Rehydrating had helped decrease the dizziness and cooled me down.

"In bed."

I twisted to make as much room for him as possible. It would be safest if no part of us touched during the night. I did not want to wake up with me straddling him as I slept through another sex dream. *Oh God, please don't let me have another sex dream.* A couple of days ago, I had thought I heard a moan from Nate's side of the wall as if he had heard me, but he never mentioned it.

Nate climbed in next to me and laid flat on his back; his intense gaze fastened to his ceiling like it was a piece of abstract art.

"Sorry for messing up your night. It means a lot that you're letting me stay here." Of course, it was more like he was *making* me stay there, considering he vetoed my other options. Still, I appreciated it. He always helped me and expected nothing in return. He helped me with Logan; he helped me with studying; he helped me have a place to sleep while my room cooled off.

"You are not messing up my night," he whispered and turned on his side to look at me. I forced myself not to cuddle up closer to him.

This was going to be tough.

Nate's hand was between my legs again. My eyes rolled into the back of my head at his sensual touch. How was he so good at this? How was he so good at everything? He exiled every other thought from my mind.

"Nate," I moaned, and he masked my sound by covering my lips with a passionate, searing kiss.

"That's my good girl."

My legs curled around his waist, and I gasped at the bulge rubbing right where I needed him. Nate pressed himself harder against me, gyrating and grinding to create delicious friction over my core.

I yelped and urged him to thrust against me even harder. My hands drifted down his toned chest, exploring him.

"Allie," Nate called out my name and bucked against me with less of a stable rhythm. Losing himself in me.

His rubbing between my legs became faster; my thighs tightened to keep him there forever.

"Yes, Nate." I panted and moaned more than I breathed. "So close. You're. So. Good—"

"Oh God, Allie." Nate's hoarse voice broke me out of my dream, and I woke up covered in sweat. "Fuck," he whispered, staring down at me.

I realized the pressure between my legs had not gone away. Glancing down, I saw my hand rubbing myself. I also saw Nate squeezing himself through his boxers.

"I-I'm sorry." Tearing my hand from between my legs, I wondered if someone could fade into oblivion from mortification. I'd had a sex dream and touched myself in *his* bed. What would he think of me now? *"I don't think we should be friends anymore." "You don't seem to understand that I don't want this."* My brain pummeled my ego with the possibilities of his response.

What he said next shocked me to the bone and turned me on like never before. "Don't." Nate groaned, his expression scrunching in pain as his eyes locked below my waist. "Please don't stop, Allie."

My shallow breathing had no chance to calm as it picked up again at his words.

"Just finish." His hand slipped under his boxers and mine moved back to the front of my lace panties.

"I-I—" What was there to do? The unbearable pulsing between my legs sped up as he looked at me.

"I need this," he grated through a tortured expression. The pleading in his voice broke me, and my hand disappeared between my legs yet again. "That's it, rub harder." His breathlessness and darkened eyes thrilled me along. "Fast little circles right over your throbbing, little clit." I did what he said, and my sex pulsed and throbbed its approval under my fingers. "Such a good girl."

My toes curled at his words. A part of me wanted to laugh at learning how professional control-freak Nate excelled in dirty talk.

"Fuck, Allie." His arm shifted faster, the muscles and veins in it flexing, tensing, and ticking. His hand stroked himself from inside his boxers. He was as close as me. "You see what you do to me?" he rasped. "Can't keep my hands off my fucking self when you moan like that."

I moaned again. Just to see if the cause and effect were real. It was.

His eyes hooded as we touched ourselves and panted onto each other's skin. "I can see your eyes glazing over, you're as close as me," he rasped. "You like watching me lose control, Parser?"

"Almost as much as you like losing control, Reddington."

He grunted, his hand stroking faster in his boxers. "You do things to me, Allie."

I sucked in a breath to respond to him. "What things?"

He released a groan and leaned closer to me. We were both still on our sides, not touching but facing each other; the same way we had fallen asleep. With his face so close to mine, all I wanted was to kiss him.

"You drive me crazy. Crazier than I've ever been." His eyes closed for a moment before he opened them again. The intensity behind them grew with each passing second. They hazed, turning desperate. "I didn't know it could be like this."

"Same." I was losing the ability to speak. Our hands moved in unison. Our noises became louder and louder. "Oh."

"You drive me wild. Out of my mind. Can't think of anything else but your sweet body." His jaw clenched, his arm moving faster under the sheet. His erection tented his boxers, jutting towards me as he stroked. "Is this what you wanted? To make me mindless for you? To drive me insane?"

"Yes," I cried.

"You want me to break my rules? Fuck, baby, you have no idea what that means. All the filthy things I want to do to you." His breathing came out in choppy, rushed breaths, puffing over my face.

"Do them," I panted. "Do them."

"I ache to own you, Allie. Your body and soul; I want it all. Every time I hear Ryan's name on your lips, I want to burn the world down."

Happiness trickled through mind-blowing pleasure. He was jealous of Ryan. Nate wanted me. "Own me," I whispered, chanting the words again and again as my fingers sped up between my legs.

"You're fingering yourself on *my* bed."

"Y-Your bed," I repeated.

"You are mine," he growled.

My head jerked up and down in frantic agreement. "Yours. Yours."

"Look at me," Nate demanded. I wanted to point out how bossy he was, but my body no longer listened to my brain. "I'm going to come so fucking hard for you. You close for me?"

My inner muscles were clamping down around my fingers, rippling. *So close.* "Yes!"

"Be a good girl and come."

Fireworks lit up behind my eyelids as we came together. My entire body shook for what felt like an hour before it relaxed.

Once we caught our breath, I feared it would become awkward, but instead of saying anything, he kissed me. His lips moved soft and pleading against mine, making the hot experience somehow a sweet one.

His mouth against mine. Claiming me. Owning me. Making promises I hoped his lips could keep.

It was a whole new world.

He pulled back to look at me. Then, as slow as a tortoise, he leaned in again and connected our lips, our souls. Touching him, being with him... I was lost. But damn, I felt found.

There were two things I knew for sure:

1. I could no longer stay away from Nate.

2. I had to break up with Ryan.

DORM MANUAL RULE #10: SEEK HELP IF YOU NEED IT

llie:

"*It's not you, it's me.*" I prepped my breakup script. "*No, really, it's me. I'm interested in someone else. More than interested. A bit obsessed. Ever since I first saw him. It doesn't make sense but it's one of those unbreakable truths.*" Ryan would not want to know the details.

The worst part of a breakup was watching the other person's facial expression change from blissful ignorance to shock and hurt. How shocked and hurt would Ryan be? We had been on three official dates, maximum. Yes, we also hung out almost every day, but it was always more friend-like than relationship-like. Still, it would be a betrayal once he found out about Nate and me.

Was there even a Nate and me? We had kissed a couple of

times, skipped the bases, and gone right to touching ourselves in front of one another. God, the more I thought about it, the more Ryan and I had something going on rather than Nate and me. Did Nate even want me? Sure, he acted like he did the night before, but was it because both of us were so caught up in the moment? Would he change his mind about me? He always listed reasons why we shouldn't be together. Did any part of him believe we might be able to work out?

"Well, the average grade on this quiz was ten percent higher than last week, so good job, but know that there is always room for improvement," my psychology professor said and disrupted my mental analyses of my love life. She handed out the quizzes. When I saw mine, I had a mini heart attack.

A *B*. I had gotten a B!

I grinned all the way back to my room, stopping to knock on Nate's door and tell him his tutoring worked. After he opened it and gazed at me with hesitant eyes, I remembered the last time I had seen him, I'd had my hand between my legs as I came on his bed. The smile on my face slipped. How was I supposed to act around him now?

"Hey." He was the first one to break the awkward silence. "Is something wrong?"

"No, um, I came here to tell you I got a B on my last psych quiz." My grin came back when he acted as excited as I felt.

"You're kidding!" He grabbed my arms and pulled me into a tight, warm hug. I jumped up and down in his thick arms. "Congratulations."

"I couldn't have done it without you. You have to keep tutoring me, so maybe one day I'll get an A." I nudged him, and he frowned. The loss of his smile was like someone dropping a live snake down my shirt.

"Yeah…" He motioned me into his room. I followed him, sensing he was about to have some kind of "talk" with me. "I've been thinking. After what happened last night, maybe we shouldn't be alone together anymore. I love hanging out with you, but I can't do this to Ryan. There's obviously something going on between us—"

"There is?" Yes, I baited him into telling me his feelings, but I needed to know.

He stared down at me. "You were there."

"I'm breaking up with Ryan," I told him. "Tonight."

He closed his eyes and sighed. "That still doesn't mean we can—"

"I'm not breaking up with him for you," I remarked, and the tension seemed to lessen in Nate's stance. "I'm doing it because I don't see him in that way, and it's not fair to him for us to keep trying while I have feelings for someone else."

There was a long silence while we both watched each other. This time I was the one to speak up.

"I just came here because, when I found out I got a B, you were the first person I wanted to tell."

He gave me a small smile.

"Will you still tutor me?" I asked and dreaded his answer. If he said "no," I might have cried. What if this was the end of our friendship too? Would he cut me off to make sure Ryan did not suspect anything? Would he act like nothing had happened, even after how close we had become?

"Of course." He leaned in, looking like he might kiss me goodbye. He didn't. Instead, he gave me a light peck on my forehead. "I couldn't stay away from you if I tried."

✝✝✝

THE WAY RYAN looked at me broke my heart. The betrayal and anger in his eyes. The sound of him grinding his teeth. I spoke in a soft tone about my feelings, but he fought me the entire way, saying things like *"feelings can change and grow,"* and *"maybe we were just moving too fast."* Once I convinced him I no longer wanted to continue dating, he got quiet, which scared me most of all. His pained eyes shook me, and I hated hurting him.

"I'm sorry," I said for the fifth time.

"You're *sorry?*" Ryan asked. "Allie, I don't understand. We were doing great."

It was not as if we had been *serious* serious. "I just...don't feel that way about you."

"You don't..." Ryan huffed angrily. "Then why the hell have you been kissing me like you have?"

"I was trying to see if I could—"

"Trying? A relationship isn't some experiment."

I disagreed with him but held my tongue. To me, dating was experimenting. It was figuring out what you wanted in the long run; it was seeing what personalities fit yours and what your *type* was. I never thought I would *like* Nate. Ryan seemed to fit what I had wanted, simple and easy. But maybe I needed something else.

"I'm sorry."

"Stop saying that and just tell me what you're really thinking!" His voice jumped, climbing louder now, and I worried for a moment Nate heard us through the walls. "Is there someone else?"

I could not lie to him. "Yes, but he's not the reason I want

201

to stop dating. I just don't see you in a romantic way." I continued, "And trust me, you don't want me, Ryan. I've got a lot of stuff going on—"

"Don't fucking do that. Of course, I want you. I don't care about your issues."

I flinched.

"That's not what I meant." Ryan let out an impatient breath. "First, you don't trust me enough to tell me personal things, and now you are blaming me for not understanding what you're going through. You have to let people in or they can't help."

He was right, but I hated his logic. It was the same logic all the therapists I had seen after Logan had told me. *"You have to trust and open up again." "You cannot go through your problems alone."* I was fine on my own. Nate was fine on his own. But we were better together.

"I know how to help myself."

"Who's the other guy?" I lost a bit of my confidence at the fire in his eyes. Ryan was such an easygoing guy; it was difficult to imagine him angry. Maybe he had issues too.

"I don't think that's important."

"Say his name, Allie." Ryan took a step toward me, and I stepped back, away from him. Ryan would never hurt me. Would he? He looked as mad as Logan had been the first time he'd hit me when I had forgotten about our five-month anniversary. But Ryan was not Logan.

"No." There was no longer any confidence or strength in my voice. It wavered, and a strange dizziness overtook me.

My back met the wall, nowhere left to hide, as Ryan strode to me. My stomach twisted into painful knots, and my lungs compressed. *Oh no. Not the time for this.* I could not have a panic attack in front of Ryan as I broke up with him.

Ryan's warm hands locked on my upper arms, and he held me as if he thought I might run away. Logan had held me the same way once or twice. Dominance loomed in the tight grip of his fingers, and I hated how scared I was of it.

"It's Nate, isn't it?"

I kept my mouth shut, less because I did not want to answer, and more because I could no longer speak or breathe.

"Tell me." Ryan shook me. Logan's aggressive face flashed before my eyes, screaming with rage, *Tell me who you slept with, you whore!*

I let out a small shriek and started hyperventilating. I leaned my weight onto the wall, applying more pressure to it as my legs weakened.

"Allie?" Now Ryan sounded scared.

Odds were I was a scary sight to behold. My pale skin paled even more. Harsh breaths came from me like I was being choked. The shivering started and my nausea worsened at every small movement. The panic I felt at having a panic attack in Ryan's presence made it more difficult to calm down.

"Allie?" I heard Nate's voice, but it was fuzzy with the harsh beating of the blood rushing to my ears. I was fading, my vision blurring. It felt like falling deeper into myself, into a blue-black dimension where everything was disconnected. Nausea made me even dizzier. "What did you do to her?"

"Nothing, I swear."

Air felt like water. Everything slowed and froze. My body was hot; my sweat was cold. The shivering wouldn't stop.

"Just get out of here."

"Is she okay?"

"Shh, Allie, I need you to breathe." Nate's warm, secure arms wrapped around me, and tension eased from my body. The fresh apple smell of him pulled me back, out of the sea of numbness. I didn't mean to shut down; I didn't want to. Cool fingers touched my overheating cheeks. "She's having a panic attack."

"What?" Ryan asked. "Why?"

"You probably scared her with your yelling," Nate sneered. "I could hear you through the damn wall!"

"Scared? I would never hurt her."

"Just get out of here." Nate's voice boomed, strong and demanding, and I was not surprised when Ryan obeyed him.

The slamming of my door jolted me, and Nate pulled me in closer. The warm crystal rain over crisp apples smell of him washed away my troubles.

"Deep breaths," he whispered in my ear and started breathing with me to help me adjust. "It's okay." He stroked my hair as I clung to him. My vision cleared, and I nuzzled in closer to his embrace. Nate protected me, calmed me. He was almost a safety blanket now. Focusing on his blue eyes made me feel better. Less somewhere else.

He put a hand on the back of my head and massaged it. His nails scratched and dug into my scalp in the most delicious way. It decreased the dizziness and helped distract me. "Don't let your anxiousness about feeling anxious build. Knock those panic bricks down."

I almost laughed. "Panic bricks?"

"You're the future therapist," he shot back.

I smiled against his chest. The relief of not having to feel guilty about my growing feelings for Nate because of Ryan was immediate. I still felt bad, but Nate holding me was all I needed to feel better.

"What did he do?" he asked, but I could hear his, "*if he hurt you, I'll kill him.*"

"Nothing," I said, but Nate's disbelieving expression led to me repeating myself. "He really did nothing."

"He didn't do 'nothing,' he was yelling at you," Nate grumbled against my head, still holding me.

"He had a right to be angry with me."

Nate did not comment, but he tightened his hold on me. Why was it when Ryan or Logan touched me or held me tight, dread filled me, but when Nate did it, my entire body warmed and relaxed?

"Anyway, it was my fault. I'm a mess." I buried my head against him in shame. "I'm literally a mess of a person."

"You are not."

"I had a panic attack just because he started raising his voice at me. Why do I have to have so many issues?" Ryan would have had no intention of hurting me, but the situation had given me ugly, vivid flashbacks to my past. Panic attacks sucked. I wanted to be over it all already. How long did healing take for goodness' sake?

"Everyone has issues. If they say they don't, they're either lying or mentally unstable."

"Nate..."

I wanted a distraction. I needed a distraction. After pulling back to look at his face, I dove in and kissed him. A single thought speared through my head.

I needed Nate.

I was on him. My greedy hand pulled him down to me by

his neck, and our lips connected within seconds. Smashing. Clashing. Raging.

I dove in deep at first, wild and rushed, but as the emotion built, my mouth slowed. I took a page out of Nate's book and took my time.

Soft. Calm. Loving.

My lips grazed his, and when he released a quiet growl, I deepened the kiss. His hands moved to my hips, and he kissed me harder and with more passion than he ever had before. Like he needed to absorb my very soul. I gasped at the intensity, my body lighting up from his touch. He was so much. Too much. He filled me up until I couldn't think of anything else. Being close to him made everything else fade. It was amazing. He was amazing.

When my mouth opened, he moved from my lips to my neck. Tingles shot down between my legs, warmth sizzling my lower stomach, as he expertly sucked at my skin in just the right places. One of his hands on my hips slithered up my side and over my ribcage, until his warm, inviting palm shifted and cupped me through my bra.

Finally. It felt like I had spent an entire lifetime trying to get this man to feel me up.

"*Yes.*" A triumphant moan slipped from me.

"Your nipples are tight little peaks," he gritted as the tips of his fingers played with them. "So fucking hard for me."

"Yes, yes."

His kiss became savage. Hard and demanding. His breath mingled with mine. "Did Ryan touch you like this?"

I shook my head, vibrating in his arms, wanting his skimming hands and naughty fingers to venture down.

"This body needs *me*. Wants me."

"You." My hand dropped between us to palm his bulge through his pants.

"Shit, you're quivering for me," he cursed. His fingers bit into my breasts, squeezing so hard it was almost painful. After an abrupt, tortured sound, Nate shot away from me, breathing hard, his expression scorching. "We—We can't," he stuttered, his eyes dark, stormy blue as he stared down at me.

"Why can't we?" I moved closer to him, and he stepped back. We switched predator roles.

"The rules," he answered, but the huskiness of his voice betrayed him.

"I don't believe in rules." Nothing stopped us now. Ryan would be angry if Nate and I got together or not. I was not going to stay away from what *could be* with Nate because of what *was not* with Ryan.

"I'm your RA," Nate said as he took a step back from me again.

"We'll figure it out." I got closer to him, my room too small to allow an escape.

"Allie." Nate's pained expression gave me pause. "You don't understand."

I could not keep doing this. He acted like he wanted me; he gave an excuse to stay away. He wanted me; he didn't. We could; we couldn't. It was the same thing again and again.

I grabbed him by the crisp shirt collar and yanked him against me.

"Nate, look at me. Look at me and tell me right now, do you want me?" He tried to avoid eye contact, but I did not give up. "Do you like talking to me? Do you like kissing me and touching me? Do you want to be around me all the time? Because that's how I feel about you. Things will always be complicated, but we get to choose what we fight for and what we end up with in life."

I wanted Nate. My life had been full of confusion, frustration, and fear, but Nate had somehow been what I needed. He did not solve everything or permanently heal me, but every minute was easier just by being near him.

"So, tell me right now..." His eyes locked onto mine as I asked, "Do you want to do this?"

"Fuck." He looked away again and let out a heavy sigh. Two lungs' worth of air. Turning back to me, he cupped my cheek in his warm, tingling palm and tangled his left hand in my hair. "Yes. I want you so fucking bad, Allie Parser."

NATE'S #8 RULE FOR LIFE: SLEEP WITH TWO EYES OPEN OR NEVER SLEEP AT ALL

*N*ate:

I HAD SLEPT with Allie again. *Just* slept. But it was so much more. It was intimate, watching her fall asleep, gazing into her eyes until she could not hold them open anymore. It took trust. My heart warmed at thinking I was one of the few people she trusted. I trusted her too. Sleeping—real sleep —in a bed with a girl broke my rule.

My relationships with women were sexual, and that was it. On rare occasions, I befriended them, though, I suppose, I rarely befriended guys either. It was crazy how Allie had somehow slipped—or rather, crashed—into my life. She had me breaking the rules I set for myself and I had never felt so right. The way she had clung to me yesterday, calming from her panic attack, the feeling that I could help her the way I had always wanted to be helped as a kid, it was more than I ever thought possible.

But as happy as I was about Allie, I could not stop thinking about what this meant for Ryan and me. We had been friends, not *good* friends, but still friends. We were RAs. Losing the friendship would far from crush me; little regret plagued me as my relationship with Allie would more than make up for it. An immature thought entered my mind: *"I liked Allie before Ryan so he was the one in the wrong."*

I was the one in the wrong.

I had told Ryan nothing was going on between Allie and me. What was I supposed to say now? Maybe if we just hid it for a while, as things blew over, it would not be—

"Un. Fucking. Believable." At Ryan's voice, my head shot up, and I froze. I had just been walking out of Allie's room, in the same clothes I had been wearing the night before, and with a smug smile on my face. Great.

I put my hands up in a surrender position. "It's not what it looks like."

"You *slept* with her the night she broke up with me?"

"We didn't have sex."

"Oh, please." His disgusted expression made me flinch. "I know how you are."

"It's not like that with her."

"I came here to make sure she was okay but, obviously, she's fine considering she switched from one guy to another in a matter of hours."

"Don't talk about her like that." Allie deserved none of his hostility. "Be angry with me."

"You're right. You're the one who said there was nothing going on and lied right to my face."

"I didn't know it would turn into this."

"You? You, the one who plans everything out and knows everything before it happens, you didn't see this coming? You can't fool me, Nate. You knew what you were doing. You have control over everything."

"I have no control when it comes to her," I admitted, and it was true. Allie had woven herself into my carefully plotted existence, and now there was nothing to be done other than keep her by my side.

"So the rules no longer apply?"

I stayed silent. Fighting with Ryan was not something I wanted.

"You're her RA. It's not allowed," he added.

My fingers tightened into fists, but I remained quiet.

"You're the one who always stressed how important that rule was but, I guess mister money bags can afford to lose his free residence and meal plan."

Not to mention, the cut from tuition. Being an RA was important to me because of the money. Hell, my father had told me we were now broke. I could not lose my position. No one would give me a loan; I would have to drop out of school.

"Oh, is that regret I see?" Ryan smirked at me, and I scowled. "What was it you asked me when I started dating Allie? 'Is she really worth it?'"

"She's worth everything."

⚑⚑⚑

ALLIE WAS STARING at me again. She had been doing it all day. Every time I caught her, she acted like she had no clue what I was talking about. She knew me well enough now that she sensed something was wrong. I loved how in tune she was with me.

"You're doing it again," I said and took a bite from my sandwich. Allie blinked for the first time in what felt like a minute. She put on her innocent, confused face, and I clarified, "Staring at me."

"Tell me what you're thinking." She changed the subject with seamless ease. I loved how she could do that as well.

"At this very moment?"

"Yup." She popped her lips on the *p*, and the action transfixed me. The talent of her lips would always continue to fascinate me.

"I was thinking about how you've been staring at me."

She pouted. "Well, that's no fun."

"What's up?"

"You answer first," she said. "You've been acting weird since this morning, and I want to know what's wrong, but I know I shouldn't just come out and ask because you probably won't tell me, so instead I've been staring at you in an attempt to either read your mind or make you uncomfortable enough to spit it out." She took a deep breath after her run-on sentence and smiled. God, she was cute.

"I'm worried about the RA rule."

"They wouldn't really fire you just for dating a resident, would they?"

I picked at the stale bread holding my chicken salad in place. "It's one of the most important rules."

She leaned closer to me over the cafeteria table. "So, what are our options?"

"We can either sneak around—"

"Hot."

I rolled my eyes, trying not to smile. "Or I can tell my direct supervisor and, hopefully, coming clean would help the situation."

"Less sexy, but the better choice."

"That's what I was thinking."

"Why is being an RA so important to you? You've never told me why you like it."

Did I even like it? I liked how there were rules. I liked how it looked impressive on a resume. But for the most part, I liked how it paid for things I needed. Could I tell Allie that? All she knew about my family was how I had problems with my father and we were one of the richest families in New York. She had trusted me and told me everything about Logan and her past; I could do the same. I owed her honesty.

"It pays for a lot."

"How much?" Her eyes widened when I told her it added up to about thirty thousand dollars a year. "Wow."

"Yeah."

"But that's not a reason to like it, it's a reason to do it. And does money matter? I thought you were one of *the* Reddingtons."

My grin weakened a bit. Here we go. "About that... The Reddingtons have been having some money problems lately."

Allie looked surprised. "Is everything okay?"

"Let's just say, if you're into me for my money, you should find someone else."

"I have no interest in your money." She paused. "Well, that's not entirely true."

I quirked an eyebrow at her response.

She laughed. "My mother approves of you because you're

richer than Logan. If you didn't have any money, then my mom would no longer like you. Which, as a result, would make you sexier."

"When I'm homeless and living on the streets, at least I'll know my girlfriend thinks I'm sexy."

"You will not be homeless." This time she rolled her eyes at me. "You're one of the smartest guys at this school, you're going places."

I continued to play with her hand, weaving my fingers through hers and rubbing my thumbs against her palm. "And what places am I going?"

"You'll be a super lawyer and travel the world." She painted a happy daydream for me. "Oh, you should go to Ireland! The color green takes on new meaning there, and— Oh! France. You have to go to France."

"I'll need a translator." I tapped my chin. "If only I knew someone who spoke French."

Allie gave me a mischievous grin. "Tu es très chanceux." Her accent caused a throb between my legs as my blood flowed south. Damn, that accent should have been illegal.

"Mm, have I told you how much I love it when you speak French? What did you say?"

"You are very lucky."

I held her hand in mine and squeezed. "I know I am."

༜༜༜

I NEEDED to tell my supervisor about my having a relationship with one of my residents. The situation sucked, but giving up Allie was not an option. I waited outside Mrs. Lun's office and fidgeted in my seat. Surely, she would not fire me. She knew I needed those benefits. She knew how serious I was about my job. She came to *me* when she needed to tell the other RAs about something. Still, I dreaded her reaction.

I tried to keep the shock out of my expression when I saw Ryan step out of her office. He glanced at me but kept his emotions off of his face. Was he angry? Angry enough to tell Mrs. Lun about Allie before I could?

The whole reason I came to tell her was because I did not want her to find out in any other way. What would happen if Ryan had told her? Would it be too late for me?

"Thanks for coming by," Mrs. Lun said to Ryan and smiled at me. "Nate, I'm ready for you now. Come on in."

I walked inside and sat on her couch as she sat behind her desk. The leathered cushion sank beneath me but did nothing to comfort me. Her office had orange positivity posters hung on the walls, and a giant stuffed animal elephant sat on her desk. The black beaded eyes of it stared at me.

"How are classes going?"

"Good." Classes always went well for me. I had stayed a straight-A student due to my work ethic and time management skills. At least all of my rules had a reason behind them. "I wanted to talk to you about something."

"What's up?" She acted like she did not know. Maybe Ryan had not told her? Why else would he have come to talk to her?

"Well." How was I supposed to tell her I broke the strictest rule of being an RA? Well, the strictest other than selling drugs or distributing alcohol in the dorm. "I kind of..."

My phone shrieked with techno beats as it vibrated in my pocket. Great.

"Sorry," I said, my face warming as I pulled out my phone to put it on silent. The screen showed Blue was calling me. She never called me. "Um, actually, is it okay if I take this?"

"Sure. I'll answer some emails till you're done."

"Thanks." I hit answer on the call and walked back into the hallway, closing the door of Mrs. Lun's office. "What's up, Blue? Is something wrong?"

"Dad sold the house and took the money."

Every molecule of my body froze. "What?"

"H-He sold the house without telling us. All my stuff is inside, Nate. There's a padlock on the door."

I cursed and strained my self-control to not kick the wall. What the fuck was I supposed to do now? Blue needed a place to sleep and food to eat. Why could I not just graduate, get hired by an amazing company, and make a million in a year? That would have solved all my problems. My grandfather made his first million at eighteen. Where was I going wrong?

"I don't know what to do," Blue cried and every hitch in her breath wrenched bits of my heart out of my chest.

"Sleep over a friend's house tonight, okay? Can you do that?"

She sniffled. "Yeah."

"Try to find someone's house to stay at till the weekend. I'll sort everything else out after that." Thanksgiving break was just a couple of days away when everyone left for a week. If I had to, I could sneak Blue into the dorms while everyone was gone and take care of her until the break ended.

"I'm scared, Nate."

"Don't be. Who do you have?"

"You."

"And who is the only person you need?" I repeated the chant we had created in our childhood.

"You."

"I love you, Blue," I said. "Just stick in there."

When I hung up, I pressed my forehead against the wall and tried to think. Mrs. Lin called from her office, "Nate? You ready now?"

I opened her door and walked back inside. Everything was different now. I could not risk Blue's safety and comfort to be with Allie. But I also could not lose Allie.

"I wanted to tell you..." I would lie and keep us secret. "I think we should be harsher about noise violations."

She blinked. "I thought we were already harsh."

"Yes, well, you're probably right." I brushed off nonexistent dust from my pants and waved. "That was all. Just wanted to run that idea by you."

"Are you sure that was all?" The way she asked, curious and suspicious, gave me pause.

Was it possible Ryan talked to her about Allie and me? If I did not come clean now, would she catch me in my lie? "Yes, that was all."

"Okay, well, thanks for stopping by." She gestured for me to leave. So, Ryan had not told her about us?

"Why did Ryan visit you?" I asked, as nonchalant as possible. Cool as a cucumber.

She gave me an inquisitive look. "He came in about a resident and RA relationship. He had met someone earlier and wanted to go through the paperwork, but he came in today to say it had ended."

"Sad," I said.

Her eyebrows shot up behind her black bangs. "Sad?"

"I mean, it's sad people can't remain professional. A resident and RA relationship is forbidden."

"It's horrible and messy for everyone involved." She nodded, shooting me a smile. "Thankfully, I never have to worry about that with you. Right, Nate?"

"Right."

❢❢❢

"WOULD you rather jump from a plane or a hot-air balloon?" Allie questioned me as we laid next to each other on her bed. Allie's roommate barely slept in their room, which meant we could always have alone time together. Considering I had not gotten approval to have a relationship with Allie, it was important to keep our relationship on the down-low. Residents always came to my room to complain, and it would cause questions and raise eyebrows for them to see Allie sleeping in my bed.

"I would rather not jump at all." I nuzzled my face into the crook of her neck and her shoulder as I wrapped my arms around her from behind. More than ever, I worried about losing her. If someone caught us together, I would lose my chance at helping Blue.

"That's not how the game works."

"Hot-air balloon." I trailed my hand along her smooth side, my fingers dipping at her waist before gliding back up to trace her hip. "Would you rather take an easy class you have no interest in or take a hard class you're fascinated by?"

She puckered her lips at me as if she was trying to pout but also trying to look adorable in the process. It worked, and I rewarded her with a small kiss. "You do realize you just described my psychology class predicament."

"Predicament? Hanging around me has affected your vocabulary."

"Oh please, I used big words before I met you." She turned on the bed until our bodies faced each other. There was not much room on the dorm beds, so—to prevent falling off—we were as close as we could get.

Bare arm against bare arm.

Warm leg against even warmer leg.

We had been together officially for a mere two days and had yet to venture into sex or anything other than making out on her mattress.

She asked, "Would you rather go skinny dipping in the winter, or wear ten winter coats and go golfing in the summer?"

"I've never gone skinny dipping," I commented.

"What?" She gaped. "How? It's like a rite of passage."

I snorted. "How is it a rite of passage?"

"We're going skinny dipping."

"It's November; it's too cold."

"We'll use the indoor pool at the recreation center."

"Yeah, because it's not against the rules to randomly swim naked."

As much as I liked her, I worried about just how different we were. I loved her spark and outlook on life, but her care-free attitude could also lead to me getting into trouble and losing everything. Even though I knew everything was at stake, saying goodbye to her was not an option. She was the person I felt closest to other than my little sister. *What if I have to choose?*

"We'll go over Thanksgiving break when no one will be on campus." We had already discussed how both of us were staying in the dorm over break, neither one of us was a big family dinner type, since my father and mother cared more about wealth and status than about their children. However, I had yet to tell Allie that Blue would stay with me for Thanksgiving break.

I shook my head at her idea to break into the pool. "There will still be workers."

"Not after hours when it's closed."

"Do you have experience in breaking and entering?"

"I have experience entering." She snorted and climbed up on top of me, straddling my waist. My thoughts slowed. "Come on, do something crazy with me." I tried to ignore the way my boxers became tighter when she bounced on my lap. Damn, did she have any idea what she did to me? "It'll be fun, I promise."

"Allie, it's against the—" She cut me off with a passionate kiss, making thinking impossible.

"I'm going to enjoy making you break the rules."

DORM MANUAL RULE #20: FOLLOW CAMPUS RULES

llie:

"Have I told you that you're crazy?" Nate whisper-yelled at me as I opened the door to the recreation building. "How do you even know how to pick locks?"

The glow from the emergency lights was just enough to see. After peering inside, I decided it was safe to enter.

"I learned things overseas." I winked at him and pulled him inside the building.

"Stop trying to make that sound sexy."

"I don't know what you're talking about, Nate. I'm not trying to do anything. If you find that sexy, then that's on you."

His neck strained as he whipped his head around, trying to see if anyone was there who could catch us. "I'd hoped you had forgotten about this skinny dipping idea of yours." He all but bit his nails.

Nervous Nate was just as cute as stern, professional Nate. I loved how we seemed to take turns at supporting each other. Whenever he was on edge, I was there to tease him. Whenever my sensitivity and fear spiked, he was there to be strong and confident. How had I not been able to see what a perfect fit we made?

However, now that we were officially together, we had been less physical and intimate than before. We shared a few hot kisses, but Nate did not push for more.

I wanted more. Did he not want more?

I had told myself maybe he waited because he did not want to have sex with me in the dorms while everyone was there. Not a solid reason, but it gave me hope of things changing between us, and becoming hot and heavy again once Thanksgiving break began and everyone deserted the campus to go home for the holiday.

We were one day into the break and had the entire dorm to ourselves. We could hook up in the communal showers if we wanted to. So why had he not made a move? Why did he break away after every kiss or caress?

Did he want to go slow? Surprising, considering the attraction between us and how we had masturbated in front of each other before we were even together.

My skinny dipping plan was to take things one step farther between us. Seeing each other naked would help. Hopefully.

"How could I forget? It was just three days ago you told me you had never gone." I had spent the next few days planning it. The pool closed at ten o'clock so we had snuck in at eleven. I had my skimpy bikini on under my clothes, and Nate wore swim trunks and a T-shirt.

"Biggest regret of my life."

"Oh, come on." I grinned at him. "I know you're loving this."

He shook his head, adamant. "Incorrect."

"You're not excited at all? We're sneaking into a pool to swim naked."

"I prefer legal dates, such as going to a movie theater or staying in with a nice hot cup of not-breaking-the-law."

"Boring."

"Morally right."

I gave him a playful tap on his nose. "You're so cute when you're scared."

"I'm not scared, I just don't enjoy the confinement and solitude of jail time."

"You're not going to get in trouble." I laughed at him and wrapped my arms around him. "Can't you just trust me?" I leaned in so close, it hurt to maintain eye contact. He had no choice but to look down and focus his eyes on my lips. He was so easy to seduce.

"I—"

I kissed him to distract him from backing out. He needed to go skinny-dipping as much as I needed a distraction. My week had been rough, and this was my official relax-and-have-fun-with-Nate time. His lips captured mine, and my body flooded with heat. Great, what had started as a distraction to calm him became a distraction for me from what we were doing.

I pulled back from the kiss with reluctance. "This will be

my date night, where I pick what we do and where we go. You can be in charge next time."

"Something tells me I'll never be in charge again," Nate grumbled under his breath, still staring down at my lips, which were now swollen from such a passionate kiss.

I grabbed his hand and led him to the heated indoor pool. The room was dark except for the lights in the pool, which illuminated it, making it look like a portal. The stillness of the water made the prospect of jumping in all the more alluring.

"See? Isn't this cool?" I ran to the edge. "It's all glowy."

"Like a tank of radioactive waste."

"But blue instead of green."

"And less toxic."

"That's the spirit!" I ran back over to him and tugged on his shirt. "Now strip."

His jaw dropped, his expression horrified. "Excuse me?"

"Skinny-dipping means no clothes." I eyed him up and down and made a gesture. "Whip 'em off, buddy."

"Don't call me buddy while trying to get me naked." He glanced back at the pool. "And don't act so nonchalant about it either."

"Oh, I see. You want me to act all in awe of your nakedness. Will do."

He sighed. "You're making fun of me."

I kissed his cheek. "No, I get it. You don't want me to make light of this moment." I kissed him again, but this time on his neck, and whispered in his ear, "I want to see you, Nate. All of you."

He swallowed, and a pulse settled between my legs. I

wanted to see him naked. I tried to downplay it with my teasing, but the truth was I was ready to drool.

He whipped off his shirt, and I whistled on impulse. He glared at me, but he smiled on the inside. He loved it whenever I told him how sexy he was. He was smug that way.

"I shouldn't be the only one taking off my clothes," Nate remarked, and my eyes widened. Oh, so now nervous Nate was transforming back into confident and bossy Nate. Good; I had missed him.

I flashed a wicked smile at him while pulling down the straps of my loose top. It fell to the ground. As I slipped out of my short shorts, I bent down and flashed him a decent amount of cleavage in the process. I stood, left in nothing but my white bikini. The sound of Nate sucking in a breath as his eyes devoured my body made all the trouble of shaving everywhere the day before worth it.

His gaze roamed, heating and heating until it blazed and burned me.

"Shall we?" I asked before I dove into the lit-up pool. When I surfaced back up for air, he still stood on the edge of the pool in front of me.

"What happened to the skinny part of the dipping?"

I giggled at his disappointed expression. "We can play a game." I swam a bit away from him, making room so he could jump in when he wanted. "We can try to take the rest off of each other in the water. The first person who is stripped naked loses...or maybe wins?"

Now Nate wore the wicked smile. "You think you can strip me before I can strip you?"

I loved challenging him. It was so easy, and he always

rose to the occasion. For someone who desired control, he sure lacked it when something needed to be proven.

"Why don't you jump in and we'll find out?" I giggled again when he dove into the water toward me. Because of the lighting, I could see him through the electric blue water, and the sight of him swimming up to me under it was somehow erotic. Or maybe it was just because it was Nate and everything about him was erotic. When he popped up for air, he was right in front of me. Mere inches separated our almost naked bodies. "Well, hello there."

Nate leaned his forehead onto mine, and it took me a minute to realize he had a perfect view down my bikini top. "Hi."

"Like the view?" I poked his chest, which ended up hurting my finger because the muscles were solid. Was he flexing on purpose?

He shifted his head against mine until his lips were at the ultra-sensitive side of my neck, just below my ear. He kissed my pulse point, and I bit back a moan. "I have a feeling I'll like it even more..." When his lips left my neck, his pesky fingers raced up to undo my bikini. I pushed him away from me, cackling with laughter, and started to swim away.

"Seducing is against the rules." I wagged my finger at him. No way would he beat me. I would dive under and get those swim trunks off him before he could ask, *where did you go?*

"So I'm supposed to just rip your clothes off at random in order to win?"

"You'd have to catch me first." I sank down in the water and swam to the other side of the pool. His hands caught my foot, but I twisted it away from him and swam faster.

We dog-paddled around the pool, avoiding each other for

a while before I risked it all and went for his trunks. I dove under, my hands slipping under his waistband, and jerked the trunks down. That's when the game became dangerous. It was the first time I had seen him naked and, damn; he fulfilled my wildest dreams. I gasped underwater at the sight of his hard cock reaching up towards me. The gasp led to me choking on water so I resurfaced, which allowed Nate the opportunity to catch me and hold me to him so I could not escape again.

"I win," I said through my coughs as my lungs cleared themselves of chlorine.

"Do you?" he whispered in my ear.

My bikini top loosened and fell into the water with a wet *splat*. His hands drifted down to my waist and played with the strings on either side, which held the piece together.

"I believe I do." I pinched his bare ass, and he grinned down at me. Nate was either playful or dominating when aroused, and I had no idea which one I preferred.

"Well, then," He kissed my collarbone and trailed his mouth down between my breasts. "I guess I can—"

He sank under the water and bent down to pull off my bikini bottoms. He slipped the piece down my legs and it floated up next to me. However, he stayed underwater and wrapped my legs around his shoulders. I moaned at the sight of his head nuzzling between my legs and yelped when he closed the distance and delivered a kiss right above my clit.

He lifted me as he resurfaced for air. Both his hands were holding me up, gripping the swell of my ass, as his head secured itself between my legs. My nipples pebbled between us from the sheer chill and thrill of Nate's touch as he held me in the air, out of the water. My hips undulated into his embrace.

"Nate," I shouted when his tongue became my new best friend.

His hot, wet tongue drew torturous circles over my throbbing bud, and I grabbed at his hair, frenzied. Desire ran through me, hard and wild like a freight train. This was not how it was supposed to have gone. I was supposed to be the seducer. My plan to skinny dip and convince him to do more than just kiss me unraveled because now he became the one pulling all the strings.

This was one case, however, where I did not mind Nate being in control. Damn, with his ability to move his tongue like that, I would give him control over everything.

He pulled back from between my legs and chuckled when my fingers tugged at his hair for him to go back to what he had been doing.

"You like that?" He delivered another sensual lick.

I groaned at his evident intent to tease me. "Yes, I like that. Who wouldn't like that?" I pulled on his hair again, making my desire known. "Now please resume."

He stared at me, appearing hungry, starving, and I wanted to hit him for pausing. "My good girl is so wet," he rasped.

"Yes, well, we are in a pool." Now I was the agitated and impatient one. If he was not going to continue where he left off, I would have to show him how much I did not appreciate being teased.

I widened my legs so the firm grip over my shoulders faded, and I slipped down his body. He raised one eyebrow, but let me change our position. I re-secured myself by tightening my legs around his waist, rubbing over his erection. The bulbous tip made direct contact with my slit, hot and begging for more. My hips rocked against him.

The tortured look on Nate's face brought a smile to mine. *All is fair in love and war.*

I arched my hips against him, aligning us until his hardness grazed my swollen bud. Shivers wracked me. Sensation took over. He moaned and moved in to kiss me, but I dodged it. I slid a hand down his chest to his arousal, curling my fingers around him and squeezing.

"Jesus, Allie," he choked.

"You like that?" I repeated his words to him. Time to show him how much I disliked teasing.

"Yes." His eyes crossed, unfocused on anything but pleasure, when I moved my hand up and down over him. My grip was firm, the water working as extra lubrication.

I leaned in and licked up his neck to the bottom of his earlobe. A bead of moisture rose on the tip of him and slickened my palm with each stroke. "Mm, my good boy is so wet." I used his words against him again, though it seemed he was no longer listening to me.

"Allie." He grunted. "Harder."

I tightened my hold on him without any hesitation. Damn it, I was finally in control again and he still called the shots?

"That's it, baby. Hard and firm." He bit back a curse, grating, "Your soft little hand is going to kill me."

A hard swallow worked down my throat as wetness leaked from my core, and I continued jerking him under the water. My fingers ran from the base to the tip of his throbbing erection.

"Ah." Nate tore my hand off of him and pulled me to the edge of the pool. He pushed himself up and turned to sit on the edge, half of his legs still in the water. He slapped on the tops of his thighs and ordered, "Up."

I shook my head and swam between his legs. "So bossy." I kissed his inner thigh, so close to the body part he wanted me to kiss, he jumped.

"Up. Now." The heavy desire in his voice resulted in an aching in my core.

I lifted my arms, and he grabbed me and pulled me up onto him. I now straddled him, and the moment I lowered myself into his lap, we both let out a loud moan at the contact. His lips crashed against mine like waves, calmly lapping and passionately crushing at the same time.

"Allie," he murmured through the kisses. "I like you so fucking much."

"I like you too."

❣❣❣

"YOU WENT skinny-dipping and you two still did not have sex?" Eliza, my friend from France, laughed, astonished, on the phone.

"I thought it might happen, or at least that more might happen, but it just ended in romantic making out the way the other nights have." I should not have been complaining. We had only been dating for several days. Still, when we weren't together, he'd had a hard time keeping his hands off of me. Were the forming emotions stalling it from happening again?

"Maybe he wants to wait?"

I kicked at my rug. "I've heard about his sex life from multiple people, even when I really didn't want to, and they all say he's a very sexual person," I commented. Why the hell could he have tons of sex with other girls but not with me? Skinny-dipping was supposed to be the night. We had both been so ready to lose control. "Do you think it's me?"

People had told me he was a dom. Was he truly kinky? Did he need to be dominating in order to have sex? Was that why he waited? Because he thought his dom traits might scare me away? He was dominating enough in normal life with all his bossiness; there was not much he could do to surprise me.

"Stop," Eliza warned. "If he makes you think he does not want you, then turn the tables on him. Seduce him."

"Me seduce him?" I repeated her plan. "Well, why didn't you say so?"

NATE'S #9 RULE FOR LIFE: HAVE THE LAST LAUGH, NEVER THE LAST WORD

*N*ate:

"Mmm, PANCAKES," Blue muttered as she stuffed the breakfast food into her mouth and chewed through her words. "This is better than cereal."

"Anything is better than cereal." I tugged the blankets over my bed, which my sister had been using since she moved in on the first day of Thanksgiving break. Just as I had thought, the dorm and campus were empty from everyone going home for the holiday. Except for Allie. Allie did not have a home to go back to and, I suppose, neither did I anymore.

I wanted to be Allie's home.

I had spent as much time with Allie as I could to not raise her suspicion, but I always had to come back and spend the majority of my time with Blue. Aka, Allie and Blue did not know about each other. Blue thought I was out doing official RA business when Allie and I had gone skinny-dipping.

God, that night had been eye-opening.

The sound of Allie laughing and splashing me played in my ears as I pictured her pressed against me, both of us bare. The deep need to thrust inside her and achieve what both of us needed. A release. But I was not about to make our first time together at a pool after hours. She deserved a bed. Or a wall. Whichever was closer in the moment. She deserved more than simple rutting.

She deserved romance.

I was terrible at romance. And even if I was not terrible— which I was—Blue sleeping in my room prevented me from doing anything. The walls were too thin if I dared to sleep over in Allie's bed. Thus, we could not go farther than a few kisses until Thanksgiving break ended and Blue went to stay at my aunt's house.

Allie would be fine waiting until then, and I would make it up to her. I just could not let her find out about Blue staying with me. I had opened up enough to say my family had money issues as of late, but I did not want her to know just how messed up everything was. According to Allie, I had already told my supervisor we were in a relationship and gotten it approved.

I had lied to her.

Two things remained true: 1. I could not tell my supervisor about Allie until everything was sorted out with Blue and my parents, or until I graduated. 2. I could not sleep with Allie until the end of Thanksgiving break, four days away.

Four days.

My cock was ready to fall off inside my pants.

Even though I slept on the uncomfortable floor while Blue took my bed, my blood flow must have been strong since it caused some thick morning wood. I had tried to wane it away with dark thoughts, but gave in and ran to the men's bathroom to take care of my problem. A few strokes to memories of skinny-dipping with Allie and I had come within minutes.

Bathroom breaks were a whole endeavor while having Blue in the dorm as well. She did not want to pee in a place with urinals, so I always had to distract Allie in her room long enough for Blue to go to the women's bathroom, do her business, and return to the sanctity of my room.

Distracting Allie for a few minutes was not an easy feat because there was no hey-let-us-have-a-quick-conversation when it came to Allie. We either discussed life, laughed for half an hour, or made out like her lips were an addictive substance.

So, when Blue told me she had to go to the bathroom, I let out a deep sigh and brainstormed a short conversation starter, lasting around three minutes.

I watched Blue sneak into the bathroom before I knocked on Allie's door with a tight smile.

She opened the door and bit her lip. Her sexy, swollen, and pink lip. "Nate, fancy seeing you here."

She had sex eyes. Eyes shining, *Fuck me and fuck me hard.* What the hell was she doing showing me her sex eyes at a time like this? She did not know I could not sleep with her for four more days, but jeez, she could have at least made it a little easier on me. She wore a thin red camisole—knowing it was my favorite color on her—with no bra—knowing it was my favorite clothing choice for her.

The tips of her breasts strained through the fabric.

"Come in?" she purred, opening her door wider. She may as well have opened her legs and said, *"Come inside me, baby."* Or my horniness was causing new levels of delusion. Either way, I needed to get control of myself. If she were shorter, the tent in my pants might have poked her eye out. For her safety, I needed to tamper down my arousal. And possibly tape it down, too. Whatever worked.

"Um, we can talk in the hallway." *Remain. Strong.* But she wrapped her hands around my forearm and tugged me inside her room. "Or not."

I rubbed the back of my neck as it heated just from being in an enclosed space with her. Allie. My girlfriend. My girlfriend whom I yearned to pleasure but could not while my twelve-year-old sister stayed in my room for four more days. Four. Fuck. Four was such an annoying number. Way more annoying than two. A little less annoying than five.

"You look tired, Nate," Allie whispered, still clutching one of my arms. The warmth from her delicate hand seeped through my shirt, skin, and right to my bones. "Want to rest a bit?" She shoved me so hard, she wrenched a surprised noise from me as my body collapsed back onto her mattress.

Creaks sprung from the bed as it absorbed my weight. "Allie, what the—"

She pulled her camisole down until her breasts fell out, swinging and aching for my touch. She crawled up my body on her bed, pausing when her nipples were level with my mouth. "I've been a good girl, Nate. Where's my reward?"

My thoughts were a chant of, *"fuck, fuck, fuck, fuck."* I

could not look away if I tried, and I did not try, because what would be the point?

"Allie," I breathed her name. In and out. Her breasts swayed above me back and forth like a hypnotic pendant my eyes could not escape.

"Don't you think I deserve a reward, Nate?" She kissed up my neck, her lips no doubt able to tell the fast beating of my heart. "I think you deserve a reward too."

"W-What kind of reward?" No. *Fight it.* Four more days. Blue would return from the bathroom any minute and be back in my room, able to hear any noise above a whisper through Allie's wall.

"That's up to you, Mr. Dominant. How do you want me? My hands, my mouth, my—"

"Okay." I raised my hands to lightly push her away, but she shifted at the same time. My palms met the bare flesh of her chest and squeezed the swells on instinct. I groaned, pressing my lips together as tight as possible. *Do not play with her nipples. Whatever you do, do not*—My fingers flicked them, and I watched them harden before caressing the tips in fast circles.

She rocked her hips down on me, rubbing against my throbbing erection hard enough for me to see not just stars but a whole constellation. All I had to do was rip off those tiny jean shorts of hers and slide my hand into her panties to feel her wetness. To prove she was as turned on as me. As lost in me as I was in her.

"I-I can't do this right now," I said, even as I continued to buck up between her legs to rock myself against her inner heat and massage her breasts.

"Why not?"

Because my little sister will hear us. Because your moans don't have a quiet setting, nor do I want them to. "I have work to do."

"Do me instead," she offered with a smile dipped in as much lust as humor.

"I can't."

She frowned, annoyance flashing in her green eyes and distracting me. "Why can't you?"

Great, now she was mad at me. "I told you I have work to do."

She sat up, removing her breasts from my hands, and paused her grinding. She crossed her arms under her heavenly cleavage, framing it. "What is more important than this?"

Nothing. Wait, no. My sister. Right. That was the correct answer. But she could not know Blue was here without finding out I had also lied to her about telling my boss about us. "School?"

"You would rather do homework than grope and be groped by your super hot girlfriend?" she asked, disbelief in her expression.

"Um." *You made your bed, now sleep in it.* Alone. "Yes?"

She tilted her head, narrowing her eyes on me. Analyzing me the way she knew I hated. "Is this a game?"

"Huh?"

"Is this some kind of Dom game where I keep touching you until you give in or something?"

"How is that a game?"

"I don't know." She lifted her arms, making her breasts jiggle lewdly in my face. "You're the kinky one."

I leaned up and yanked the neckline of her tank top back over her bare chest, so it covered the biggest distraction as to why I could not sleep with her. "I just think we should... wait." For four days. Then go at it like animals. With the same amount of biting.

"Wait? Why? We did more before we were even an actual couple." True. She shifted off of me on the bed. "I know you want me because that is not a phone in your pocket." She pointed down at my erection, and I frowned. "Why do you always pull back and stop?"

"I didn't know you wanted sex so much." Lies. Blame. I wanted sex just as much as her, if not more. I was dying from not touching her or hearing her moans in my ear. But I had to wait until Blue was gone. "We've only been going out for a few days."

"I'm not some sex maniac," she said, and I wanted to bang my head for making her think I saw her that way. "I just thought you would want to, so why don't you want to?"

"Allie." She thought I did not want her? "Of course, I want to. I just—I haven't been in a relationship in a while and neither have you. You said before that you have one-night stands because you're uncomfortable being intimate."

Great, Nate, put the blame on her some more. The only reason my tongue was not circling her clit at this very moment was because my little sister might hear Allie screaming my name and be scarred forevermore. This sucked. I did not want her thinking she was the reason I kept stopping us from going forward.

"It's not like I can't wait for some action," she said. "I just want you to act like you want it too."

It was not possible for me to want her more than I did. *Think up some explanation. Put the blame on me.* "I've done a lot of things with girls, and I've never gotten into the emotional side of things. It was just sex." *Great, just what every girlfriend wanted to hear.* "I wanted to go slower with you. You're special to me."

"And what about handcuffs?"

My body twitched on her bed at the image of her cuffed. "Allie…"

"Do you want to try stuff like that with me?"

"I don't like talking about this."

"Just tell me how you feel and where you stand, and I won't bother you about this again." She wanted to know I wanted her.

"Really?" My voice came out rough. "You want to know all the things I want to do to you?"

She clapped, and I rolled my eyes at her childish excitement. "Please," she exclaimed.

I leaned in to whisper in her ear, "I want to tie you to my bed and lick every inch of your body." Her breath caught at my sentence. "Every moment I'm with you, I have to fight an internal battle with myself because I don't want to treat you like other girls, but I also want to pull you to me and kiss you until you think I'll never stop. I want to fuck you against the wall, on my desk, in my bed. I want you all the time, but I stop before we go farther because what I need from you is more important than what I want. And also because I know the longer we wait, the more everything will build up until neither of us can take it anymore. And some things, Allie, are worth the wait."

But I was not.

Because I still lied to her. And I had no plans to stop.

Then the door to my room slammed shut.

ALLIE'S #2 RULE FOR LIFE: DON'T BEAT AROUND THE BUSH; LIGHT IT ON FIRE

llie:

"WHAT WAS THAT?" I asked after the sound of Nate's door closed while he laid on my bed as I sat next to him. Was someone else staying in the dorm during the holiday break? Were they breaking into his room? Why did he not appear more concerned? There was a robber, a thief strutting around—

He knew who was in his room. Another girl? I would kill her. He was cheating on me? I would kill him. We had been together for just a few days, and he could not keep it in his pants long enough for a one-week anniversary? I *wanted* him to take it out of his pants. For me.

So he would not sleep with me because he wanted to wait, but he would sleep with other women?

I growled, my body tensing more and more with each second ticking by. My DNA transformed into that of a tigress as I stared down at him.

He opened his mouth and inhaled. "It's not what you think."

I leaped off the bed and sprinted out of my room.

"Stop!" he yelled, running after me and grabbing my waist.

From our opposing forces coming together, we spun and fell into the wall of the hallway. I escaped his warm hands and ran to Nate's door. My palm hovered, about to connect with his doorknob, when he tackled me to the tiled floor, turning us midair so his body absorbed most of the blow.

"You're cheating on me?" I shrieked, tears coming faster than my thoughts could. I should not feel so broken up. All men were monsters. Except for Gavin. "You're no better than Logan."

Nate froze beside me on the ground. His arms snapped away from me, uncaging me as he sat up on his knees. "What the fuck did you just say?"

I clenched my teeth but spoke through them. "I said you're no better than Logan."

It was his turn to growl. "Never compare me to him ever again."

"He cheated on me too."

"I didn't—" Nate dropped his head and let out a frustrated sound. "That's it. I'm never lying again." He stood up and offered me his hand. "Come on."

I slapped his palm away and got up by myself. "How dare you?" I pounded a finger into the hard muscles of his chest with each word.

241

"Shut up," he said. "I'd never cheat on you. Don't be stupid."

Red clouded my vision. "You think I'm stupid?"

"If you think I could even look at another girl after you've fucking blinded me, then yeah, I think you're stupid."

The bubbles of rage pooling in my stomach lightened into butterflies so fast I almost became nauseous. "What?"

"Just come on." He pulled me to his room, knocked on the door, and walked me inside.

On Nate's chair, at his desk, sat a young girl with the same shade of dark brown hair as Nate. This was the sister Nate had mentioned? He was not cheating on me. His sister was here. And by the look of the two stuffed suitcases, she had been staying here for days.

And I was just now meeting her?

I whacked Nate's ass hard enough to make him jump, yelp, and make his sister giggle.

He cradled his stinging cheeks. "Why did you do that?"

"That was for not introducing me to your sister and for making me think you cheated." I stepped closer to the girl. "I'm Allie." I waited for recognition to light up her bright eyes, for her say to Nate, "*So this is the girl you've told me so much about.*" But she did not react to my name.

Instead, she reached out a hand to shake like the middle-aged professional she was not and said, "Nice to meet you. My name is Bluebell—uh, Blue—Reddington." Of course, the sister of Nate would not just say, "*I'm Blue.*" She needed some fun just as much as he did. "Are you one of Nate's residents?"

"Yes." I glanced at Nate, who speared nervous fingers through his hair.

He had not told her about me at all? She was the person

closest to him; what did it say about us that he had never mentioned me? At all? A bit of rage came back, but hurt was what leaked into my stomach and burned the inner lining.

"Allie is…" Nate trailed off. "She's, um…"

"Need some help?" I asked, lifting my eyebrows as he dug his own grave.

"We're um, well, we're together," he spat out.

Blue's mouth dropped open. "You have a girlfriend?"

"And a gorgeous one," I added. "Shocking, I know."

"Wow, Nate hasn't had a girlfriend since—"

"Okay," he said. "That's enough. Allie, Blue. Blue, Allie. Blue is not supposed to be here, so we have to keep her secret until the end of break." Why was she staying here instead of at their home? Also, awww, Nate let her stay with him.

No wonder he did not want us to have sex. It was because Blue was here. Not because he wanted to wait. The heat in his eyes was unmistakable. Oh my God, he had lied to me.

Why? I did not care about the lie, but I was curious as to his reasoning behind it. He knew I could keep a secret. Well, I could attempt to keep a secret. Okay, yeah, I was a bad secret keeper. Still, why had he not told his girlfriend about his sister staying next door?

A light bulb went off in my head. "She is why you come over with stupid questions every other hour?"

"I needed to use the restroom." Blue's cheeks went pink as she gestured to her abnormally tall water bottle. "I drink a lot of water."

My heart inflated two sizes bigger at the cuteness of Bluebell Reddington. "You are so adorable." I cupped her warming face in my hands and squeezed her cheeks like an overexcited grandmother. "I'm adopting you."

A strange noise came from Nate as he stumbled into his dresser.

"What?" I asked him.

"N-Nothing," he answered.

"Nate plans to adopt me once he graduates and has a job," Blue explained.

"Well, I will adopt you first if I can. Nate would make for a boring parent. You need some excitement."

"Excuse me?" Nate scoffed. "You were the one who said I wasn't boring."

"You're too sexy to be boring."

He appeared confused.

"Don't question me," I told him and turned back to Blue. "Let's have a makeover. I have every color—"

"I don't like nail polish."

I was falling in love with this girl. My arms wrapped around her as a grin curved my mouth. "I was going to say every color hair dye."

Her lips curled up into a wicked smile.

Nate threw himself between us, pushing Blue behind him as if he needed to defend her from me. "No," he said.

I leaned around him so I could meet Blue's eyes. "How old are you?"

"Almost thirteen."

"Old enough not to let your older brother make your decisions for you," I commented.

Nate gave me his classic glare, but I had become immune. "You are not coloring my little sister's hair."

"It's temporary dye. Only lasts a week. It's how I do my

highlights." I touched the red strands. Typically, I changed the color every month or so, but Nate loved red so much I had yet to switch to something else. "Oh, blue highlights to match your name. How cute would that be?"

"So cute," his sister replied.

♀♀♀

THE REST of Thanksgiving break was spent hanging out with Blue. She was a cock-blocker, sure, but she was a cute one. Her professional demeanor had melted once I applied blue highlights to the bottom tips of her hair. I prided myself on her liking me. We teased Nate together, and he turned red every time. Nate was not used to being teased. It was strange, but we almost resembled a family unit.

Nate and I never got a chance to be alone after I discovered Blue. She filled up our free time. We ate meals together and did random fun activities together. By the end of our week, she left with new hair and a new at-ease smile. She was set to move in with her aunt for the time being due to his parents being unreliable.

The second Blue left on the last day, I went to my room and got dressed for a much-needed seduction. Innocent schoolgirl was supposed to be a fantasy every guy had, right? I searched my closet for my black skirt and found a perfect low-cut, lacey white top to go with it.

When I knocked back on his door, I readied myself for our "study session." With Blue gone, I did not plan on doing any real studying. Upon seeing my outfit, Nate's reaction was a grunt, a nod, and a quick kiss. After days of foreplay and not being able to touch each other, all I got was a chaste kiss and a grunt. What the hell?

I wanted more from him. Making him lose control had become addictive. *Time for a seduction.* Again.

"What are you doing?" he asked me several minutes later after we had cracked open our books.

"I have no idea what you're talking about," I said, trailing the end of my pencil up my throat and the eraser along my lips. Step one in seduction: draw attention to your lips. However, a pencil had not been the best idea because some of the eraser had not so erotically rubbed off on my lips, and I had to wipe it off with my hand.

Nate stared at me like I was crazy, and I shrugged at him.

Nate pointed at the study sheet for the history class we shared. "Let's just focus on question five."

This was our usual tutoring time where we met in his room to go over whatever we needed help on in class. Nate never seemed to need any help, so instead, he had taken on more of a teacher role in the study time we spent together. Sure, he helped tutor me in psychology but, as the days went by, his interest in teaching grew. Maybe because he enjoyed having authority. I had told Nate he should look into becoming a teacher, but he was dead set on going to law school.

I pulled my chair closer than normal to his, claiming the textbook font was too small for me to see without the sides of our thighs pressing together. He did not comment on the change, but the way he glanced down at the cleavage my white top put on display gave me confidence. Thank God for push-up bras.

Now, however, he was back to his professional tutor

façade. I needed to break down the no-touching trend established between us while Blue was there. I needed to seduce the living daylights out of him. What would an out-of-a-fantasy school girl say in this situation to get his attention?

"Oh, wow." I pushed my chest against his arm and masked my smile at the way his body tensed. "This question is so *hard*."

"Seriously, what are you doing?" Nate inquired, appearing unaffected. Damn, maybe seduction was not one of my skill sets.

"What should I be doing?" I batted my eyelashes. "*Sir?*"

Still unaffected. "Allie?"

I slapped him on the arm. "Well, what the hell? I thought you were into the whole dom-submissive thing? Isn't naughty school girl supposed to turn you on?"

"I'm fascinated by how your brain works. Where do you get these ideas of yours?"

"Why are we not having sex right now? Blue is gone. I thought we would jump each other as soon as she left, but it has now been two hours of nothing."

That shocked him. "What?"

"I know you were lying about wanting to wait so I wouldn't find out about Blue. So let's get to it." I clapped my hands together as if the action of palm against palm was a universal symbol for sex.

"Get to it?" Nate quoted me in a disbelieving voice. "How romantic, Allie."

"I don't need romance." I was horny. I needed touching. I needed him.

"But you deserve romance."

"People deserve to eat and yet eight hundred million people go hungry each year."

He blinked. "How do you know the number?"

"Rough estimate," I said and stood up from his desk. He thought he could control himself around me? Fine. Didn't mean I couldn't tease him. "You know what, maybe I'll just find another man to satisfy me." I checked my nails, acting nonchalant, but it was as bluffy as a bluff could be. "I wonder if Ryan is available…"

Nate's back stiffened from his seat at his desk. His head whipped over so he met my gaze. His eyes bored into mine, flaring.

The room's atmosphere shifted to cold. Chilly. Frozen. I would have thought the air-conditioning kicked on, but we were approaching winter and the dorms only had heat.

"What the fuck—" he gritted out each word. "—did you just say?"

My heart stuttered, but the nervous excitement swirling in my lower abdomen forced me to push him harder. To make him snap. "I said maybe I should find someone else—"

He shot up from the desk, taking two long strides, before tossing me onto his bed. I fell back with a gasp of surprise before his body crawled over mine, looming above me. His expression was tight, angry, and threatening. Yet I wasn't afraid. I wasn't afraid of him.

My chest lightened with the feeling of freedom from my anxieties left over from being with Logan. Nate would never hurt me.

He bit out, "You want to repeat what you said?"

"Um, no?"

"You need to be fucked so bad, you'd go to someone else?"

His left hand inched down the side of my white top and black pencil skirt. His fingers clasped the hem of the skirt but made no other move.

"I was teasing," I explained, the back of my neck slickening with fresh sweat.

"Has anyone ever told you you're like a little kitten?" he asked. "Teasing and scratching and destroying things if you get bored."

"Kittens are adorable, so I take that as a compliment," I muttered under my breath as his expression darkened, and he lowered his head to the side of my face.

He drew in a deep breath of me before his lips dragged down my cheek, down, down, and he nipped at my jaw. "My little Alley Kitten."

I snorted at his new *Allie* nickname for me. "Never heard that one before."

"What do I have to do to get my kitten to focus on studying?" he whispered onto my neck. My heart thundered in my chest as I awaited his next move. "Do I need to make her purr?"

Fuuuuuuuuuuucccccckkkkkk. "Yes," I pleaded. "Some petting. She likes petting."

"I bet she does." His free hand skimmed down the back of my thighs. His fingers trailed up and down the tender skin. "But where to pet you?"

My teeth sank into my bottom lip.

"But where to pet my. Pretty. Little. Pussy," he punctuated each word with a nip, lick, and suck to my lips.

My body shook under his on the bed. "Nate," I cried out as his hand granted me mercy and sank between my legs, rising to touch my panties. "Yes."

His fingers dug into the fabric covering me and yanked it to the side until he could run the pads of his fingertips up and down my slit. Up and down. Up. Down. Just barely grazing over my throbbing bundle of nerves, where I ached for him. *He* teased *me*.

He dipped his head for a kiss as I whimpered onto his lips.

He gave a dark chuckle. "You needed a good little petting, didn't you?"

"More. Please." One of my hands fell to lock my fingers around his wrist, pressing his hand harder to me. He evaded my grip and continued teasing me so softly. So slowly. *"Please."*

"You think you can go to another man?"

"No, I was joking," I swore, breathless. "It was a joke."

"You were pushing me," he said, watching me shiver and fall apart with a small wicked smile. "I do not like to be pushed, Kitten."

His long, thick middle finger buried itself inside me, and a broken yell escaped my throat. I babbled incoherently as he sank the finger as deep as it would go and withdrew it. Then breached me once again. Again and again. Pulling out and ramming back inside.

In. Out.

"Nate," I chanted through broken breaths.

"My little Alley Cat goes docile when I pet her like this," he said in a low, pleased voice. "The next time you misbehave, maybe I'll just have to finger fuck you like this again. The next time you break a rule or push me, I'll have to take it out on this pretty, wet, hot as fuck, pussy." He thrust his finger harder, adding a second one. "How about that?"

"I love—" My breath caught in my throat, and his eyes widened. I added, quickly, "—your plan."

He shifted his hand, using his thumb to swipe over my clit back and forth, thrumming me like a freaking guitar. Music melted my ears.

He said, "I wanted to wait because you told me you have a hard time thinking of sex as intimacy instead of an act. I don't want you to separate your feelings for me with what we do together."

"I won't," I promised, mindless and—if I was honest—not listening as he fingered me in fast, expert strokes.

"But you had to push me and dress like some naughty school girl."

"Mmhm, mmmmmm."

His fingers moved faster still. "You're always trying to make me lose control."

"More—oh—more fun that way." My toes were curling, my fists bunching his sheets. "*Nate.*"

"Beg me for it, Kitten."

"Please." I wouldn't be surprised if tears were falling down my face. I needed it so badly. I needed him to take me there. A familiar tightening occurred in my lower stomach, my muscles contracting, winding up.

"Will this satisfy you for a day or just an hour?" he asked huskily. "How often will I need to pet this perfect pussy for you to obey me?"

"Always," I shrieked.

"Come for me," he demanded. "Right. Now." He burrowed his fingers inside me, curling them to hit my special spot.

My eyes rolled back, and my body gave a violent shudder as he held me down. My cry of pleasure also required him to peel his hand from my panties and clamp it over my mouth so no one heard us. I could smell myself on his fingers.

As the climax faded, my body returning to normal, a deep sigh climbed out of me. "Wow."

His pained grin twitched as he shifted on the bed. A stiff bulge pressed from behind the crotch of his pants. I reached for his erection, but he grabbed my wrists. "No," he reminded me. "Like I said, I want to wait."

"For what?" I whined, drunk on my orgasm and wanting to give him the same.

"For you to know this is real for me too. I want it to be special, not at three o'clock on a random day of the week."

"Do you require candles and roses as well?"

"Allie."

I blew out a breath, pouting. "Fine. We'll wait a bit longer. But, Nate?"

"Yeah?"

My lips inched up and gave him a hard, sensual kiss. "You feel free to call me when you want your kitten to lap up some cream."

He snorted. "Gross."

"You loved it."

DORM MANUAL RULE #26: NO LOUD PHONE CALLS

llie:

I WANTED HIM. Bad. The only thing to distract me from Nate was Gavin's arrival back onto campus after Thanksgiving break.

The college campus was once again overrun by students as I sat to eat with Gavin. Through a crowd of people waiting to pay for their food, I made eye contact with Ryan. He did not appear happy to see me.

I frowned, ripping up some of my roll, and Gavin sighed. "He's mad, Allie."

"He has a right to be." I nodded and hated how dramatic my life had become. I had wanted easy and simple, but Nate had destroyed my expectations and I would not give him up for anything. Still, I hated how I had hurt Ryan's feelings in the process.

"He thinks you slept with Nate the night you broke up with him."

"What? Why would he think that?"

"He saw Nate leaving your room the next morning." Why had Nate not told me?

"We just slept. I have…nightmares, and it's better if I have someone with me to wake me up."

Sleeping next to him granted me a sense of calm and safety, and I had not had a nightmare in a while. In fact, now the sex dreams were the problem, but Nate always enjoyed waking me up from those. Yet, we still had not had sex. What was the hold-up? He said he wanted it to be special and wanted me to see it as intimacy—something I struggled with —rather than a hookup.

Of course, I did not see him as a hookup. I freaking liked him. We were together.

Was he still mad I highlighted his sister's hair and talked her into getting a tattoo when she turned eighteen?

"Your roommate couldn't do that?" Gavin asked.

"She never sleeps over. Should I talk to Ryan?"

"I would say no. Let him calm down first."

"It's been over a week." How long would he stay mad? We only went on a few dates, for goodness' sake. Kissing was as far as Ryan and I had gone. Would he hold such a grudge against me?

"He liked you, Allie."

"Yeah." I was starting to think his ego was hurt more than his feelings.

"But you're happy with Nate?"

"Shockingly so." Other than the unanswered horniness. "I never thought we would work so well. I've never felt this way before."

♀♀♀

I OPENED NATE'S DOOR, about to tell him his kitten needed some petting, and regretted it when I realized he was in the middle of a serious phone conversation. He had his back to me, so he did not notice I had entered. I closed the door back to give him privacy but not before hearing, "Steal my money again and I swear to God, you'll regret it."

I waited thirty seconds before knocking, and he opened the door for me. Apparently, he had hung up after his angry comment.

"Were you on the phone?" He shot me an inquisitive expression, and I explained myself, "I thought I heard you talking through the walls."

"Yeah, my dad called me."

He had been talking to his dad? With a threatening voice? Wait, his dad was stealing money from him? Nate's family had money troubles, but I never imagined it would be that bad. Then again, Blue had snuck into a dorm to be with her brother, instead of her parents for the holiday break, and now lived with their aunt. How bad was it?

"Is everything okay?" I did not want to push for more information than he wanted to give me. He had been patient with me when discussing Logan, and he deserved the same.

"No, but I don't want to talk about it."

"I thought I was the one who avoided problems." I

nudged him, trying to make him smile. I hated it when he frowned.

"I guess you're rubbing off on me."

"Mm, sounds kinky." I kissed him, our lips joining and moving together. He wrapped his arms around my waist like it had become instinct by now. He also kissed me harder than he had before, his tongue coming out to play. His hands wrenched me tight against him, molding me to his hard body. Hard. *Hello, erection.* I pulled back and quirked an eyebrow. "As sexy as that kiss was, maybe this isn't the best time."

"Why not? I thought you wanted to *get to it*," he said as he walked me to his bed, making me even more suspicious and also turned on. He could transition into make-out mode after a fight with his dad?

"Well, that call obviously made you tense—"

"No more talking." His lips captured mine, and I forgot what I was going to say. He threw me onto his bed, and I had zero time to gasp before he jumped on top of me. "You wanted to know how much I want you." He nibbled my earlobe, and I squeezed my thighs together to try to ease some of the ache he had started. "Let me show you."

He grabbed my hair and tangled it around his fist, yanking me into an all-consuming kiss. Damn, how was he always able to surprise me? This forceful Nate was just as sexy as any other. The expert talent he had with his lips turned me into a melted puddle. He sucked my bottom lip between his and growled, proving to me how he was a bit of an animal. When he pressed himself against me, grinding, my head fell back on the pillow at the new sensation. We both moaned.

In the past, this was when he stopped. Why wasn't he stopping?

He pulled down my strapless dress, and the material fell without much hesitation. He smiled at my red bra, and sparks raced through me as he stroked a warm finger over the lace cups. *Yes.*

"You were wearing red the first time I saw you."

"Mmhm." It was hard to think when he kissed right above the curve of my breasts like that. Damn, was he going for it this time?

"Did you know it's my favorite color?" His fingers reached beneath me and unhooked the clasp. He tugged off my bra and—

There was a knock at his door.

Really? Now?

Why did this keep happening to us? *Kitten needs her milk, dammit.*

Nate groaned, his expression going cold and angry at the interruption, and pulled my dress back up to cover my chest, leaving my bra off. "Damn." He trudged to answer the door, grumbling under his breath, "They better have a real fucking problem going on." He opened it. "Damn."

From his reaction, I got up out of bed and hide my bra in the covers just in case the person walked in. I praised my instincts because Jennifer, the blonde who had friend-ghosted me during my first week, strutted in within seconds. Her interest in Nate had been prevalent since day one.

"That's no way to greet me—" She saw me. "What is *she* doing here?"

"She—"

"I had a roommate problem." I covered for him. "We were talking about it."

Jennifer did not look at either of us; instead, her gaze locked onto the disheveled bed. "Forget to make your bed this morning, Nate? Kind of unlike you."

Nate had on his angry, impatient face. A part of me relished how much he wanted to get back to kissing me. *Yes, kick her out of your room and throw me on the bed again.*

"So you're fucking her already?" Jennifer just came right out with it. My jaw made an audible clicking noise when it dropped.

"Stop."

"You said you didn't want to be with me because RAs can't date residents." She raised her voice, and I dreaded anyone in the hallway hearing her. "But you're with her?"

"Jennifer."

"What makes you so special?" She got in my face, and I stepped back. If she tried anything, I could take her. Ever since Logan, I had learned multiple self-defense moves.

"Nothing," Nate said.

I exhaled from the emotional punch to the gut. "Ouch."

Now Nate glared at me too. "That's not what I meant."

"I thought you always said what you meant."

"You're special because you're not special."

I crossed my arms. "You have such a way with words."

"Damn it, I'm not good at stuff like this." He ran a hand through his hair, appearing distressed. "Jennifer, why are you here?"

She flipped her hair over her bare shoulder. "I'm here because I have a roommate complaint."

"Contact the RA on duty like normal. You don't need to come to my room."

"Rude."

Nate opened the door for her to leave, and she sashayed out like a professional seducer.

"So, I'm special because I'm not special, huh?" I half-joked, half-complained about his comment.

He let out a deep sigh. "This day just..." He shook his head and jumped onto his bed, stretching out. I decided to join in and lay next to him. I smiled at the way his arm went around me like a reflex.

"It's okay." I trailed my fingers over his shirt, tracing his muscles. "I don't think you're that special either."

Nate looked down at me, and his stressed face melted into a smile. "You're not special, you're...idiosyncratic."

"I hate you," I responded.

"What? Why?"

"First off, that word is obnoxious. Secondly, you just called me weird."

"It does not mean weird."

"Do you want me to look it up on my phone right now? Because I know for a fact, weird is a synonym for idio-syncratic."

"You want to know what else is a synonym for it?" He leaned in and kissed my head while he continued to stroke my hair with tenderness.

"No, but I know you'll tell me, anyway."

"Distinctive, unique, individualistic, remarkable, quirky—"

"Stop listing synonyms. You're not a thesaurus."

"Tell me what I am." He rolled on top of me, hovering his

head over mine. The lower half of his body brushed and pressed into mine. "Tell me how much you like me." This guy and his ego.

"No." I tapped his nose before running my hands down his chest and stopping at the waistband of his jeans. "I think..." My fingers undid his button and slid the zipper down. "I'll show you." Slipping my hand into his pants, I gripped him through his boxers and he moaned.

His eyelids fluttered shut. "Fuck."

"I heard you had a *hard* day." He was still on top of me, so I rose and landed a hot kiss on his lips, before sinking back down and focusing on the growing bulge in his boxers. I squeezed, and he let out a loud, strangled noise of pleasure. "Maybe I could do something to soothe you, ease you. Maybe a kind of *release*."

"Allie," Nate said, sounding desperate as he thrust hard into my hand.

A knock at the door had both of us falling back and groaning with agitation.

Who was interrupting us now? God himself?

My body was on the verge of crying.

"I swear to God..." Nate pulled up his pants and buttoned them back as he walked to the door. I followed close behind him, ready to tell Jennifer to leave and never come back.

Instead, there were two men in suits.

One stepped forward and reached out a hand to Nate. "We're with the FBI. We have some questions regarding your father's disappearance."

ALLIE'S #3 RULE FOR LIFE: IF IT SCARES YOU, DO IT

llie:

"WE'RE WITH THE FBI. We have some questions regarding your father's disappearance."

Any sexual tension disappeared after hearing that. Well, not all of it. But most. Nate's dad had disappeared? Where? Did he know? His dumbfounded expression told me the answer was no.

"Excuse me?"

"For the past few weeks, we have been investigating your father for fraud and embezzlement. We found out today that he has escaped the country."

Nate stood, dumbfounded. "I just talked to him on the phone like an hour ago."

"Can we see your phone?" The taller, paler agent asked

Nate, and he handed it to him. The agent called the number Nate had and frowned. "The number has already been disconnected. Do you have any idea where your father could be, son?" the agent questioned him. With one glance at Nate's face, I could see he wanted to run and hide.

The younger, shorter agent stood there, watching me. I shuffled to the side, and the younger agent continued staring at me with those dark, prodding eyes. I did not like it.

"He transferred ten thousand dollars out of my account this morning," Nate growled the information out at them. I put a hand on his back in an attempt to comfort him. His father had stolen money from him for real? Ten *thousand* dollars? How had Nate gotten that money to begin with? Had he started working when he was a kid? The image of a baby Nate in a suit became much less cute in my mind. "He stole money from me before, but I was able to get it back. This came from an old joint account with his name still on it."

"If he had that much in cash, he could have gone anywhere." The taller agent turned to the other one, the one who still stared at me. "How did he get access? I thought we froze all of his accounts."

"It was *mine*," Nate repeated. "My account."

"Are there any countries you know your father is fond of? Maybe somewhere he once traveled to and enjoyed well enough—"

"I have no idea where my father could be. I'll answer any questions you have, but I can assure you, there will be no helpful information for me to give you."

The tall agent sighed, and the younger one frowned.

"We'll contact you with any more questions we may have." They nodded at each other with understanding.

The younger, shorter agent tilted his head, *still* staring at me. "Why do you look so familiar to me?" he asked.

"I guess I have one of those faces." I laughed it off. "I don't know anyone in the FBI."

The agent would not let it go. "I'm new to the FBI, I was a cop before that."

I shrugged. What did he want me to say? I did not know him.

"Are you from Meadowville?" I froze at the name of my hometown. He noticed my cringe and nodded, raising his finger at me. "Yeah, I do know you. You're Dally Allie."

"What did you just call her?" Nate was still angry about his father, so his defensive and annoyed voice crackled, chilling the room to ice.

"Dally Allie," the agent said again, though in a less confident voice as he took in Nate's evident attitude. "She had Logan *Garth* go to trial after she made up some story about him hitting her at prom—"

"What's wrong with you?" Nate was now steaming. I kind of loved how protecting me was more important to him than finding out his father had left the country.

"N-Nothing." The agent hastily tried to explain himself. "At the station, we used to call her Dally Allie, because she wasted our time, and it rhymed and such. That's all. Just fun—"

"Wasted your time?"

"You don't know Logan Garth. He's the mayor's son. He would never—"

"I do know him, and he put my girlfriend in a fucking

coma and never went to jail because of people like you. Now get the hell out of my room." Nate glanced at the tall agent who had not said a word after the shorter one recognized me. "I'll answer your questions, but I never want to see or talk to this man again." Nate slammed the door on them and leaned back against it, huffing.

I was looking down at my feet when he walked over and lifted my chin, forcing me to meet his eyes.

"They called you Dally Allie?"

I flinched at the nickname and shrugged. "No one believed me. The bat with my blood and Logan's fingerprints was never found. They said anyone could have jumped and beaten me, and the coma affected my memory."

"The whole town wouldn't listen to you?"

I laughed bitterly, reminiscing. "Not after my mother told everyone I was lying."

"Why would she do that?"

"My dad does business with Logan's father. I guess money ended up being more important."

Nate shook his head and yanked me into a tight hug. The warmth of him soothed me as he rubbed my back.

"We have messed up lives."

I hugged him back, needing to give him the same comfort he gave me. "Your father just stole ten thousand dollars from you and fled the country."

"What do you do when you want to forget about everything? Something crazy?" Nate let out a stressed noise. "Well, I can't believe I'm about to say this, but let's go do something crazy."

❦❦❦

"CHUG, CHUG, CHUG," I repeated, slamming my fist on the bar for dramatic effect.

"Allie, you can't chug a shot." Nate glanced at me, amused, before he bent back and drank down the liquid courage also known as vodka.

"I was doing my impression of a drunk frat brother," I explained my pleas for chugging. "How was I?"

"Good, but you needed to add at least two 'togas, togas!'" Nate mock cheered, and I grinned at him.

Tipsy Nate was about to be my new best friend. He was much more open, and after a couple more shots, he might spew his every secret. Plus, when he drank, he was bolder too. I loved the way, at all times, he kept one of his hands on me. Since we sat at the crowded bar, our legs were already close to each other, but he still had a thrilling hand secured on my thigh.

"I'll remember that next time." I waved the bartender back over to refill our drinks. I sipped on a margarita while Nate attempted drinking his emotions away with shots of vanilla vodka. The situation started feeling less "crazy" and more sad. We needed to do something.

"Refill of the same?" the bartender questioned us.

"Can we have two shots of tequila and a bowl of lime wedges, please?"

The bartender smiled and nodded at me, while Nate raised a brow at my choice.

We were going to have fun.

I grabbed one of the salt packets from two seats away from me and positioned myself on the barstool, aligning myself with Nate. Facing him, I picked up his hand, which had been on my thigh, and licked it.

"What are you—" Nate began, but stopped and groaned when I twirled my tongue over the back of his hand.

The bartender placed the bowl of cut limes and two shot glasses full of tequila down in front of us.

With Nate distracted, I ripped open the salt packet and dusted the now moistened part of his hand with the salt crystals. Mm, he looked delicious. I could lick salt off him for hours. Salt, icing, whipped cream…. Our relationship would give me high blood pressure or diabetes in ten years. Make that five years.

"Put this in your mouth," I told Nate, pressing a lime wedge against his lips.

"Allie—" His mouth opening to speak gave me the perfect opportunity to shove in the tart fruit. His lips curled back, but I gave him no time to respond.

Within seconds, I licked the salt off his hand and tossed back my shot. Grabbing his head and pulling him by the hair down to me for a lime kiss was the best decision I had ever made. I bit down on the lime to rid my taste buds of the burning taste of the tequila and reveled in the hot pressing of his lips against mine. Nate groaned as I pulled the lime out of his mouth.

"Your turn." I winked and laughed at him as his face became utterly determined.

"You know, there's a better way to do this…" The confidence in his deep voice turned me on.

"Oh, yeah?"

He leaned in and pushed my hair back, whispering in my ear, "Yeah." He dipped his head down. A wet tongue dove between my cleavage and trailed up to the base of my neck. My head tipped back in abandon. Shivering, I held in my moan as he sprinkled the rest of the salt packet on the line of my skin where he licked.

"You better get all this salt off me."

He moved back up to the intimacy of my ear. "Say the word, and I'll lick every inch of you."

"Say what word? What's the word?" I asked.

Images of him teasing me burned in my brain, and all the sexual tension I had been feeling during the week rose yet again. I wanted him so much. We had both been building toward something big; we just needed that last jump off the ledge to satisfy us.

"If you want me to go all the way…" He nibbled on my earlobe, and I gasped. He was comfortable seducing me in the middle of a crowded bar? Note to self: tipsy Nate transformed into frisky Nate. "Just say…" I was on the edge of my seat for him; ready to say any word he could think of. "Persimmon," he said.

Time stopped.

I pushed him off me as he laughed. He knew I hated the word persimmon. "You are obnoxious." Nate was always hot and cold. He would tell me he wanted me then crack a joke, continuing to tease me instead of giving me what I wanted. Damn him, he knew just how much it frustrated me. "Now hurry up and lick this salt off me."

He pointed at the second lime wedge. I sighed, picking it up and holding it in my mouth for him.

"Good girl," he grinned, and I cursed the throbbing between my legs when he said those words.

He licked the salt off my chest, dragging his tongue over me and not caring about the watching bystanders. After swallowing down his shot, he bit into the lime I presented him with between my lips. The tart juices from it dripped down my chin to my throat, where he gave another lick. When he pulled back and saw my deep blush, he chuckled.

He yelled over to the bartender, "Two more, please."

☥ ☥ ☥

"Do it!" I squealed in excitement, clapping my hands.

Nate glared at me, which had me giggling louder. "I will not."

"Please," I whined, attempting puppy-dog eyes. The tattoo artist laughed at us.

"You're not convincing me to get a tattoo; I'm not that drunk."

I poked his nose. "You're pretty drunk."

"Not as drunk as you."

"Getting a drunk tattoo is a rite of passage," I exclaimed louder than I needed to in such a quiet, empty shop. "Don't you want to live?"

"Yes, I want to live not having to pay to go through multiple expensive and painful tattoo removal procedures."

"Fine." I pouted and pushed him out of the black reclining chair. His seat became mine. "I want a bear," I told the tattoo artist.

He gave me a small smile. "You are obviously intoxicated, and we're not supposed to—"

"Give me a bear," I repeated. I realized it might have sounded rude, so I added, "Please."

"I—"

I pulled up my dress, too drunk to care about how I flashed Nate and him my red lace panties. Tattoo artists

268

dealt with way worse than partial nudity. I pointed at the tattoo I had hidden on the side of my hip and the one on my foot.

"See?" I put my foot in his face so he could see the small Japanese symbol on it. "I'm not new to this."

"Allie, put your dress down." Nate fumbled with pulling the skirt back down to cover me. He also grabbed my ankle out of the man's face. "Don't spread your legs in front of strangers," he scolded.

"My bad."

The tattoo artist smiled while he put his tools away. "If you come back tomorrow and still want a tattoo, I'll be happy to help you."

"Well, damn." I frowned and got out of the leather chair. "What do we do now?"

"Take an Uber home?" Nate suggested.

I shook my head. "Where is your sense of adventure? Let's walk."

"It's like two miles away." Nate followed me out of the tattoo parlor. I half fell into him when dizziness consumed me. "I don't think you're okay to walk that far."

I waved off his concerns and took his hand in mine. If he was worried, I would hold on to him the whole way. No complaints here.

We walked at a normal pace, only stopping when I got distracted by a pretty tree or flower.

"Nate, look!" I pulled his arm over to the massive fountain. The fountain was well known at Beckett University. Big, mysterious, and luscious looking. No one could see the bottom of it so there were rumors as to how deep it went. Night cast a dark sheen over the water, the liquid reflecting the sky like a blanket of silver silk over onyx waves. Beautiful.

I wanted to jump into it.

"Yes, very pretty, now let's get you home."

I pulled on his arm again and ran over to it. "But I wanna go in."

"Allie." I heard Nate shout, and wide arms encircled my waist and stopped my running. "Don't. One guy jumped into it my freshman year and cracked his head against the side. He almost drowned."

"Oh, please." I tried to escape him, but he wouldn't let go. "I'll be fine."

"It's deeper than it looks, and there could be stone ledges you can't see in the dark." I stopped my wiggling and cupped his cheeks with my hands. With my gaze on him, he spoke with less strength as he said, "You'll get hurt."

"I really like you." I smiled and stole a quick kiss. With this distraction, I escaped his grasp and ran for the fountain. Once I stood on the step, I spun back to him, throwing my arms up and feeling free. "Daring to do what you shouldn't, that's living," I yelled before jumping in.

Cold water surrounded me in seconds, and bubbles escaped my nose. After opening my eyes in the dark water and seeing nothing, I freaked out for a moment, thinking I had gone blind. I blinked to make sure my eyelids were open. All I saw was blackness. Abyss. It was haunting.

I stretched my legs down to find the bottom, but there was nothing beneath me. Deciding to swim back up for air, I kicked my legs but went nowhere. Something held me down. I felt my dress being pulled; the fabric caught on one of the stones.

Shit, I needed to breathe. Why hadn't I listened to Nate? What was wrong with me? Doing crazy things just to feel alive. Was I going to drown? Was death that easy to find? Where was Nate? Would he—

A body pressed to mine and tried tugging me up out of the water, but it still did not work. Nate must have realized the problem because his fingers brushed down to my legs where he ripped the thin fabric to free it from a sharp stone. We swam up for air, him not letting go of me for a second.

We surfaced and gasped together. He pressed his forehead to mine, hard enough to give me a headache. "Never. Do. That. Again," he growled.

"I'm sorry."

He swam me to the ledge to pull myself up and get out, helping me along the way. "You scared the shit out of me."

"I'm sorry."

"It's my fault for approving of the crazy things you do." Once he got out of the cold water too, he picked me up and carried me back in the direction of the dorm building. "That's not what living is."

I stayed quiet. It was how I lived. It was how I survived. I loved doing wild things I never planned for. That was who I was. Who I had no choice but to become after everything that had happened to me. I lived for distractions. For heart-racing experiences, the ones that proved I was still alive. That Logan had not killed me.

"Living isn't about doing what can kill you," Nate said.

Part of me disagreed.

NATE'S #10 RULE FOR LIFE: NEVER BE SOMEONE'S FAVORITE OR LEAST FAVORITE PERSON

*N*ate:

BY THE TIME we got back to Allie's dorm room, we were frozen by the cold. With soaked clothes in the late fall at night, I worried we would get hypothermia. Placing her down on her bed, she was already half asleep. Was I supposed to take the wet dress off her? Could she do it herself?

"Are you going to get this thing off me or not?" She tapped at her wrists as if she wore a watch. "I don't want my bed to get wet."

Okay. I could do this. Was I drunk? Yes. Did she turn me on just by breathing? Yes. But taking off her dress was for her safety, not for me to ogle her.

I turned the light off in her room and strode back over to

where she laid down. Closing my eyes, my hands felt around for her dress. Instead, my right palm connected with her breast and a hard nipple poking through. Fuck, was she not wearing a bra? Right, I had taken it off of her earlier in the day.

She had been braless the whole night? I bit back my groan as my pants became tighter, my cock twitching to life. No, this was not the time for that. She was drunk and half asleep. So was I.

I moved on and grabbed the material of the dress, sliding it off her and thanking God it was sleeveless to make the act easier. I threw her wet outfit into her hamper of dirty clothes and stood there, not sure of what to do next. She stretched out on her bed, lying seductively in a pair of see-through red lace panties with her hair still damp and drying in soft, wavy curls. She was a Goddess.

No, Nate. No ogling.

I closed my eyes again, which added to my confusion about what to do next.

"You could at least pretend to like what you see," she mumbled in a harsh tone. Hurt.

Like what I see? I almost laughed. I fucking loved what I saw. Too much. Her nipples pointed up as if saluting me and those long, sexy legs of hers were spread across the mattress like an open invitation. A sheen slickened her skin from the moisture of her dress, adding to her irresistibleness. She was hypnotic. I would have done anything she asked while she looked at me like that.

"Come here," she whispered from her bed, and my legs moved of their own volition.

Still, her stunt at the fountain bothered me. I had made it

clear how dangerous it was, and she just ran for it like a lunatic searching for a way to get killed. When she jumped and did not resurface within a minute, I had never been so scared in my life.

The idea of being without Allie.... How had someone become so important to me in such a short amount of time? We were constantly together, how did we not get bored of each other? The feeling I had when I saw her smile, when I touched her skin, when I kissed her.... Was this love?

"Hold me," she said as I stood in front of her.

Every molecule in my body softened when she turned on the bed to make room for me. She calmed me like no one else. My brain always worked in overdrive, over-analyzing everything, and stressing about every consequence of every action. That part of me shut down when I was around Allie. Everything felt simple. Well, simpler.

I laid down next to her and held her close in my arms. Her skin was still chilled from walking home in cold, wet clothes, and I moved my hands over her to warm her.

"That's nice," she said as she drifted asleep.

It was nice.

☙☙☙

WAKING up the next morning was one of the most painful moments of my life for many different reasons. First, the hangover I had qualified as severe. An evil beam of sunlight streamed through her window and sucker-punched me right in the face. It felt like I had been hit in my cerebellum, my skull cracked open in the process. Now I remembered why I never got drunk; the migraines were literal Hell.

Second, I woke up with the most painful, raging hard-on I had experienced since high school. The kind a cold shower would not defeat. Opening my eyes, I took in Allie's presence as she lay stretched out on top of me. No wonder I had an erection.

She moaned in her sleep as she rubbed up against me, her wetness pressing against my thigh, so close to my aching cock.

She sighed, dreamily. "Nate."

I forgave her for her torture. Damn, I loved it when she said my name in her dreams. I loved it in real life too, but something about knowing her subconscious liked me—as much as her conscious self did—made me even happier. She was adorable when she slept. Well, adorable until she had a vivid sex dream. Sleep was impossible for me without touching her and waking her from one of those.

Her hair lay in huge, crazy curls over my chest. Since it had been damp and dried while she slept, the auburn strands were messy and tangled into big poofs. She looked wild, which was what she was.

Her eyelids opened, revealing the mystical green I got lost in. "Nate?"

I attempted smoothing out her hair but held in a chuckle at the way it bounced back with a vengeance. "Good morning."

"Last night was fun," she said.

Not what I expected. I wanted her to regret jumping into the fountain. I worried *"doing something crazy"* meant endangering herself. She needed to acknowledge the danger she put herself in. If she had been alone and I did not jump in after her, she could have died. She needed to take more responsibility for herself.

Though I loved being around her, I hated how sometimes I acted more like a parent than a boyfriend. For instance, I believed she spent too much time going out and doing things or hanging out with people when she should have been studying and doing homework. I had not told her this, and it worked out that now we studied together twice every week, fixing the problem.

Still, the way she viewed life concerned me. Her wild side was a vital part of her personality, but almost drowning in a fountain should have been enough to make her have some regret or some reluctance to do it again.

"It was fun until you almost died," I remarked. Honesty was the best policy, and I needed to tell Allie how I felt. I needed her to be safer.

She ran her finger over my chest. "I wouldn't have died."

"You were stuck. Underwater. That's how drowning works."

"Yeah, if you want to be literal about it."

"Allie."

"I could have just slipped out of my dress." She leaned in and kissed my cheek. "After all, you know how fond I am of skinny dipping."

"This isn't a joke." I hated how she flinched from the sternness of my voice. "Allie... I'm worried about the way you handle things."

"What's that supposed to mean?" She rose on her elbows and inched away from me, hurt. *Great.*

"Before you jumped, you said something about how 'this is living,' doing dangerous things—"

"Living is about being daring," she corrected me, her defenses coming up.

"It's great to be daring as long as you're not reckless."

"Reckless?" She snorted and shot up out of the bed. "At least I'm not boring."

I moved off the mattress and stood. Hurt panged inside my chest. "What?" She knew I hated being called boring. Sure, I enjoyed planning things and being organized. It was called being smart, not boring.

"You think *I* have problems handling things? You're scared of everything you can't control, Nate, and you know what? That's life."

She walked around the mattress so she could get closer to me. I did not miss the way her eyes dropped down to scan over my body before shooting back up to fight with me. I wore only my dark blue boxers, and she was still half-naked. Her breasts were bare under my hungry gaze, and it became harder and harder to focus on what she was saying. My erection came back at the worst time.

"It's full of unexplainable and unavoidable situations," she said. "You can't plan out everything."

I tried to gather my thoughts—thoughts not involving throwing her back on the bed and devouring her. Fuck, did she have to stand in nothing like that? With only see-through red panties on her, I could see pretty much everything I had been dreaming about seeing for months. And damn, I was not disappointed. She was stunning. Her pert breasts and strong thighs had me pausing for a minute to remember our conversation.

"Life also isn't about doing crazy things just to feel something," I shot back, but my voice lost its confidence as she walked even closer to me. Her bare skin was mere centimeters from mine. Her nipples poked against my chest. *Focus.* "It isn't about finding new ways to run away from your problems."

"You want to know what life is about?" Her eyes held a challenge as she placed her hot palms on the muscles of my chest and clutched them, digging her nails into me. "It's about finding what you want."

She trailed her hands down, getting closer and closer to the waistband of my boxers. I attempted to ignore the straining of my erection, but the heated look in her eyes had me questioning what was happening. We had just been in the middle of a fight. What was she doing?

"And fucking—" she whispered hoarsely and slid a hand inside my boxers. Her fingers wrapped around my cock and squeezed, making me go cross-eyed. "—taking it." She finished and all I could think of *taking* was her.

Her lips met mine in a rush as she battled me for control over the primal kiss. Her hand was still on my cock, stroking up and down, successful in making me lose my mind. When her thumb circled the sensitive head, I bucked into her fingers and grabbed her. After I lifted her, she took the lead again by wrapping her enticing legs around my waist. She replaced the stroking of her hand with the rocking of her hips.

There was no more fighting. Only madness.

The kiss was so intense; I was afraid our lips would bruise from it. We moaned into each other's mouths as she picked up the pace of her grinding on me. I pushed her body up against the wall so I no longer needed to support all of her weight. My hands wanted to explore. Her bare chest rubbed against mine, and I took my time dragging my fingers over her luscious thighs.

"I love these legs," I told her and resumed the kiss. Everything felt raw. New. Insane and irresistible.

"They love you too."

"I love the way they part for me and squeeze around me." I groped the back of her thigh. "They tell me exactly what you want."

When we fell back on the bed, my body was in overload. I put some space between us in hopes I might calm myself down and not end things before they had even started, but she clung to me.

"Don't you dare stop this time," Allie growled, and the aroused, animalistic sound of it turned me on even more. "I need you." She pushed her hips up against me, rocking them, and I groaned, my cock throbbing with need.

"I won't stop." I kissed down her neck to the swells of her breasts. My tongue flicked out before I sucked one of her nipples. My thumb played with the other one, giving attention to where attention was due. Overdue.

One of her hands captured mine and pulled it down to between her legs, where she burned for me. She shuddered as my fingers trailed over her lips and dove to circle her swollen little clit.

"Is this what you needed, Kitten?" I whispered to her.

"No. I need you," she shot back, squeezing my erection. She grabbed onto my boxers, yanking them down before I could stop her. My shaft pulsed and twitched at the freedom. "Let's go," she demanded, gesturing for me to enter her.

"What's the rush?" I continued with my strokes over her bud and moved my fingers to slide into her at the same time. She spasmed around the intrusion and moaned into my ear. God, she was wet. Soaking my hand. "I like playing with you." I curled my fingers inside her, and her eyes rolled into the back of her head. "I think you like it when I play with you too." She always made me lose control, so seeing her so lost made me feel like an erotic sex God.

"You know I h-hate teasing. N-Now stop it," she gasped, unable to finish her sentence when my thumb accelerated its circles on her.

"What's that saying?" I continued to tease her. "Enjoy the journey, not the destination?"

Her glare faded into an expression of ecstasy. Her brows unfurrowed, and her limbs splayed out on the mattress. "Th-That's a stupid saying."

I licked up her neck and planted a kiss right below her ear. "I think you're liking this."

"You know what I'd like more?" she asked, and before I knew it, my back met the mattress, her on top of me. She straddled my waist, rocking down on my bulge. "Mm, nothing left to say?" Words struggled to form in my mind with her grinding against me like that. Her wetness slammed over me, rubbing. "God, I want you so much," she moaned out, her hips speeding up.

So. Close. And I wasn't even inside her yet.

This time needed to be slow. I needed to show her how I felt about her. I would never let her go after this. Any fight or disagreement in the future would mean nothing after this.

Fuck, I...I loved her.

"Allie." It sounded more like a prayer than a name. My

large hands gripped her waist, and my thumb moved over the small heart tattoo she had there. A red border created the shape, and inside it was the word *mine*. "What does this mean?"

I had wanted to ask her about her tattoos for a while, and now I was using the subject to distract both of us. If we went on like this any longer, I would snap. She rolled a condom onto me, and I almost surrendered at the pressure of it.

No, hold on for her. But I was only so strong. I had not had sex in months, and she was about to make me explode.

"I'll tell you what my tattoos mean later. This is not the time." She guided my sheathed cock to her entrance, pushing down onto me. My shaft slid into her heat and all air escaped me. She felt like liquid heaven. Wet, hot, and so fucking tight. Nothing had ever been so good. Damn it, *don't come. Don't. Come*. Not yet.

"Tell me." I needed the distraction. "The heart that says 'mine.' Why?"

"It means my body is mine, and my love is mine, and—" We both moaned at the way her hips slammed down on me as I went deeper than before. "A-And that they're mine to give."

My hot grip tightened on her waist, stopping her from moving above me. I bit the inside of my cheek, trying to ignore the way my balls tightened and my limbs tingled at the sensual sensation of being inside her. She was magical to me. All-consuming.

I rolled us over on the bed, so I was once again above her. My hips pumped at a slow pace, absorbing every second into my skin. She threw her head back on the pillow and called out my name again.

"And will you give me them?" I questioned, sweat dripping down my chest as I held back from pounding into her with all my might.

She looked at me like I was crazy. I suppose I was crazy for talking during such a pivotal moment. "What?"

"Your body." I moaned as her inner muscles fluttered around me, clenching. "Will you give it to me?"

"I-I kind of already am."

"And y-your…fuck—" I cut off again with a groan. My thrusts became all the more primal, losing rhythm as the sensations rose. "Your love, will you give it to me?"

Her eyes glazed over, and her jaw hung open as my pounding grew hurried. Did she even hear me?

"Allie?"

"Yes," she yelped. "Yes, *yes*."

It was the point of no return. My rapid slams into her sped up until my thrusts were faster than my racing heartbeat. White-hot heat slithered down my spine, shooting to my groin. My hips grew frantic.

Hard thrusts.

Panting.

Her pussy gripping me in spasms.

"You're squeezing me so fucking tight, Parser," I told her, breathless. "I can feel you rippling around me. So close. You want to come for me?"

"Please," she cried, clutching my back and digging her nails into the skin.

I dipped a hand between us to play with her clit. I needed her to come already because, by the tingling sensation in my balls, I did not have much longer to hold back. "Then do it. Be a good girl and come. *Come*. Come now."

She screamed and threw her head back as she convulsed around me. I grunted my pleasure before we both collapsed onto the bed, exhausted.

My mind was hazy post bliss, but I remembered telling her I loved her.

DORM MANUAL RULE #27: LIMIT CUSSING IN THE DORM

llie:

NATE HAD SAID he loved me. He acted like he did not remember saying it, and maybe he hadn't meant to, but those words had traveled out of his lips, through my ears, and burned themselves into my brain. He loved me? My experience with love was friendships, cold parents, and an abusive long-term boyfriend.

Yes, I loved being around him and I was often concerned for him, but was this feeling love? Could I love someone whom I held a secret from?

The final paper for my psychology class would be due soon, and I was almost done writing it about Nate. He had shared everything about his life, and the guilt I now felt for analyzing him was crippling. I wrote about him like he was an experiment instead of a person. Wasn't that why I wanted to be a psychologist? Because I wanted to help people as people and not as labels. Was I losing myself and my reason for studying psychology by writing the paper on someone I cared about?

He would think of me as a monster for the things I wrote. Stating how an abusive relationship with his father severely affected his ability to adjust to change as an adult. Stating he suffered from overthinking and over planning everything, a common trait of mild obsessive-compulsive disorder.

I hated keeping a secret from him, but he would hate me if he found out about the paper. Guilt and regret consumed me, but I was also *proud* of the paper I had written. Nate fascinated me, and the final product could be enough to help me pass the class with a somewhat good grade.

My grade in my women's history class was higher than I had expected it to be. There were two short weeks left of school, so final projects, final papers, and final exams were soaking up all of my personal time. Thankfully, Nate enjoyed studying with me. It was strange being around him and not talking to him or teasing him, but it was also nice to sit in comfortable silence. Sometimes he even held my hand and quizzed me.

I was addicted to him. We still slept in the same bed every night. Touching him was a drug. Talking to him and making him laugh felt like winning the lottery. Maybe I did love him. It had been a week since he said it and everything had been going so great; I didn't know if I should bring up the subject or just forget about it.

"You look good," Nate said in a low voice. His blazing eyes ate me up as I sat next to him in our History class.

Three fresh pieces of lined paper and two pens sat in front of him on the desk. My little overachiever.

"I'm wearing a puffy winter coat." I laughed at him, and he smiled. Winter had come, and now my walks to classes were freezing. My wardrobe full of dresses transformed into thick, wool stockings and heavy coats.

He leaned in and kissed my cheek before nibbling on my ear. "Mm, but puffy in all the right places."

I blushed but loved it. "Don't be ridiculous." Ever since we'd had sex, he had gained confidence with his flirting and sneaky touches. I loved that too.

Did I love him?

"All right." The history professor clapped a couple of times to get the attention of all the talking students. "As you know, the final exam is coming up, but before then, there will be a group project due. You can choose whom you work with; groups have to be at least four people. The description of the project is in the syllabus."

"I hate group work," Nate mumbled.

"That's because you hate people."

"I do not." Nate scoffed and whispered so we would not disrupt the teacher, "I like *you*."

"Don't you mean you *love* me?" I teased him. It might have been the wrong time to bring up how he said he loved me a week ago by accident, but it slipped out.

Instead of replying with a witty comeback, as usual, Nate stared at me. My skin tingled as he made no move to correct my statement.

"You love me?" I asked again.

Nate gave me a small smile and wrapped a finger in my

wavy hair. That was the extent of his response. He focused on the teacher without speaking a word.

WHEN THE CLASS ENDED, two students, who sat near Nate and me, asked if we wanted to be partners with them for the group project. I readily agreed, and Nate gave a reluctant nod. Later, when we were studying in a personal room at the library, he explained why he hated group work.

"Every time I have group work, I end up doing all of it myself."

"Well, not this time, because I'm going to be one of your partners." I leaned in and whispered to him, "And I take work *very* seriously."

"Why did that sound like an innuendo?"

"I think you just find everything I say sexy."

"I think you might be right."

"You know what I find sexy about you?" That he loved me.

"What?" Nate questioned, flipping a page of his textbook as he half-read it and half talked to me. God, he was so cute. Cute and hot. A perfect combination.

If only we were in the privacy of my room instead of a random study room of the library.

"How bossy you are."

A disbelieving sound came from Nate. "Oh, please."

"Really," I assured him. "I love the way you tell me what you want me to do." My hand crept from the book in front of me to under the table, on his upper leg. His body jolted at my touch. I tried not to grin. "Do you think you could tell me what you want me to do right now?"

"Allie." He used his warning voice, and his confused expression just made me want to do this more.

He loved me, and I wanted to show him my feelings. He thought he liked me more than I liked him because he pretended not to say the "L" word after I didn't say it back. I wanted to show him how much he meant to me. A little worshipping would help ease his doubts.

My hand moved over the growing bulge in his jeans.

"What are you doing?" Nate looked around the room, concerned. It was a private study room, but the glass wall allowed people in the main library to see through it. It somewhat added to the thrill. The large table blocked most of our bottom halves, and I used that to my advantage.

His eyes widened as he realized what I had planned. "We're in public." He swatted at my hand for me to stop groping him, but with one well-placed squeeze, he groaned and let me touch him.

"From the rumors I heard about you, that's never stopped you before."

"Rumors mean nothing. It comes from the Latin word for 'noise,'" he ceased from telling me more dictionary facts as he grunted when my fingers tightened around him.

"It also comes from the old French word 'rumur.'" I rolled my "r."

His eyes darkened. "I love it when you do your French accent."

Since he no longer attempted taking my hand away from him, I decided to step it up a notch. I unbuttoned his shorts and unzipped him. He never broke eye contact with me as I maneuvered him out of his boxers, but I could not help myself from glancing down. I had seen him many times before, and yet he always stunned me with how perfect he was.

His hard cock jutted out, the bulbous head a dusky red, glistening at the tip.

"Magnifique," I whispered, and his erection twitched at my voice. Damn.

"Say something in French again," he commanded me.

He did not have to ask me twice. If I had known it turned him on *that* much... Again, I repeat, *damn*.

"Je voudrais une glace." I giggled at the way his cock moved again, as if searching for me. My hand wrapped around him and stroked from the base to the tip. Up and down.

"Damn, that's hot." Nate closed his eyes but reopened them as if he did not want to miss a moment of this. "What did you say?"

"I would like an ice cream."

Nate chuckled then moaned as I quickened my hand on him. "How do you do this?" Nate asked in a hoarse voice.

I tilted my head to the side. "Well, first I hold it like this." I demonstrated. "And then I alternate between stroking up and down, and squeezing the—"

"*Not* what I was asking." One of his arms stretched around me, pulling me closer as I jerked him. "How do you get me to break rules like this?" The amazement in his eyes caused me to smile.

"I think I just awaken the part of you that always wanted to." I worked him in my hand and nibbled on his neck, watching in awe as his taut muscles jumped under his fitted, dark shirt. "I think deep down you've always fantasized about losing control." He hissed when my grip on him tightened, and I pumped faster and faster. So fast. "And damn, nothing turns me on more than when you do," I told him.

"*Allie.*" He sucked in a breath and bucked into my hand. A dark, mischievous gleam claimed his eyes. "I'm not the only one about to lose control." He slipped his hand between my thighs and rubbed me through my clothing.

We panted for breath and yet we could not stop kissing even with the lack of oxygen. I was close just from touching him and watching his pleasure, but now as his fingers circled over me, I was ready to fall over the edge.

"You're like a fantasy," he rasped against my mouth, and we both sped up our stroking. Our eyes locked onto one another's as if it was a challenge as to who would break first. "Drenching my fingers. I think my little kitten needed this."

"Always." My core throbbed. Soon the tremors of release would claim me.

"You have no idea the things I want to do to you," he groaned. "So many things. Bad things."

"How bad?"

"Filthy." He bit at the nape of my neck as my panting accelerated. "Jack me off faster, Kitten," he added. "Before I decide rules don't matter and I fuck you against the glass wall where everyone could see us."

"*Nate,*" I cried out, so close. My head fell onto his shoulder, my neck too weak to hold it up. A bolt of lightning shot through my belly.

He whispered in my ear, "The next time you come after this, I'll be inside you as you're handcuffed to my bed."

"Fuck!" Lights erupted behind my eyelids, and he moaned

into my neck as my orgasm triggered his. His agonized and ecstatic expression caused my core to clench around his fingers harder.

We fought to calm our breathing.

Two thoughts crossed my mind. *Nothing could be better than this.*

And *I might love him too.*

❡❡❡

"Can't. Get. Enough. Of. You," he growled into my ear. It was happening, just as he had said. Handcuffs chained me to his bed's headboard as he thrust between my thighs.

"Same," I groaned, and he lifted my legs to slam into me at a deeper, better angle, hitting my g-spot on each stroke inside. "Oh!"

"The sounds you make..." Nate trailed off as he changed the rhythm to his pounding. "And you look so fucking good in handcuffs."

"I look good in everything."

"My girl is so modest." His dazzling smile, while he propelled inside me, made my inner muscles clench down around him. His eyes rolled back for a moment, and he stopped thrusting. "Do that again."

I did, and he resumed gazing at me like I was a Goddess straight out of some kind of sexual Heaven.

"Again," he demanded. I vowed then and there to never deny him anything. When I tightened around him, he somehow felt even bigger, filling me to the absolute hilt.

"Nate," I gasped and bucked. I wanted to run my hands down his chest or grab his back, but my arms were behind my head and firm handcuffs secured my wrists. "I've decided I don't like handcuffs."

He frowned, slowing down the pace of his thrusts. "They shouldn't hurt."

I inclined my head to kiss him. "They don't. Though I would rather have a fuzzy, soft pair instead."

"Hot pink?"

"You know I love bright colors." He flexed his hips against mine, causing a grinding sensation that had me holding in a scream. I pulled on the handcuffs again, trying to get free. "I want to touch you, damn it."

"So impatient." One of his hands went down between us to rub me. I forgot what I was complaining about. "Just enjoy what I'm doing to you."

"I want to do th-things—*oh, right there*—to you too."

"There's no rush." Nate slowed down his rocking motions, and I nearly cried. "We can go as slow as we want. We have all the time in the world."

"Move those hips faster, or I swear I will kill you." He chuckled and did not listen to me. "What did I tell you about teasing?" I cried.

"You want it fast tonight?" His skin slapped against mine, loud and slick. Flesh pounded against flesh. My jaw dropped at the new speed at which he pistoned into me.

"Yes!"

"Hard?" He doubled the force behind each thrust, and my toes curled at the depth he reached.

"Yes!" After shuddering for the third time that day, a shriek ripped itself from my mouth.

"Come, Allie," he ordered and nothing could have been sexier. After I came around him, squealing my pleasure, he called me his "Good girl." Damn, that was sexier.

❦❦❦

"That wasn't too bad—"

"It was horrible," Nate said, and I laughed at him. I rubbed a hand down his face to try to soothe away his frown, but he just looked at me like I was crazy.

"They helped." The two partners we had for the history group project had agreed to meet up with us to choose the topic and work on the project. The two hours we were all together counted as wasted time as they did not pay attention and played on their phones.

Nate and I walked into my room to set up by my desk and put the final touches on the group assignment.

"They literally Googled the questions we asked them." Nate, of course, had glared at them the whole time. He had also attempted again and again to take charge of the project, but I fought with him; it was *group* work for a reason. He was the type of guy to complain about having to do all the work but also fight to have control over every bit of the process. He was such a grump.

I loved a grump.

I smiled to myself, and his frown faded when he saw me.

"What are you thinking?"

Kissing him seemed like the appropriate response. I loved kissing him. I loved him. Coming to the realization was like sinking underwater, inevitable, ear-popping, eye-stinging, and consuming. I never thought feelings and love could be like this, like...home. My home had turned on me when my parents said I lied about Logan, and I had never come close to the feeling of such comfort as I had when I was with Nate.

He pulled away from the soft, emotion-filled kiss to say, "We need to finish the project."

Ever the professional, my Nate. Mine.

"Yes, sir." I winked at him, and he grunted. He took my bag from me and got my laptop out. "Go ahead and open the Word document, I'll be right back," I said.

Running to the bathroom, I moved as fast as I could because of the strong desire to be back with him. The level of *need* to be near him all the time was insane. Maybe it was because I had lacked loving affection and an amusing comrade for so long. Lucky for me, he would be an addiction I might never have to experience withdrawal from.

Walking back into my room, I found him staring stoically at my computer screen. Always the worker.

"If you think that hard, you really will break your brain," I joked at his solemn and serious expression. This time he did not smile. I tilted my head and moved closer to him, glancing at what he had up on the screen.

It was my psychology paper starring his every issue and insecurity.

"What the fuck is this?"

NATE'S #11 RULE FOR LIFE: FORGET
BUT NEVER FORGIVE

$\mathcal{N}$ate:

"DID YOU HEAR ME?" My voice came out gruffer and more aggressive than I meant it to, but nothing could change it. How could she have done this?

She had frozen at my original question; her eyes glazed over as she stared at me as if in a trance. *Time to wake up and give me a God damned explanation.*

I motioned to her computer. "I said, what the fuck is this?"

When she had left to use the bathroom, I had tried to pull up the group project document. Instead, *this* had popped up first. It was titled "Reactive-Detachment-Disorder Reddington." I never knew a context existed for when alliteration was distasteful.

"It's, um, my psychology paper," she responded.

"You wrote about me?" Just like my ex. Using me and my secrets and my past for her own selfish gain.

Allie took a deep breath before letting out a quiet, "Yes."

Betrayal stabbed me in the chest, making it hard to even breathe. "What's reactive detachment disorder?" *Breathe. Be calm.* My fists clenched so hard, one of my knuckles cracked under the pressure. Anger. Hurt. God, the *hurt.*

"It's caused by a lack of attachment to your guardians as a kid. It causes the child to have problems forming normal relationships when grown-up—"

"Problems with relationships?" Did I do something to her? "Did I make you think—"

"No." She shook her head so quickly, I wondered if she grew dizzy from it. "No, you've been the perfect boyfriend. Perfect."

"Then." I ground my teeth on each word. "What. The. Hell."

"The symptoms include issues with control, anger, and also having realistic expectations."

"And you think I fit all of those?" Realistic expectations? How was that a problem? Sure, I liked control, but it was just what I preferred. But, anger? I had never shown my anger to her—other than beating up Logan.

"Given the complicated history you described with your parents, I believe I came to the best-fitting conclusion."

Like I was an experiment.

Like none of this had mattered to her.

I tore my gaze from her and skimmed more of the paper. Dear God. She had written about my father. She had written about his abuse of me when I was young, and how he had stolen my money and was wanted by the FBI. What the fuck? I had trusted her, and she had taken all of my secrets and put them in a paper. *Just like Abbie.* Except different. Because Allie had not done it for a fat paycheck. She had destroyed me for fucking free.

"I can't believe this." Shock still strangled me. How could she have done this to us? Everything had been going so great. I loved her. I *loved* her. She had ripped out my heart and turned it in for a grade.

"I'm sorry. I didn't want you finding out like—"

"A fucking paper?" I stood up from her desk, not wanting to read any more of it. "You used me for a fucking paper?"

"I think I'll get an A on it if that matters," she replied, her head down. Hell no. She would look at me as she revealed her betrayal. I deserved that much.

I lifted her chin so her eyes had nowhere to go but on me. "So, I was just some nut job you thought you could fix? This whole time?"

"No."

"Was all of this just some kind of experiment?" I had never spoken so loudly.

My brain worked in overtime, and I strived to remember anything to help me understand. She had told me before how she loved playing with me, making me lose control, and how she wanted to fix me. Had all of this been a game? Did my feelings mean nothing to her? I risked my position as an RA for her. I risked my future, Blue's future. For her. I broke my rules for her.

"It was, wasn't it?" It all clicked in my head. "Trying to see how far you could push me, how much you could get me to admit. You never said you love me; this was all a lie."

"It wasn't," she cried, and every molecule of my being wanted to comfort her. No. I was the one who should be broken. How could she have done this? "I-It started as me wanting to learn more about you and help you. You fascinated me, and when my teacher described the paper, I thought you were perfect for it. But Nate, getting to know you—"

"Don't." I could not stand to hear anymore. She moved closer to me, putting her hands on my chest. My heart beat faster at her touch, and I hated it. I almost hated her.

"I fell in love with you," she said.

"I said, don't." I raised my hands to run them through my hair to calm myself, and she flinched and jumped away from my action. Something flashed behind her eyes, but her expression gave nothing away. Yet, I knew what she thought. I knew her. "You thought I was going to fucking hit you?"

This was proof she did not trust me as much as she had let on. It really had all been an act. I turned to stone at the realization. All my life I had acted and put on mask after mask. Now I had gone and fallen in love with an A-plus actress, just to have my heart broken. Never. Again.

"Do you fuck all of your experiments?" I sneered.

"It wasn't like that." She fought with me, gaining her confidence again. She never did give up. It had been something I loved about her.

"So you weren't calculating and diagnosing me while you stroked my cock?"

She flinched again. "Don't be so crude."

"If you had stayed with Ryan, would the paper be about him?" Why did that thought fill me with even more anger?

Why was I jealous at the prospect of her breaking anyone's heart but mine?

She placed her hands on my chest again, attempting to comfort me. "It would have always been about you."

I groaned in agonizing frustration and backed away from her, to the other corner of the room. I needed space.

"How could you do this?" My voice cracked on the words as my heart cracked on the feelings.

"I had always planned to write about you and then we... I felt guilty—"

A bitter laugh shook my chest. "Well, that's something at least."

"It was too late to write about anyone else. Nate, it's my *final* paper. It counts for most of my grade. I chose you because you're the person I know best. I see myself in you."

"This is the last time I put my trust in someone."

"No." Allie's eyes widened, and she closed the distance between us again. "Don't say that."

"I don't want to be with you anymore."

"No." Tears slipped down her cheeks. My skin was ice. I had never been so numb. "Nate, I love you. I was going to tell you—"

"When?"

She looked down, and I read her like one of my history books.

I said, "You never would have told me because you knew what this would mean."

She clung to me, crying onto my arm. "I'm sorry."

I peeled her off of my body. "Goodbye, Allie."

"This can't be goodbye. Nate, it can't be."

"You wanted to fix me? Congratulations. You fucking broke me."

♊︎♊︎♊︎

"You don't look good," Joey, my only friend who was not a real friend, commented while I attacked my pasta with an aggressive fork.

Joey was another RA in my dorm, and we ate together at the dining hall on occasion, but once I had been with Allie, I had spent all my time with her instead. Ryan used to join us for lunch, but now it was down to Joey. He was the only one I had left, and I barely had him.

I felt alone.

Still, him agreeing to meet me for dinner to distract me from my thoughts about her was extremely welcome. "Tell me something I don't know," I bit out.

"The capital of Ghana is Accra."

"I already knew that," I told him, and he grinned at me.

"And that's why you're a freak."

"I'm sure Allie would agree with you."

My mood had been horrible for two days, ever since I had broken up with Allie. She had tried knocking on and opening my door, but I had locked it. She tried talking to me through the wall we shared, but I blared music for the first time in my life just to drown her out.

I could not forgive her. She had taken my family's secrets, *my* secrets, and used them for a grade. Diagnosing me like I was mentally ill. Like I was less stable than her, the girl who put herself in danger just to feel something. The *nerve*.

Joey frowned and let out a deep sigh. "Man, you need to get over this."

"Excuse me?"

How did he not understand? He sided with her? Her over me? After what she had done?

"Maybe it started as a paper, but then it became more. It's not like she didn't tell you all of her secrets in return."

"She used my personal life to analyze for a class."

"It's not her fault your personal life is so interesting."

"I'm serious."

"So am I." Joey's tone lost all of his amusement. "Ever since you two broke up, you have been pissed like nothing I have ever seen before. I thought you were tied up tight before, but damn, Nate, now you're even worse."

I hid my hurt at his words, keeping my expression blank as I was used to doing. Why did everyone have to judge me so harshly? I worked hard to fit in with everyone's humor and expectations. Allie had been the one I did not have to work for. *Damn it.*

"When you're with her, you're better. I'm sorry, but it's true."

"I can't trust her again."

"Trust is earned—"

"And she broke it." I slammed my hand against the table, which shook under us from the assault.

"You know what they say, love mends all wounds—"

"But she didn't love me." I was grateful to him for trying, but he was wrong. "She never loved me."

"How do you know that?" Now Joey sounded as agitated as I felt.

"Because I know her better than I know myself."

❡❡❡

GOING to the gym had been a great idea. Pumping iron to the point of pain, meant no ability to think about Allie, to worry about how she was doing, to remember how good it felt to be with her. Going to the gym had been a great idea. Too bad she was there in her hot pink sports bra and spandex shorts. I almost passed out from looking at her. Knowing what was under those clothes somehow tortured me more. I wanted to rip them off her, flick my tongue—

Fuck.

She was killing me. Staying away from her was hard enough, but now she had to be right in front of me in barely anything, sweating, with her hair up in a ponytail I instinctively wanted to pull.

Again, I repeat, *fuck.*

She stared at me, so I went to the other side of the gym where her treadmill had no view of me. I lifted weights on a machine when Ryan appeared right in front of me.

"Trouble in paradise?" he asked.

"I don't have time for this," I grunted, continuing to stress my muscles with the weights. I came here to not think about Allie, not see Allie, and especially to not talk about Allie. I regretted how my friendship with Ryan had ended after I began dating her, but she had been worth it. At the time she had been worth it, worth everything. Had she even cared about all the things I had given up for her?

"I expected you two to work out together like those sickening couples, but instead it's like you're putting as much distance between yourselves as possible." Ryan tilted his head and smiled. He was such a jerk. "Did you throw her away just like the girls before her?"

I stayed silent, ignoring him as much as I could. *Just lift up and set back down.* Up, Down.

"You stole her, used her, and now it's all over? She no longer fits what you want? I have to say, I never imagined Allie as a submissive—"

"Shut up."

He did not take my advice to stop questioning me. "Was it just a game to you?"

"It wasn't a game to *me*."

She had been the one to play me, using me for information. She had probably planned to throw me away once she submitted the paper. Would she have ever even said she loved me if I had not found the paper and confronted her?

"Well—"

"Why are you pestering me, Ryan?" I snapped and set down the weights, moving threateningly closer to him. Sleep evaded me, my hair was fussed, and I knew I appeared a bit wild. The fear in Ryan's eyes was warranted. "Do you still want her? Is that why?"

"I—"

"You can have her." The words burned out of me with the sour taste of regret.

If he ever laid a hand on her, I would break all twenty-seven bones in it.

❦❦❦

DAYS WENT by in a haze without Allie. It was not until I walked down the hall to my room, when I saw her in nothing but a damp towel, that I realized a week had passed since our breakup. Her wet hair dripped after coming back from her shower and the way the small towel draped over her, cinching and accentuating every curve.

"Fuck," I said and wished I could have shoved the sound back into my mouth. Her head snapped up, and her expression became one of horror. Apparently, cornering me in the hallway wearing a towel like a seductive temptress had not been her plan. "What are you doing?"

"Um." She refused to make eye contact with me. "Marissa must have come in while I was in the shower and left. She locked me out." She stood right in front of her door, staring at it as if her mind had the power to open it. I almost felt bad for making her look so miserable. Wait, she *should* feel guilty. It was her fault. I had loved her, trusted her.

"I have a master key." I unlocked the door to my room to go and get it for her. Now I knew why being an RA and dating one of the residents was a terrible idea. Not only did it break the rules, but it was awkward as hell when the relationship ended.

"Here," I said, unlocking her door for her.

"Nate—"

"Allie." That was all I could say.

"I'm sorry." The heart-wrenching tone of her voice made me second-guess my claim of it always having been about the paper.

What if Joey had been right, and she had grown to care about me? What if it was all real? What if I was throwing away the chance of a lifetime?

But it could not have been real. She would not have

written those things about me if she had loved me the way I loved her.

I was stone. "Me too."

"Can't we just go back to the way things were? Before." She asked, "Can't we just pretend this didn't—"

"That's not how it works."

"I miss you," she said. The pained expression on her face and the fact that she was still clad in her towel made me want to wrap my arms around her and never let her go.

"You can't just have everything you want." I stuck to classic, dry sarcasm, hoping to sting her as much as she stung me. "Welcome to real life. May I take your order?"

"Yeah." She met my eyes with the same confident look I knew so well. "I'd like to return your sarcasm. It's too dry for my tastes."

"I'm not going to get over this."

"I think you will."

I raised my eyebrows. Oh, so now getting back together was a new challenge? Our relationship before was based on a charade, and now she planned to start new as a dare?

"I was passionate about you, Allie."

She appeared surprised by my admittance. "I-I was too."

"But passion is being excited about something. Tenacity is the ability to stick with it." I moved swiftly to her, giving her no time to react. My lips pressed against hers, not as a kiss, but to mumble against them, "We're done."

I heard her as I walked back to my room.

"We haven't even started."

DORM MANUAL RULE #24: IF YOU GO TO A PARTY, BE SAFE

llie:

THE SEMESTER WAS COMING to an end, and Nate still refused to give me the time of day. I had sworn to myself I would win him back and prove my loyalty again, but it was hard to accomplish when he hid from me.

Finals week commenced, and I had not told Nate about my submitting the paper. I had also not told him I threw away the one I worked on all semester writing about him and had spent three sleepless nights rewriting one about a random girl I had met in my film class instead.

Revealing Nate's secrets and analyzing him—like a product of experiences instead of a person—was unforgivable. While writing it, I knew it would crush him if he found out. Of course, he not only found out but read it and broke up with me. I did not blame him. It had broken his trust and his heart.

He thought our entire relationship had been an act. It had not been.

Breakups were a lot like war. Deserters got out unscathed, and fighters could lose limbs or lives. It felt like I had lost a part of myself. Like my arm was gone, but I could still feel it. I would try to reach with it, only to realize it was no longer attached to me. Nate was a ghost to me. I missed him like what I imagined homesickness to be like if I had ever liked my home enough to miss it. Thinking about him hating me made me nauseous.

I had been fine without a guy before, but now I was weak from the withdrawal of him. Real love was a drug I had not known was addictive until I tried it. I hated being dependent on anyone, but Nate had become everything I wanted. I loved him.

Even if my plan failed and he never took me back, I would have no regrets over the time we shared because love, even the painful or destructive kind, should not be regretted.

Everything that happened to me with Logan and my parents and my town messed me up. But if I had never been burned, I would have never risen from ashes. I would not have been strong enough or complicated enough to fit with and understand Nate as well as I did. That did not mean I was glad over my harsh past and that if time machines were real I would not splurge on one and buy a steel baseball bat to rival Logan's wooden one.

No one deserved what had happened to me, but Nate made it better.

"Girl, stop," Gavin said, pausing his video game and nudging me on his beanbag chair in his room.

I had been hanging out with Gavin constantly since Nate had created a massive hole in my heart. I was used to talking to Nate, eating with Nate, sleeping with Nate. Now everything felt lonely. Gavin helped me be less depressed. I needed to be less depressed to scoop Nate back up. I needed to be classic Allie: confident, fun, and colorful.

"Stop what?"

"Turn that frown upside down," Gavin instructed me.

"You should really be studying right now instead of playing video games. Don't you have a final tomorrow?" Now I sounded like Nate.

"Oh, I'm sorry, I forgot you are my mother," Gavin said. I threw a piece of popcorn at him, and he caught it and ate it. "But you're right," he added. "We should be doing something else. We should go to a party."

"Are you serious?" I questioned him. He hated going out. He had once said, *"Why would anyone go outside if they did not absolutely have to?"*

"Aw, come on. We need to celebrate the end of the semester and get your mind off the end of something else."

"Nate and I are not over. I'll get him back." Losing him was not an option. Not after everything we had been through.

"I have full and utter confidence in you." Gavin tapped my head with affection. "But we should still go to a party together. I won't see you again until the start of next semester. This can be our big friendship boom before we don't see each other for two months."

I raised my eyebrows at him. "Friendship boom?" Gavin

was the only thing in my life capable of making me smile without Nate around.

"It's a real thing."

I laughed for the first time since losing Nate. "I guess I could go to a party."

I missed getting dressed up. Drinking my problems away sounded bad, but it was just one night. I deserved a little fun. Every day since the breakup, I had studied until my head hurt: "pulling a Nate," as I called it.

I had become dedicated to an academic schedule of homework, studying, and sleeping enough hours to not be a walking zombie. Of course, I still felt like a walking zombie, due to my inability to sleep well without Nate next to me in addition to my emotional turmoil of being without him. Still, my new habits had helped my grades go up by at least three percentage points in all of my classes. Maybe Nate had it right. Maybe I had needed to work harder.

"It'll be fun."

"Promise?"

"Promise."

***

"This is the worst," I mumbled like a grouch, reminding myself of Nate. My sexy grump. No, not mine. Not anymore. But soon.

Drunk college students screaming at the top of their lungs and dancing—correction, gyrating—to the pounding music packed the house. The temperature straddled the line between boiling and tropical rainforest, caused by the heaters and damp humidity from people's beer-breath and sweat. Gross. It was gross.

"Oh, come on, it's…" Gavin began, but when someone threw up next to him, he did not continue.

"Ryan has been glaring at me for an hour now." I had spotted Ryan across the room from the moment I had stepped into the small, off-campus house. Even in the hot crowd, I felt his chilly reaction to seeing me.

"Maybe he's not glaring," Gavin suggested, shrugging.

I gave him a look of disbelief. "Then why are his eyes narrowed on me while his lips curl down into a scowl?"

"Maybe that's his smolder. His sexy smolder look. You don't know." Gavin tried to comfort my guilt over how things went down with Ryan.

First Ryan, now Nate. Was there a reason behind my rough pattern with relationships? Was I the problem? Damn, maybe I was. I should have never said yes to go on a date with Ryan in the first place.

I should have never finished writing the paper on Nate once we had gotten together. Mistake after mistake. *That* was classic Allie. Who was I kidding with the confident, fun, and colorful demeanor I put on? I was a mess. And, without Nate, I was an even bigger mess than before.

I could not keep doing crazy, wild things just to feel alive. I could not keep pushing everything I had been through down, deep inside. I needed to grow up. Nate needed me to grow up. I would take responsibility for my actions.

"I'm going to talk to him," I told Gavin and stepped forward.

His hand wrapped around my arm and pulled me back. "I'm sorry, what?"

"I need to apologize to Ryan about how things went down."

"I mean, it's messy, but, Allie, you do not need to apologize to him. He chose to date you. You chose to end it. It's not your fault you felt less than he did. You went on like three dates max and kissed Nate once. You did not cheat on him; you are not a bad person; you are just a freshman trying to date. College is a tricky time."

"You're such a great friend." I hugged him and smiled. "You're like the brother I never had."

"If I had been secretly in love with you this whole time, that would have stung, but I prefer blondes."

"I'm still going over to talk to him. The animosity from his staring is making me jumpy."

"Fine, but meet me back here ASAP before one of these blondes steal me away."

I giggled as he mimed gazing through binoculars, looking for his next conquest.

Gavin's conquests were light flirting followed by leaving without a number or name, and telling me all about the person the next day like he or she was his soul mate.

I was just glad Nate was not at the party, because there were far too many beautiful girls with low-cut tops to compete with. Even broken up, I would be jealous. Hell, *especially* since we were broken up.

"Hey," I said to Ryan once I stood in front of him. His glare had lessened on my walk over to him, and now his vexation appeared more mild than spicy.

"Hey."

He leaned against the fridge in the open kitchen, so I

moved to the side and poured myself a drink while talking to him. "How are you?"

"Nate said you two broke up. Is this you trying to get me back?"

Oh, jeez. "No." What else could I have said?

"Good. I'm taken." His words came out in a harsh tone, as if he wanted his statement to hurt me, but it had the opposite effect.

"I'm glad." This was not going the way I had hoped. I just wanted to ease the tension between us. We had been friends once before.

"Speaking of Nate," Ryan grumbled, deepening his glare to somewhere behind me.

I turned around to see Nate sliding through the tight crowd to the kitchen. His gaze lifted and locked onto mine the exact second I saw him.

I forgot how to breathe.

Nate looked good enough to eat whole. No chewing required. His dark jeans clung to his muscular but slender thighs. Instead of his normal dark button-up, he wore a black T-shirt. Mr. Professional had become Mr. Casual? Had I broken his brain that much?

The dark brown of his hair shone even in the dim light, and he seemed…angry. Because I was talking to Ryan? Was he jealous? Was that the key to him realizing his feelings and me getting him back? We were both possessive people, and if jealousy would work on me, maybe—

Nope. Nate turned away from us and went into a different room.

"As cold and antisocial as ever," Ryan remarked.

"You have no idea what you're talking about," I said, my

icy voice dripping with icicles. "He is the least cold person I know, and maybe if you cared enough to really get to know him, you'd see how funny and personable he is."

Ryan coughed with an incredulous look. "You think Nate is funny?"

"I first thought I should apologize to you for how things went down, but, honestly, I'm not sorry. You lead me to Nate, so instead, I'd like to thank you. But, other than that, you have acted immaturely and rudely." My mind went on a tangent, the words escaping my mouth without much thought. "Nate loves his rules, but he broke them for me. That's how important I was to him—"

"And yet he just frowned at you and walked away? That doesn't seem like—"

"I love him."

Ryan's mouth clamped shut.

"I love him and I hurt him, so if you'll excuse me, I have a guy to win back."

After a couple of minutes of searching the house, I found Nate. He had ended up walking outside. Had he given up on being social because he had seen me? Before I slid the glass door open to join him, I put my drink down on the side table at the edge of a sofa. I needed my hands free so I could grab his hair if I kissed him. I missed kissing him.

"Hey," I said and shivered as I walked out into the cold where he stood.

He stared out at the night sky, not looking at me. "Back with Ryan?"

"If you have to ask me that, you don't know me at all."

"Maybe I feel like I don't." His words hit me harder than the winter chill.

"You do. I made a mistake, writing that paper. I should have never done it or I should have talked to you about it."

He squinted at the sky as if looking for a specific star. "I'm sure your teacher will enjoy reading about my private life."

I did not tell him I had written a new paper and not turned in the one about him because it would not have helped the problem. The problem was trust. I had broken his. I needed to earn it back.

"The first time I met you, I thought you were fascinating," I said.

Surprised, he shifted his weight onto his less dominant leg at my statement. Trying to find his footing to face me? I wanted to shake the earth at his feet. His gaze flickered over to me.

"Frustrating, sure, but fascinating," I said, the wind humming like background music to my confession. "It was like everything about you called to me. On the first day of class, the teacher described the assignment. A final paper analyzing someone I knew. You were the first person I thought of."

"Thanks?"

"No one captured my attention like you did. Even Ryan saw that in the beginning. I worked on that paper and got to know you, and everything changed. Nate, I saw myself in you, and, suddenly, writing the paper was about analyzing myself too."

I stepped closer to him, and he did not inch away. He stood like a stone sculpture, eyes frozen on me and ears helpless to listen.

"You crave control. I crave chaos," I said. "It stopped being something my teacher would read and started being a way for me to understand our relationship better. It was like a diary. When you found it, in that moment, I realized how much trust I had broken. I felt guilty before, but seeing your face... Nate, I'm so sorry. I never meant—I would never—"

Tears stabbed my eyes like pinpricks, blurring the image of him standing before me. "Every day without you sucks." I moved right in front of him now, inches separating us. "It feels like I'm no longer living because living isn't about going on wild adventures or always knowing what will happen next. Living is loving." I reached a hand up and touched his cheek. "And I love you."

"Allie," Nate rasped in a pained and breathless voice. He sounded hurt. I hated how I made him feel anything but happy. "I can't."

My heart shattered all over again, self-destructing in my chest like an over-excited grenade. I had professed my love for him and it had done nothing. Right. Time for a distraction. *Remember, Allie, you are ice: cold, hard, unbreakable.*

"Well." I swallowed my pride. Was there anything left to do to win him over? He would not even give me the chance to earn back his trust. Maybe things were really just...done. "Have a good holiday break."

The second I stepped back into the house, I found my drink and tossed it back, guzzling the liquid down, hoping it could lessen my feeling of being broken. I willed myself to feel better. I willed myself not to cry. *Cold, hard, unbreakable.*

The rest of the night blurred. Literally. I could barely remember stumbling around for an hour before a redheaded guy came up to me and helped me stabilize, also known as not falling into walls. I had thanked him, and he had said something funny. I remembered laughing. The next thing I recalled was him giving me a tour of the house. Was it his house? What more was there to show me? My thoughts lagged and dragged, and he told me to "relax."

He pushed me into one of the bedrooms, and my hip hit the wooden desk hard enough to bruise. I fumbled to pull my shirt up to look at the wound, but I could not see it in the pitch-black room.

The redheaded boy ignored my yelp of pain. He suddenly seemed less nice. "I'm dizzy." I slapped at the wall while the room spun.

"Rohypnol does that to a person."

Even the sound of his words blurred in my ears, distorting. "I need to lay down," I said.

He pointed. "There's a bed."

I sagged onto it, my legs unable to keep me up any longer. Every one of my muscles seemed to power down like a dying phone losing its charge. I couldn't move. Why couldn't I move?

"So easy."

"Hmm?" A noise rumbled from me, through the pillow my cheek laid on. My face went numb.

"You're not supposed to leave your drink unattended, you know. You're lucky it was me instead of some sicko."

One of his hands trailed down my backside, and I closed my eyes. I wanted to cry but had no energy to do so.

White light shot behind my eyelids, and I heard a roar.

"Who are y—" The redhead's question cut off to the sound of a loud, cracking punch.

"Allie?" It was Nate. Nate's voice. My Nate. "You fucking

drugged her?" There were a couple of more violent sounds followed by whimpers.

All I could do was groan against the mattress.

The violence stopped. "Leave," Nate growled.

"Look, I—"

"I'm going to report you no matter what you say and will not stop until there are charges and you're expelled and hopefully jailed."

"I didn't even do anything!"

"I'm sure she wasn't your first try. Now get out before I break every one of your ribs."

The door opened and slammed closed. Nate's warm hands picked me up off the mattress. He cradled me against his chest, and I wanted to cry again.

"Saved me," I said and hoped he understood my mumble in his ear.

"There's nothing I wouldn't do for you."

I leaned my head against him because holding it up any longer was not an option. "False."

"I may hate what you did, but no matter how hard I try, I can't hate you," he said, his voice low in my ear.

"Love me?"

I heard him sigh as he nuzzled his chin over my hair.

"Irrevocably."

I did not ruin the moment by commenting on his obsession with big words. Instead, I passed out in his arms.

DORM MANUAL RULE #13: NO GOSSIPING

llie:

I WOKE up confused as to how I had gotten into my bed. My memory was fuzzy from the party the night before, and my body felt like it had run four miles. After Nate had rejected me, I had grabbed my drink and....

Horror filled me, but I calmed myself down just in time. No. A friend of mine had been raped in high school and she said a person would be able to tell. Feel it.

Nausea still flooded me, and I grabbed the trash can by my bed. Worst day ever.

A harsh ringing pounded against my ears, and I groaned. Who would dare call me this early in the morning? I found my phone and hit *"answer,"* raising it to my ear.

"Allie?" A low, gruff male voice sounded on the other end.

"Dad?"

"Allie, I need you to come home."

"Dad, what's this about?" I still had two days left of studying before my last final. "I'm at school."

"You need to come home." He still did not give me an explanation. His tone, however, scared me.

"I can't just leave. I have a final on Thursday."

"Your mother…" His voice cracked. "She passed away last night."

I blinked twice before absorbing his words. "What?"

"She passed away, honey. She had a heart attack."

How? I had just seen her a month ago. My father had looked in worse health than she did.

I waited for the tears.

But tears did not come to me the way they did when I thought about losing Nate. Tears did not come to me the way they did at the end of *Fault in Our Stars* or *Titanic*. Was I that unfeeling? Was I a horrible person? No. No, I was just numb. But the numbness would fade at some point.

"I need you," Dad said.

Statements flooded my head like liquid poison. *I needed you when it came to Logan. I needed you when it came to the entire town turning against me. I needed you when the therapist had said the best cure was medication to calm my panic attacks but never learn from them. You never stood by me, helped me, or protected me—the way I needed you to.* I had needed my dad.

Now he needed me.

"Okay."

❢❢❢

319

I STILL HAD NOT CRIED. After emailing my professor about what had happened, he told me I could take the final exam online instead. Then I packed what I needed for winter break and left everything else in the dorm room for when I came back for the spring semester.

After taking a taxi, a plane, and another taxi, I still had yet to cry.

I had loved my mother. Well, I had loved her in the way one loved someone who raised her. She had always been cold to me, or seeking her own best interest in my decisions, but still never seeing her again hurt. Stung. Echoed. We would never have a chance at the best friend relationship mothers and daughters often had later on in life. If I ever had children, they would not have a grandmother. My mother would not be with me when I bought a wedding dress. All of those things saddened me, but my eyes stayed as dry as ever. Maybe I was just dehydrated.

Seeing the *"Welcome to Meadowville"* town sign as the taxi driver passed it, I realized I had not been home in over a year and a half. I had vowed not to come back here.

The last time I had been shopping at the local grocery store, a grown man had spit at me and grumbled about how my lie could have cost *Logan Garth* his scholarship. My "lie" being the assault and battery charges.

No one had believed me about Logan being the one who beat me in the school parking lot after the prom. Then again, it had been my mother who told everyone I was lying and darling Logan could never do such a thing. My own mother.

And now she was dead.

And there were still no tears.

The taxi pulled into the driveway of our large house, the

house I had grown up in, feeling lonely and misunderstood. The house had been a symbol for me, a prison. Now I was going back to it as a free woman. I just had to remember not to put on the shackles.

I would not stay long. After attending the funeral and comforting my dad, I would live somewhere else before school resumed. This small town still felt like something I needed to run away from. The police here had never enforced my restraining order against Logan, and I could not assume they would now, years later. Would I see Logan at the funeral? My mother had loved him and his parents. They had to be invited.

Logan's parents were just as scary as he was. Instead of hitting me, they had simply destroyed my life, ruining my image for every employer in the state. Logan's dad was the mayor, after all.

Stepping out of the taxi and grabbing my two suitcases, I marched up to my front door and knocked. It took a minute for someone to open it and, instead of it being a house-keeper, it was my dad.

"Thank you." His bloodshot eyes closed as he pulled me into a tight hug. He smelled like an ocean of salt tears. "I wasn't sure you'd come," he said.

"You said you needed me."

"I do." He ended the hug and took one of my suitcases from me. "Come in, come in."

Inside, there were hundreds of white flowers in vases on tables and even some on the floor. I assumed they were there for the funeral.

"A lot of flowers."

"A lot of people loved your mother," responded my father as he led me to the living room.

"I'm sure." My mother had been the town gossip as well as voted "Ms. Meadowville" and prom queen back in her high school days. She was beloved by everyone but me.

My father talked to me for two hours before he let me go to my room to unpack. When he asked me about school, I answered. When he asked me about Nate, I skirted around the subject, telling him, "He's fine."

My father had not talked to me in such an open, interested manner in a very long time. His eyes focused on me, his body leaning to mine. Once I had started dating Logan near the beginning of high school, my father had stopped asking me about my days or my goals.

Dad told me he needed help to plan the funeral according to my mother's will. Apparently, she wanted more than the typical gathering. She wanted us to throw a large, fancy dinner party in her honor, inviting almost everyone in town, including the Garths. She had even been so specific as to have the dinner menu already planned. Roasted duck, and lemongrass and ginger tea-steamed vegetables. Classic rich people meal. My family was wealthy, but my mother had never stopped trying to appear even wealthier. It was her motive behind pushing me to date the son of the richest man in town.

A part of me wondered how she was so prepared for her own funeral. It was a heart attack, after all. Was it not a surprise?

I spent most of the next day calling caterers to find a chef who could cook the meal, and a store for the ice-blue blown glass decorations my mother wanted for the centerpieces at the long tables. Going to pick up the glass sculptures was embarrassing enough without people seeing me and whispering to each other.

One woman approached me. "Will you be at the funeral?"

I rolled my eyes. "No, I'm just back in town to pick up these glass things for fun."

She looked shocked. She should have been.

When I had left town, I had been reduced to a meek and quiet version of myself. Broken. The unenforced restraining order against Logan had been my one push back to the way people treated me. Some people approached me, telling me I never deserved Logan in the first place and I should have never woken up from my coma. When I left, I grew. I stopped wearing black and gray loose clothes and embraced every bright color known to man. I wore dresses, got tattoos, and let my hair grow long. I was different. I was me.

"No need to be rude," the woman said.

"Me? You implied I wasn't going to my own mother's funeral." I took a step closer to her. Her eyes widened, and she glanced over to her friends, who were inching away from us. "I'm the one planning it, so actually, you're no longer invited," I told her.

"B-But—"

"But it's the biggest event in town this year? Sorry, you'll have to miss the gourmet meal and entertainment of depressing stories full of material for your gossiping. There will be a guard and I'll tell him exactly who not to let in."

She gained confidence and raised her head defiantly. "You don't even know my name." As if my not knowing her name meant she could slip in any way. She was wrong.

"My mother didn't know your name because you were

unimportant." I tilted my head and stared down at one of the women in the high school book club I used to belong to. "Amelia."

"You..." She blinked, surprised again at my remembering her. I remembered everyone. A person tends to remember the names of people who wronged her.

"I'm not my mother." I spun around and wheeled my cart to the cashier. However, Amelia had to have the last word.

"Are you going to uninvite the Garth family too?"

No. My mother had loved them. Still, Amelia's question echoed one I had been asking myself since coming back to town.

What would I do when I saw Logan and his parents again?

"WELCOME. WELCOME... WELCOME." After saying the word so many times, it started feeling like a weird sound with no meaning against my tongue. It was the same with, "Thank you," as a response to, "Sorry for your loss."

Repetitive. Stale. Fake. Those words should have been the Meadowville town motto.

"Did mom even know all these people?" I inquired to my dad, and he gave me a small smile.

"They knew her."

"You sure married a popularity queen."

"Your mother had her faults," he said. "But I hope one day you will be able to forgive her for them."

"It's hard to forgive." The moment I said it, Nate popped into my head and my chest ached. I missed him so much. Now I could not even see him in a hallway or hear him on the phone through my wall. He was gone from my life...like my mom. Both were ghosts.

"We know," a grating, hard-hearted voice stole my attention from my own thoughts. Gazing up, I saw Mrs. Garth, Logan's mom and my mother's best friend, standing in front of me.

Here. We. Go.

"Excuse me?" I tried to keep my tone civil. *She* was saying forgiveness was hard? They were the ones who should have been asking for my forgiveness after everything they had put me through.

"You've put our family through a lot." Hell. No. "But we have forgiven you."

I now recalled why I had nicknamed Mrs. Garth "Ice Bitch" in my head.

"Have you?" A growl escaped me.

"Allie," my father warned, but nothing could cool me down from her fierce glare.

"Yes. I believe Logan is even interested in taking you back." She continued making me want to scratch her eyes out. "It was your mother's last wish. Are you going to deny her what she wanted, even in death?"

"Hell, yes." I would never go back to Logan.

"So disrespectful."

She was in *my* home at *my* mother's funeral after her family destroyed *my* life, and *I* was the one being disrespectful? My nails dug into my palms.

"Me?"

"Enough." The severity in my father's tone shook me and for a second I thought he was talking to me, but his eyes were locked onto Mrs. Garth. He was defending me?

At that moment, Logan and his father stepped inside, behind her.

"Allie." Logan moved so quickly, my body mimicked a deer in headlights when he leaned in and wrapped me into a hug as if he had permission to touch me. A panicked noise clawed its way out of my throat, and he released me. "I've missed you. I see that guy isn't here. Single yet again?"

My scowl did not scare him away.

"Like another guy in the picture would stop you." Mr. Garth chuckled and slapped at his son's back with pride.

"The police certainly didn't," I commented.

Mrs. Garth did not laugh at my hilarious and dark joke. "Are you still lying and making up stories for attention? I would have thought you'd grown up. It's very unbecoming of a young lady."

"You know what else is unbecoming? Being put in a coma. Eating food from a tube is very unflattering, but none of you would know that since you never visited me in the hospital. Didn't even send flowers or a fifty-cent 'Get Well Soon' card. *That* is pretty unbecoming."

Mrs. and Mr. Garth gaped at me, while Logan tilted his head and looked at me like he just now noticed me there.

"Now if you'll excuse me, I need to say a couple of words to the audience before the free meal starts." I trotted into the packed grand living room where the guests waited for the dining hall doors to be opened to them. The two servers nodded at me, and I nodded back. They were not allowed to open the doors until I finished my speech. "Can I have your attention, please?"

Everyone turned away from the doors and scanned me

with hesitant but intrigued eyes, as if I was a price tag and they were deciding whether to purchase me or not.

The whispers began. I heard bits and pieces of "daughter," "Logan," "lied," and "awful."

Perfect. Now I was being gossiped about in my own home at my mother's funeral dinner.

A numbing, cold, and calm rage slipped through my veins and pumped along with my blood to reach my every limb.

I took a deep breath and read from the notecard. My mother had written my speech about her for me. It had been stapled to the will along with the details of the dinner menu, decorations, and guest list. Again, I wondered if she had known she was going to die soon, or if she had just been that prepared.

"My mother was one of the most beloved people in this town. She was smart, funny, and beautiful, and as close to perfect as a human could get—Jesus." I cut myself off and flinched. *Just read from the cards, Allie. Then dinner will start and it will be over.* "She was a mother, a friend, an idol—" *Idol?* Wow, mom. Very modest of you to write this for me. "She inspired us all."

I looked up from the cards to give a fake smile, as she had written, *"smile sadly at the audience"* on it. I did not see watery eyes, however. What I saw made me furious. They were still fucking whispering into each other's ears and glaring at me. What the hell?

Meadowville would never change.

I threw the cards down.

"My mother was a strong person. Stronger than any of you."

Now their whispering became loud comments. "The

nerve of her to come back here after all the problems she caused the Garths."

"Should have stayed wherever the hell she was."

My gaze wracked the crowd for anyone not insulting me, and my body froze when I saw Nate leaning against the wall in the back of the room.

Nate. Nate was here. Why was he here? How? How did he even know?

He looked amazing. This was the first time I had seen him in a suit, and he now fit my fantasy of a sexy New York businessman. He was frowning. Not at me, thank God, but he frowned at all the people talking while I gave my speech.

When our eyes met, his expression told me everything was going to be okay. For some reason, I felt like a princess spotting her knight, ready to take her away from the dreaded tower. Or maybe I was the knight performing my last quest before I could go lift the princess off her feet.

"When will dinner be served?" a random person in the crowd asked.

I lost it.

Nate saw my expression and strode to me as if he planned to take charge and save me, but I put a hand up to stop him. I could save myself.

"When will dinner be served? It no longer matters to you because you're leaving." I motioned to one of the guards to escort the person out and, sure enough, he did. I smiled at the audience. My first real, free smile in a while.

"I hate you people." My grin widened as the gasps sounded around the room. It felt a little twisted, but I was done with them. "I find you disgusting. You come to my mother's funeral and talk badly about her daughter, the one who planned and put it all together. And during her damn moving speech, you whisper about her. When I think of you, one word comes to mind." I looked right at Mrs. Garth. "Leeches. You suck on whoever you find important in this town and drain them of everything good. You stick to the rich, no matter what kind of people they are. And don't think for a second I haven't seen a few of you searching around for gift bags like this was some kind of goddamn birthday party."

I continued, "I used to be afraid of you. I used to try to run from you when I wasn't even on the same continent." My gaze ventured over to Nate. "I used to think I needed to distract myself from everything that had happened to me, to live dangerously to feel alive again because you all dug me a fresh grave every day and tried to bury me." My smile grew. "But I am alive and I don't need to prove it to people like you."

I clasped my hands together. "So, if you did not know my mother personally or don't have anything good to say about her, leave now or Dally Allie will kick you out herself."

I turned my attention onto Nate because now, he was all that mattered.

NATE'S #12 RULE FOR LIFE: UNEXPECT THE EXPECTED

*N*ate:

IT HAD TAKEN every bit of my willpower not to kill the guy who had drugged Allie. If he'd had the chance to touch her…. Thank God for my instinct to search for her at the party. I had been harsh, shutting her down after she had explained herself and confessed she loved me. I had been trying to find her again to talk. When I had not found her downstairs, I checked the upstairs bedrooms.

By the time I got her back to her dorm room, she had passed out in my arms. Everything clicked in my mind while watching her sleep, so peaceful and calm. Peace leaked into my tense disposition when I was with her. The pang of loneliness I felt every day without hearing Allie's laugh shook me to the bone. I loved her and I could not stop loving her.

It had broken me the way she had written about me, but what if her explanation was true? What if it had started off as a paper, but our relationship became real? What if she realized she loved me after she wrote it? What if we still had a chance? I could forgive her.

In the beginning, I had shut her down again and again. After every stolen kiss, I would backtrack us with a *"We can't."* Yet, she had continued to fight for me. Every time I pushed her away, she fought for me, which was more than anyone else had ever done. What she had written had hurt me, but I loved her too much to let her go. Hell, it was not as if she had exposed my secrets to a fad magazine for money, like someone else I knew. I admired how she had linked me to a true academic project she worked hard on. It showed her dedication and determination, and, in a way, I was proud of her. I had shared just as much with her as she had shared with me. We were equals.

I forgave her.

Staring down at her sleeping face, stroking her hair, I let out a little laugh at how simple it was to release my fears. I forgave her because she regretted it and she would not do something like it again. I forgave her because I loved her and she could have just let me go like so many others before her, but instead, she declared she would earn back my trust.

I left her dorm room at six o'clock in the morning because I had to get ready for my early final. I scanned through my notes one more time and went to the classroom to take the test. The entire time, I thought about getting back to Allie. Being with her. Seeing her every day again, talking with her, laughing with her, sleeping with her, and then *sleeping* with her. I craved everything with her because she had become my everything.

She was it for me.

After my test, I ran back to her room and knocked and knocked, but no one answered.

"Allie?"

She had to have woken up already. Lunchtime was around the corner. Dread filled me. Could the drugs have knocked her out for even longer? How much stuff had the guy given her? Should I have taken her to the hospital instead of letting her sleep it off? If anything happened to her, I would never forgive myself.

I grabbed my RA keys and opened her door, pushing inside.

She was not there.

I frowned. Where was she? Why was some of her stuff gone? Had she left? No, she had another final. She would not have moved out for winter break already. Why was she gone? Where did she go?

I stomped over to Gavin's door across the hall. As her best friend, he had to know something. *Please, let him know something.*

My emotions were going haywire. Where was she? I could not go another day without her. I had already gone too long without kissing her and telling her what she meant to me. She did not know. I had been so rude to her, shutting her out of my life when she had been one of my damn lifelines. Had she left because of me? Would she even want to take me back anymore?

Gavin opened the door and—upon seeing me—looked around, confused. "Nate?"

"Where's Allie?" If she had gone back to France, I would buy the next plane ticket. *With what money?* Any money.

"What?"

"She's not in her room. Do you know where she went?"

At Gavin's pained expression, I prepared myself for the worst. What if she left with plans to never come back? "It's rough."

"What is?" I would squeeze the answer out of him if he hesitated any longer.

"Her dad called her this morning to tell her that her mom died." What? "She packed what she needed and got on the first flight home. She said she'd see me next semester."

Damn. She had gone back to that hateful little town. The one full of people who had mistreated her and allowed Logan to walk free. Plus, she had just lost a parent. She needed me. My girl needed me.

I did not say another word to Gavin as I rushed back to my room and packed a suitcase.

☂☂☂

STEPPING OFF THE AIRPLANE, I realized I had no idea where to go. I had remembered she lived in Meadowville because the name of it had sounded so fake and contrived; it burned into my memory. From what Allie had told me, it should have been called Weedville because it had taken a lovely flower and drained the life from her. I took a taxi there and got out, hoping to ask the townspeople where the Parser residence was.

"Do you know Allie Parser's address?" I asked a random woman walking on the street.

She frowned. "Last I heard, she had done us all a favor and left the country." She flinched when she glanced at my expression. I was well known for my signature glare. "Th-The Parsers live on Gale Street."

I did not want to have to knock on the door of every house, but I would if I had to. "Know the number?"

"It's the blue house."

I would have thanked her if she had not insulted Allie in the first place.

Once I found the blue house, I stared in wonder. It was huge. Not quite big enough to be a mansion, but Allie had never let on that her parents were wealthy enough for this. What was the reason her mother pushed for her to find a rich boy? Just to keep money in the family?

Allie had never liked her mother, but the death of a parent hit someone harder than a WBA fighter. It creates a hole in a life, which could not have existed without someone to fill that role.

Her house had a sign in the yard reading, "Reception at 4:00." Was the funeral today? With the plane ride, the taxi, and the search, it was already close to the time of starting. I could not just walk in wearing jeans and a T-shirt. It was disrespectful enough to go in without an invitation, let alone wearing casual clothes.

Fifty minutes later, I had walked back into town, purchased a cheap suit, and journeyed back to the house. I assumed all the guests had arrived because there was no guard at the front door preventing me from getting in, and the long driveway and street were filled to the brim with parked vehicles.

I slipped inside and blinked to get used to all the bright

colors in the room. There were light blue decorations everywhere, thousands of white flowers, and most of the crowd inside wore bright pastels. Was I the only one wearing black? Wasn't this a funeral?

A giant golden chandelier hung from the ceiling above where people gathered. While I searched the crowd for Allie, someone's voice boomed over the others. A strong, powerful, and vulnerable, feminine voice. Her voice.

"Can I have your attention, please?"

She would always have my attention. She stood in a long, regal black gown, looking like a queen. Exquisite. Her head sat leveled, chin held up with confidence, as she gazed over the crowd. I moved to a back corner of the room, not wanting her to notice me yet.

She started the speech with note cards, but as the guests continued to whisper over her words, insulting her, she threw the cards down and insulted them right back. Their comments triggered my anger as well, but she handled it like a strong, defiant princess. No, a queen. She pointed out their twisted loyalties and gross gold-digging habits, and she even went so far as uninviting all of those who did not know her mother personally.

I had never been prouder. What was I thinking earlier? That she needed my help to return to this town? She did not. She was fierce. Just like one of her tattoos, she was a flame. Fire burning so bright, any other light was meaningless. A flicker in comparison. She stood up for herself and shut down the gossipers.

She had once told me she never wanted to go back to her hometown because she feared she would turn back into the person who let what happened to her happen again. Now, she did not let any of them speak another word. She faced her fears. I never knew it was possible to love her more.

When she ended the speech and spotted me, we met each other in the middle of the room, which cleared out as people left, grumbling.

So beautiful. A wild thought ran through my head. *If she looks this good in a black gown, she will be stunning in a white one.*

"You're here," she whispered and touched my face as if to make sure I was real.

I kissed her palm. "And I'm never leaving you again."

Her green eyes watered, lily pads floating in a clear pond. "You forgive me?"

"You wrote a paper about me, Allie." I chuckled. How had I never thought how small and meaningless it was compared to what we had together? "That's not a reason to throw away love."

♀♀♀

"So…" Allie's father began, but stopped.

After Allie had kicked out most of the guests, only Logan and his parents stayed with us for the fancy meal. Allie had told me her mother loved Logan and his parents, and I was proud of her for sacrificing her own comfort to honor her mother. But damn, it was terrible. Still embarrassed from when I had given him two black eyes, Logan glared at me over the dinner table, sitting right across from me. Awkward as hell.

"The duck is good," Allie commented through a sly smile. She couldn't care less about the obvious discomfort of everyone. She had told me, *"None of this matters now that I have you."* She had proceeded to be at ease in front of the people she despised the most. It was comical the way Logan's parents were put-off by her newfound confidence.

Allie's father nodded. "Delicious."

"Very duck-like," I added, and Allie snickered.

Another round of silence stretched over the long, wide mahogany table.

"Two ex-boyfriends sitting in a tree." Allie joked to the tune of the rhyme, spelling out the letters, "A-w-k-w-a-r-d."

I grinned while Logan radiated nuclear waves of anger.

"What the hell is he doing here, Allie?" Logan snapped. It had taken him long enough.

"He's my boyfriend; this is my house. He has more reason to be here than you do."

"Honestly." Logan's mother sighed. "Peter, when are you going to control your daughter?"

"I think she's doing fine on her own." Allie's father smiled at her. Maybe this whole thing would bring Allie closer to him. I hoped it would.

"She's brought a random boy here to Erica's funeral." Logan's mother continued to scowl at me with disapproval. I couldn't care less about what she thought of me.

"He's not a random boy, I've met him."

"My name is Nate Reddington, ma'am," I said with the same fake smile I had used since I was six years old. Her eyes widened as she recognized my name. Anyone with money on the East Coast knew the name *Reddington*.

"So, Allie, you've snagged another rich one," she sneered.

I stiffened. How dare she?

"I would love Nate just as much if he had zero dollars to

his name," Allie answered, shrugging as if she hadn't just said something I waited my entire life to hear.

"You're such a selfish child. You truly have no plans to follow your mother's wishes and marry my son?" She wanted Allie to marry Logan, the guy who had put her in a coma?

"None at all."

Logan's mother stood up and motioned for her husband to follow her. "We're leaving." They exited the room, but not before she turned to see Logan still sitting down. "Logan?"

Logan stared at Allie. My glare did nothing to stop him. "In a minute, mom," he said.

"I think you should go too," Allie remarked, but Logan continued gazing at her.

"I still love you, Allie," Logan said. I released a scoffing noise, and he turned to me. "What?"

"You love her?" I questioned him.

"Yes."

I leaned back in my chair. I wanted to hear this. "And why do you think you love her?"

"Because she makes me feel—"

"No," I cut him off. He already got it wrong.

Logan's face grew red. "What?"

"You don't love her because love is not about how the person makes you feel, it's about how you want to make *her* feel. You've hurt her emotionally and physically. You don't love her."

Logan gaped at my words. Allie grinned at me with green eyes so bright, they could blind.

"The cooked vegetables are quite good as well," said Allie's father, smiling.

❦❦❦

"You can stay in this room." Allie led me through the hallway of the upper level of her house. I carried my bags into the room and bounced down on the bed. She leaned against the doorway and watched me.

"What?"

"Can I ask you a question?" She walked into the room when I nodded. "Are you here because Gavin told you I rewrote the paper on someone else?"

"You did?" I had no idea she had done that.

"I want you to trust me again, and if it's just because I ended up changing it before submitting, I still think we have things to work on—"

"Allie, I came here thinking you had submitted that paper. That your professor had already read it and judged me and sold it to a magazine. I'm here because I love you more than you writing an assignment on me could ever change, and forgiving you became easier with every day I was without you. You've become a part of me."

I stood up and cupped her cheeks in my hands. "I used to be cold and closed, and you have warmed and opened me. You've taken me rock wall climbing and skinny-dipping, and I know I will never have as much fun or live the way I want to without you. Life isn't only dull, but it's painful without you. You're the light to my darkness."

"Gross." Her face scrunched. "Next you'll tell me I'm the peanut butter to your jelly."

"You're the salt to my cracker."

"But am I the drip to your faucet?"

My grin was unstoppable. "And the pink to my Flamingo."

"Stop being cliché and kiss me."

A lightweight cloud of emotion settled in my chest and rose like a balloon.

I leaned forward, but I must have moved slower than she wanted because she yanked me down by my hair and slammed her lips against mine. The kiss was as sweet, sexy, and addictive as ever. Controlled yet wild. The kiss spoke to our strengths, our flaws. It was the kind of kiss people spent their lives trying to find.

Falling in love with her was like falling into a ball pit. Bumpy and soft and colorful and childish. And all I wanted to do was jump in again and again.

I would never be able to get enough of her. Not in a lifetime.

EPILOGUE

 *a*llie

I HAD BEEN with Nate for three years and I still could not keep my hands off of him.

"Hey," I said, coming up from behind him. He bent over in nothing but underwear and an apron as he pulled a tray of cinnamon rolls out of the oven. My hands groped his backside through his boxers as he straightened and placed the hot tray over the stove.

"Allie." His warning voice made me want him more.

"You know I can't resist you when you wear your cooking apron." I had bought it for him for Christmas last year. It said, *"Kiss the cook? I'd rather fuck him."* I had found Nate's scandalized face when he had read it hilarious. He wore it to please me. Damn, he always pleased me.

"You need to pause your fondling when I'm near a hot oven. You could get hurt."

Always thinking about me before himself. God, I loved this man.

"Oh, but honey, don't you remember?" I hugged him from behind, settling my hands on his stomach. "You're hotter than a third-degree burn." My fingertips slid under the waistband of his boxers and he swatted them away.

"We don't have time this morning," he said but still kissed me, his lips rough against mine, as if he was trying to get rid of all his passionate feelings in one kiss, so he could focus on the task at hand. The idea backfired because our kiss continued well over three hot minutes.

"I'll make time."

"What if Blue sees us?" he asked.

"She's gone full-blown teenager and locked herself in her room. Plus, knowing her, she won't be up before one o'clock."

My hands drifted down between us, back to his boxers, and he groaned. "Don't think I won't tie you to the bed again," he threatened.

I moaned at the memory. "Mm, please."

This time he kissed me on instinct, betraying his words of *"We don't have time."* Heat washed over me as he nibbled on my bottom lip, and I groaned against him.

He pulled back and swatted my butt. "No distracting me when I'm baking."

"God, you're so hot when you talk domesticated to me," I teased him.

"Is it safe to come out?" Nate's sister Blue yelled from her bedroom in our small apartment. Ever since she'd come home early one day to find Nate and I covered in whipped cream and sprawled out on the kitchen table, she'd become dramatic about entering any room unannounced. The whipped cream had been delicious.

"It's safe," Nate called out to her, grinning at me like the naughty minx he thought *I* was. My man was just as mischievous.

Blue walked into the living room and toward us in the kitchen. I held my breath as Nate glanced at her before turning and staring.

"What the fuck is that?"

"Oh, this?" Blue gestured to her newly dyed hair. Rainbow because neither of us could choose a color. "Allie did it for me last night while you were sleeping."

Nate released an animalistic sound and faced me. His narrowed eyes burned into the back of my skull as I pretended to pour a glass of milk without a milk carton in my hand. "Allie?" His breath caught like he was holding back.

"Yeah, babe?"

"You dyed my baby sister's head every color in the rainbow?"

Confrontations had never been my strong suit. "I mean, if you think about it, it's your fault for going to bed at eight-thirty like a ninety-year-old man."

He quirked an eyebrow, but his stance remained tense and threatening.

But when Nate got threatening? It was crazy hot.

His eyes darkened, his breathing became light panting, and his fists clenched and unclenched like he did not know whether to spank me or pin and kiss me against a wall.

343

"All the cool kids are doing it," I whined like I was the teenager in the room.

"My sister isn't a cool kid," he shot back.

Blue placed her hands on her hips. "Hey."

"Blue, go to your room."

"Oh, no." She shook her rainbow head. "You guys are going to your room. I know how you two settle arguments by now."

I giggled, but Nate yanked me by the wrist to the privacy of our bedroom. He slammed the door closed behind us and towered over me.

"I can't believe you did that without telling me," Nate said.

"You were asleep; we didn't want to bother you."

"She's got crayon hair, Allie!"

"I love crayons. Are you saying you don't love crayons? Because your childhood must have been *sad*."

"Next you're going to take her out to get a tattoo."

I bit my lip because he read my mind. That was the exact plan Blue, and I had for her upcoming sixteenth birthday. "Now that you mention it—"

He threw his arms up in frustration and walked farther into our room, distancing himself from me. "I feel like I'm living with two teenage girls."

"If that were true, what we did last night would land you in jail."

"Babe, you've got to tell me things before you do them."

"Uh huh," I said, not really listening as I approached him, a predator gliding up to a gazelle.

"She's about to be sixteen; she's still a kid."

"Yup." My feet guided me to stand in front of him, and he moved his hand from his hair to look at me.

"I'm serious."

"Mmm, yeah, you are." My sentence came out breathless. God, I wanted him so badly. "Hey, babe?"

"Yes, Allie?"

I fell to my knees, ripped down the elastic waistband of his gray sweatpants, and dove to lick at his cock.

"*Fuck*," Nate shouted.

My wet mouth stretched around his length, sucking as my hands moved to stroke the rest of him. I flicked my tongue against the tip of him, laving him. *Suck*. His deep, broken breaths shook his chest behind the cooking apron. "Babe?" I asked, my lips spread around him, muffling the sound.

"Ye-Yeah?" he stuttered. "Oh fuck, that's good." His fingers slid into my hair, tugging me onto him. He set my pace with those tugs until I matched what he wanted. He moaned as I sucked him deeper.

I pulled back to whisper, "Tell me again what I can or can't do." His cock jerked for more of my mouth. "Come on, Nate. Do something crazy with me."

The man was putty in my hands.

And playing with him was the greatest joy of my life.

ABOUT THE AUTHOR

M. K. Hale writes romance novels starring dirty-talking heroes and the witty women who leave them tongue-tied. She specializes in romantic comedies and has dabbled in comedy for years, including standup, improv, and sketch comedy. She believes laughter is the best medicine, except for, you know, actual medicine. "Hating Him" was her first new adult romantic comedy, and "Disobeying Him" was her first dramatic romance novel.

She obtained her English degree from the University of Maryland and spends her free time reading as many romance novels as humanly possible.

Follow her on Instagram, Twitter, & Facebook:
@mkhaleauthor

HATING HIM

Mandy has a plan to move on from her cheating ex by seducing her best friend's brother. Instead, she mistakenly seduces a stranger with a body from an erotic fairy tale. For Mandy, an art major who only paints in black and white, Brandon adds a dangerous splash of color to her life.

Brandon Gage is used to getting what he wants, so he won't give up his pursuit of her despite her telling him she's been in love with his roommate Jake since high school. After a sports injury, he becomes her patient at the health clinic where she works and hatches his own plan to make Mandy forget about Jake and fall for him.

He soon learns that pretending to date her only makes him want her more. Who will be the winner in "Operation Mandy"?

COSTUME MISCONDUCT

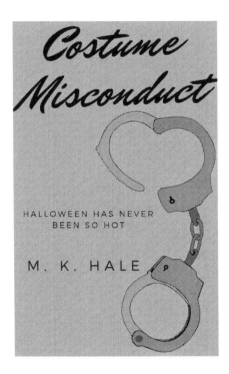

Some like it cop.

Tara Callihan's plan to save money this Halloween by wearing her father's old cop uniform unravels when she gets mistaken for a real police officer while breaking into her friend's ex's apartment. She could have come clean, but instead she rolls with the lie because the chemistry between her and the officer who caught her is enough to make the cold October night feel hot.

He wants her help to catch the culprit? He has already caught her.

She just hopes he won't throw her back in the water once he finds out she is not a real cop and has been lying to him the whole night.

Halloween has never been so hot and so hilarious in this steamy, contemporary rom-com novella.

Made in the USA
Middletown, DE
12 July 2021

44038797R00199